Hostage to Fortune

BOOK TWO IN THE TEA AND TAROT COZY MYSTERY SERIES

KIRSTEN WEISS

This book is a work of fiction. Names, characters and incidents are either the product of the author's imagination or are used factiously. Any resemblance to actual persons, living or dead, is entirely coincidental and not intended by the author.

Copyright ©2020 Kirsten Weiss. All rights reserved, including the right to reproduce this book, or portions thereof, in any form. No part of this text may be reproduced, transmitted, downloaded, decompiled, reverse engineered, or stored in or introduced into any information storage and retrieval system, in any form or by any means, whether electronic or mechanical without the express written permission of the author. The scanning, uploading, and distribution of this book via the Internet or via any other means without permission of the publisher is illegal and punishable by law. Please purchase only authorized electronic editions, and do not participate in or encourage electronic piracy of copyrighted materials.

Cover artist: Dar Albert

Visit the author website: www.kirstenweiss.com

Misterio Press mass market paperback edition / May, 2020
http://Misteriopress.com

ISBN-13: 978-1-944767-49-5

CHAPTER 1

I owed Razzzor.

I was also, possibly, going to kill him.

"Is the Tesla too obvious?" Razzzor crumpled the bag of organic dried cherries. Before I could object – because you don't steal a woman's stakeout snacks – he reached into my bag of tortilla chips. Razzzor jammed a fistful into his mouth.

My ex-boss choked, sputtering. "Augh. Abigail! What are these?"

"This is why I partitioned our food. They're chemical-coated, lime-flavored tortilla chips. And no, a Tesla is not too obvious." God help us all. We'd already spotted three of the luxury sports cars zipping past the high-end wine store we were watching.

Across the street, the shop's windows glowed. Its interior overhead lights sparkled off the wine bottles. Twilight cast purple shades across its white stucco front.

The shadows seemed to shift, and I forced myself to relax. Nothing was going to happen. This was just for fun. A way to reconnect with an old friend outside of an online gaming platform. A way to repay a debt I never really could repay.

"Not organic?" Razzzor wiped his mouth with the back of his hand. "How can you eat this garbage?" He motioned at the bags littering the front of the sleek car.

"It's easy. I don't want to go through life thinking about all the good food I missed."

"You make organic tea and scones and you eat this?"

"I'm complicated."

"You're not thinking this through." He patted his abs through the front of his hoodie. "You've only got one body. Gotta take care of it."

My gaze traversed his lanky frame, his pale face. "You're one to talk. The only parts you exercise are your fingers."

Razzzor shot me his cheerful, boy-next-door grin. "Untrue. I have a personal trainer now."

"Meh. Flat abs are nice, but have you tried these donuts?" I raised a pink box. "They put candy bar pieces on top."

He frowned.

I sighed and set the box on the burled wood dash. After nearly a decade working as his executive assistant, I knew how far I could push.

As if reading my mind, he said, "You should come back to work for me. I've got a great new project—"

"No."

"It's world-changing tech—"

"No."

One corner of his mouth quirked upward, his expression softening. "We haven't done so badly together, have we?"

I didn't respond. When he'd sold his tech firm, I'd done well. Without him, I wouldn't have been able to open Beanblossom's Tea and Tarot.

But I owed him for a lot more than that.

Hence the stakeout.

Also, I hadn't exactly had any better offers this evening.

Tourists in board shorts and tank tops wandered east, away from the beach. Whirligigs and windsocks fluttered beneath a nearby awning. Lights twinkled on the hillside, cascading down to the Pacific.

San Borromeo was tiny but had a to-die-for location, just south of Santa Cruz. The tourists crowded in. As a new small business owner, I said *huzzah* to that. Tourists meant afternoon teas and Tarot readings. But it was starting to feel a little crowded.

"How did you know the bottle was counterfeit?" I asked, changing the subject.

Razzzor, in addition to being my best friend, ex-employer, and favorite gaming partner, was now a proud winery owner. In Silicon Valley, a vineyard was the ultimate accessory. Aside from the latest Tesla.

"Because I tasted it." He adjusted his wire-frame glasses. "It wasn't my pinot." The twilight deepened, setting his handsome face in shadow, but I could see the angry set to his mouth.

"Huh." He'd sent me a bottle once, as a gift. (There was no way I could afford his wine.) The bottle had been near-black, elegantly mysterious, and damned heavy. "Explain again why you haven't gone to the police?"

"I just want to check things out a bit first," he said vaguely.

I shifted in the Tesla to get a better look at him. There wasn't a whole lot of room for moving around, and I banged my elbow on the window. "Ow." I winced.

"What are you doing?"

"Trying to figure out what you're hiding." Because he was definitely hiding something. His reluctance to talk to the cops was about more than his libertarian tendencies. And when my ex-boss got sneaky, all sorts of bad things happened.

He straightened, then abruptly slumped lower, his knees jamming beneath the wheel, his hoodie riding up over his neck. Another weird fact about Silicon Valley rich dudes? Being able to dress down is a sign of success.

"Someone's going inside," he said.

I pressed the binoculars to my eyes. A willowy blonde with long, coiling hair and a leather portfolio strode into the wine store. She looked a lot like me, but taller. And her fashionable but no-nonsense red pantsuit looked expensive.

I glanced down at my own outfit – a rose-colored split skirt and loose white cotton tank. Mine looked more comfy.

She stepped outside a few minutes later, still carrying the portfolio. The woman strode down the street.

"Suspicious," I teased. "She didn't buy any wine."

Razzzor grunted.

"And what *was* in that portfolio?" I asked in a deeper, TV-announcer voice.

He stared after the blonde, his mouth compressing.

I threw a handful of organic popcorn at him. "Earth to Razzzor."

A bike messenger skidded to a halt in front of the store. He ducked inside. The man emerged even faster than the blonde, hopped on his bike, and cycled off.

Frowning, I leaned across Razzzor and watched the messenger disappear down the narrow street. "That's weird."

His head whipped toward me. "What?"

"He didn't take anything into the store, did he?"

"I don't know," Razzzor said. "I wasn't watching that closely."

"Because he didn't take anything out either."

"Do you think—"

"That I've figured out the flaw in this stakeout? Yes. There's nothing odd or unusual about people going into a wine store. What exactly are we watching for here?"

"Fine," Razzzor huffed. "I can see you're not taking this seriously." He opened the Tesla's door and stepped out.

"Where are you going?"

"Inside."

"Wait." I scrambled to escape the sports car. This was harder than it sounded. Tesla's don't have handles. They have buttons. But it's hard to remember that when you're not used to riding in one. My hands fumbled, gliding across the door's smooth surface. Finally, I found a button.

The window glided down.

"Oh, come on."

Razzzor strode across the street. His long shadow vanished beneath a streetlight. An unreasoning panic flashed through me.

Grabbing a lamp post for balance, I scrambled out the window and bolted after him.

"I'm sorry." I panted. "I am taking this seriously. But if you really think someone's counterfeiting your wine, you should call the police."

He grabbed the wine shop's door handle and pulled it open. A bell jangled overhead. We stepped inside.

Long aisles lined with wooden shelves stretched toward the back of the narrow store.

"The pinots are over there." Razzzor turned a corner and vanished down an aisle.

An oversized, black paper tag dangled from a bottle, pulled slightly out of one of the shelves. Since it looked like something out of *Harry Potter*, I glanced at the tag. In neat, silvery script, it read: "This inky Cot pairs well with barbecued pork and burgers with blue cheese."

"Not with *my* burgers." I shoved the bottle deeper onto the shelf. Razzzor had disappeared, and I suddenly felt very alone. "Razzzor?"

"Over here."

I turned a corner.

Razzzor rotated a black wine bottle in his hand. "It's one of mine."

"Is it fake?" I asked.

"I don't think so, but I'd have to taste it to be sure. It's a different year than the counterfeit bottle I found last week."

"Does that matter?"

"Maybe. I don't know." He started to put the bottle back onto the shelf.

I laid a hand on his. "Hold on. Why don't we ask the owner where he bought this one?"

"You know I hate direct confrontations."

Boy, did I. I'd spent the better part of my twenties helping him evade them. "Who said anything about a confrontation? You're a vintner. He's a wine seller. It's just a friendly chat."

We walked to the rear of the shop, where an old-fashioned cash register stood on a glass-topped wooden counter. A bell sat beside the register. I tapped it, and it pealed through the wine store.

"So," Razzzor said in a low voice. "Who should we be?"

"Be?"

"Our stakeout personas. Should we be boyfriend and girlfriend?"

"Maybe we should stick with something closer to reality," I whispered. "I can be your admin assistant."

His head dipped, his shoulders hunching. "Whatever you say."

We waited.

Razzzor frowned and dinged the bell again.

We waited some more.

Razzzor rubbed the back of his neck.

"Something could be wrong." I grinned. Even though I was just a lowly tearoom co-owner, I kind of liked playing detective. "As good citizens, we should check." Good citizens and totally not two gaming geeks.

He canted his head. "Maybe we should wait some more."

"I'm your fake assistant, remember? It's my job to make sure your time isn't wasted." I strode around the counter. "Hello?" I called.

A door behind the counter stood open. I peered inside. Cases of wine made unsteady towers on the floor and blocked a simple wooden desk.

I stepped into the doorway and stopped short, sucking in a harsh breath.

Razzzor bumped into me. "What? What's wrong?"

A man lay prone on the wood floor. Blood pooled around his head, turned toward the desk.

I gaped like a koi fish, my heart knocking against my chest. "Oh my God." I hurried forward, cursing guiltily. Dammit. I hadn't *really* thought someone was hurt.

"Call an ambulance," I said.

I stepped around the odd arrangement of boxes to the fallen man's side. "Sir?" I asked loudly and pressed two fingers to the side of his neck. I didn't feel a pulse, but I wasn't exactly a pulse-taking expert.

I glanced at Razzzor, standing behind the wooden desk. His fists clenched at his sides.

"Fine," I said, "*I'll* call an ambulance." I rummaged in my purse for my phone.

"No." Greenish, Razzzor steadied himself on a stack of wine boxes.

I paused, phone gripped between my hands. "No? What are you talking about?"

He gulped, his Adam's apple bobbing. "His eyes..." He pointed. "Call the police. He's dead."

CHAPTER 2

"Ms. Beanblossom, fancy meeting you here," Detective Tony Chase drawled. The Texan transplant wore his usual California cop casual: jeans, massive belt buckle, button-up shirt, and navy blazer. "Where's your business partner?" he asked. "Don't you two usually find trouble together?"

"Hyperion couldn't come," I muttered. The night air smelled of suntan oil and suspicion—mine.

Detective Chase and I had met before. So far, I had no evidence to suggest he was anything but a good cop. But I don't like authority figures, and that includes handsome detectives. That was why I'd photographed the office and everything else I could before the cops had arrived. I didn't want anyone complaining I'd messed with the crime scene.

Red and blue lights flashed weirdly over the narrow, curving street lined with pastel, stucco buildings. Tourists stared from restaurant windows and beneath awnings. Razzzor stood a bit away, talking to a policewoman.

Tall, lean, and blond, the detective watched me, his expression bland. "And how did you come to stumble across another body?"

I jammed my hands into my skirt pockets. Had I imagined he'd emphasized another?

I cleared my throat. "My friend, Razzzor—"

"That can't be his real name."

"It's with three z's."

"That makes it perfectly common then."

"It came from his gaming handle, but he legally changed it."

The detective didn't respond.

"Check the business pages," I said stubbornly. "He's in them."

"Moving on."

"Right." I smoothed the front of my split-skirt. "Um. He owns a winery—"

The detective snorted.

"And he discovered someone's selling wine that isn't his in bottles that look like his," I finished.

"Wine fraud? How much do this Razzzor's bottles go for?"

"Over a thousand bucks." Most wineries were money sucks. Not Razzzor's. But everything he touched turned to gold.

Maybe I should have asked him to invest in Beanblossom's Tea and Tarot.

"Who buys thousand-dollar wine?" the detective asked. "That seems plain ridiculous."

"In Silicon Valley?"

"So, you thought the fake wine was being sold from this shop?"

"Razzzor did. We sat outside for a while, watching–"

"A stakeout?"

My cheeks warmed. "We saw a tall, blond woman in a red suit go in and come out a few minutes later without any wine. And right after her, a bike messenger went inside. I noticed he didn't have anything to deliver, and he came out empty-handed too."

"Recognize the uniform?"

I shook my head. "He was wearing a neon-yellow top with a blue logo on the back."

"And the blonde?"

"She had long, curling hair, like mine, but I didn't get a good look at her."

"See anything else?"

I opened my mouth, then bit my bottom lip. "Something seemed... wrong about the office."

"Aside from the dead body?"

My face heated again. "Aside from that."

"What exactly was wrong?"

My skin grew hotter. "Um, I'm not sure."

"Not sure?"

"I don't know," I admitted. But something had been off. I'd noticed it as soon as I'd walked inside the room. But what was it?

He snapped shut his old-fashioned notepad. "Thank you, Ms. Beanblossom. I'll be in touch." He sauntered off.

The muscles between my shoulders unclenched. Chase wasn't a bad guy. He'd saved me once from a killer.

Okay, twice. He'd saved me twice.

It was getting embarrassing.

But it did seem kind of weird that I'd found another dead body.

What was going on with our small town's crime rate?

I walked to Razzzor's Tesla.

Scowling, he joined me a few minutes later. "Let's get out of here."

We drove from the tiny downtown, up the hill into residential areas, thick with eucalyptus trees.

"Did you notice anything odd about that office?" I asked.

"Yeah. A dead guy."

I rolled my eyes. "I meant, besides that."

"No. Why, what did you see?"

"I'm not sure. It's just... Never mind." It was probably "just" the body.

"There's, uh, something I should tell you," Razzzor said.

"I know you didn't kill that man and then set us up to find the body."

"No, of course not. But, um, that blond woman we saw go inside, I, uh, know her."

"Good," I said. "That will make it easier for the police to find her."

He didn't respond.

"You did tell the police." I swiveled in the leather seat to look at his angular profile. His Adam's apple bobbed. "Didn't you?"

"Not exactly."

My heart dropped to my sandals. "Not exactly or not at all?"

"Well..."

"Oh, for heaven's... Razzzor, that's withholding evidence. You have to call them." I fumbled in my slouchy purse for my phone.

"Deva and I used to date."

I groaned. "The blonde is your ex?" And then I realized what that meant. Razzzor didn't date much. He was private, introverted. His relationship with her must have meant something. And... "Hold on, you think your ex is faking your wines to get back at you?"

"How did you–?" He grimaced. "She's a wine distributor. And it did seem a little weird that one of her clients is the wine shop where my fake wine was sold. I mean, not my fake wine. I didn't fake it, but–"

"I get it." Too well. Growing up in foster care had left Razzzor with an extreme distrust of government authorities. He'd want to be certain he was right before accusing anyone to the authorities. The idiot.

"You have to tell them," I said.

"No."

"Razzzor–"

"She was dating the wine shop owner."

"How do you–?" I tasted something sour, the puzzle pieces tumbling into place. "Oh, no. This wasn't your first stakeout, was it? Were you stalking her?"

"No. You know I wouldn't do that. Not after— I was watching Whitmore."

I slumped back in the leather seat. "Who's Whitmore?"

"Whitmore Carson. The dead guy."

I swore. "You were stalking the guy who was dating your ex?"

"Watching, not stalking. I didn't know they were dating until after I started my stakeouts. But what was I supposed to do? He was selling counterfeit wine. It could ruin my brand."

"The police are going to think you're a suspect."

"Yeah," he said glumly and turned onto my street. "Now you see why I couldn't tell them. They'll just go after the easiest target, the simplest explanation—me."

"This is not the time for your libertarian tendencies to kick in."

"Someday, I'm buying an island," he muttered. "Forget wineries."

"The police are going to find out, and you'll look worse."

He slowed at a speedbump. "After everything you've been through—we've been through—do you really trust the cops?"

I opened my mouth to tell him, yes. Tony Chase was smart and honest. Besides, this was the San Borromeo PD, not some corrupt, big city police force. We had no reason not to put our faith in the justice system. But something—honesty, I guess—stopped me.

He shot me a sideways glance. "I didn't think so," he said quietly and slowed again in front of my yellow bungalow.

"It's not the same."

But my response was lost in a wall of sound. The ongoing party that is my Saturday night hell rattled the Tesla's windows. My neighbor's parties were also my Sunday night hell. And my Friday night. And...

"Whoa," he said. "You weren't kidding about the parties. Is that–?"

I growled. "My neighbor." Brik.

He squeezed the Tesla into my driveway.

I fumbled for the button. He leaned across me and opened the door.

I stepped from the car. "You need to talk to the police." I shouted over the roar of the heavy metal.

"What?"

"I said, you need to talk to the police!"

"Okay," Razzzor said. "We'll talk tomorrow."

Giving up, I shut the door. Razzzor waited while I climbed the wooden steps to the cheerful yellow bungalow I rented. I let myself inside and waved from the open door.

He reversed from the driveway, and the Tesla glided down the street.

I shut the door, muffling the sound from the party. Leaning against the wall, I surveyed my domain.

The bungalow's soothing blue walls failed to soothe. The inviting soft couches failed to invite.

I kicked off my sandals and walked across the bamboo floor to my kitchen. Gray granite counters. Glass-fronted cupboards. A butcher block work island. It was my favorite room in the house. And still my stomach jittered.

Detective Chase was no dummy. He'd figure out Razzzor at best knew more than he was telling and at worst was a suspect. And if I knew Razzzor, he'd flee the country before colluding with cops. His lone-wolf passion for creating was what made him great, but it was also a flaw.

I just hoped it wouldn't be a fatal flaw.

And who was this Deva woman?

Blowing out my breath, I scraped my hands through my hair. I needed to chill.

I glanced at the white, bi-fold doors to the pantry, filled with tea canisters and drying herbs, and shook my head. Tea wasn't going to fix this headache.

I needed peace. I needed Zen. I needed quiet.

My life used to be simple. Selling tea on the pier. Online gaming with Razzzor. Dinners with my grandfather and his best friend, my honorary uncle Tomas.

I walked through my living room toward the deck's French doors and froze. A man lounged on one of the patio chairs.

I yanked open the glass-paned door, and the music from next door roared. "Hyperion, what are you doing here?"

Hyperion Night was my business partner and the Tarot half of Beanblossom's Tea and Tarot. He wore elegant gray skinny pants and a lightweight turtleneck that flattered his dark skin. But everything flattered him. He had a face made for the cover of a magazine—high cheekbones and startlingly light-colored eyes.

He yawned. "Hey, girl."

A muscle in my left eyelid twitched. "Why are you in my yard?"

"Brik's got a weird crowd tonight." He motioned negligently to the redwood fence, and my neighbor's house behind it. "I thought I'd stop by."

In other words, he'd gotten bored at my neighbor's party. And why was it so annoying that he'd been there at all?

"What are you doing out so late?" he asked.

"You wouldn't believe me if I told you." I dropped into the cushioned deck chair across from him.

"Ooh, have you been up to no good? Tell me everything."

"Howdy, Hyperion." My grandfather ambled down the path beside my house, his duck, Peking, waddling beside him. His best friend, Tomas, followed.

I hurried down the steps and hugged the two men. Tomas climbed the porch steps, but Gramps hesitated.

"Is everything okay?" I asked.

The mallard quacked.

"I got a postcard from your mother," my grandfather said in a low voice.

A tiny flame of anger sparked in my heart, and I wasn't proud of it. When I'd gone to work for Razzzor, we'd discovered we shared a darkness. We'd both been abandoned by our parents. But unlike Razzzor, I'd had loving grandparents who'd stepped up to fill the void.

I'd been lucky. But I still hadn't gotten past it. It's not something you get past easily.

I shook my head. "I don't need to know what it said."

My grandfather's face spasmed.

"Unless... I do need to know?" I asked slowly.

He hesitated, then patted my arm. "No. It can wait."

We joined Tomas and Hyperion on the porch, and Gramps flopped into a chair. Peking fluttered into his lap and eyed Hyperion.

"Sorry," I said. "No cat today." Peking and Hyperion's cat, Bastet, had one of those weird animal-kingdom friendships you see on internet videos. Since

Bastet's initial instinct had been to try to eat him, Peking was clearly more forgiving than I.

"What are you doing here?" Tomas asked Hyperion.

"Brik's got a strange crowd tonight. The vibe felt off. I wanted a change of scene."

"Really?" Gramps fiddled with the zipper on his khaki jacket. A stain marred its collar, and an ache stirred in my heart. But I didn't say anything about the stain. Gramps would feel like he was being treated like a child, and neither of us wanted that.

"What's wrong with it?" my grandfather continued.

"Crowd too rough for you?" Tomas's leathery face curved into a grin. "Bet none of them ever killed a man with a bottlecap."

I rubbed my head. Not that war story again.

"Abigail was just telling me about her latest adventure," Hyperion said. "Go on, Abs."

"Razzzor asked me on a stakeout," I said, "and—"

Hyperion raised one hand. "Hold on. Razzzor exists?"

"Of course he exists," I said.

Gramps rubbed his chin. "Come to think of it, I haven't met him either."

"Does Razzzor exist IRL?" Hyperion arched a brow. "That means in real life."

"I know what it means," I said, waspish.

"I didn't," Gramps said.

"Yes," I said, "he's real. He bought a winery a couple years back, and it's doing really well, except—"

"Now I know this is a gag," Hyperion said. "Who ever heard of a profitable winery?"

I plowed onward. "And he found a bottle of counterfeit wine with his label on it in the Wine Merchants—"

"Have you ever met him?" Hyperion asked Tomas.

My uncle shook his head.

"This is a little too convenient," Hyperion said, "don't you think?"

The older men nodded. Peking quacked.

"The fake wine's probably being sold in other stores too," I said. "Razzzor just happened to be here…"

Brik climbed the steps and leaned against the porch railing. My neighbor crossed his arms, his biceps bulging. Which I totally didn't notice. Or I wouldn't have, if he didn't insist on wearing tight white t-shirts and jeans that…

Never mind.

"What are you doing here?" I asked. "Aren't you hosting a party?"

"Crowd's a little off tonight." Brik ran a hand through his mane of thick, blond hair.

"That's what I said," Hyperion said.

"Can I finish my story?" I asked.

Hyperion rolled his eyes. "So, you and your imaginary friend went on a stakeout, and...?"

"And the owner of the wine store was dead."

"Oh. My. God." Hyperion pointed an accusing finger. "You saw Tony, didn't you?"

"He might have been there," I admitted. Hyperion had a thing for the detective.

Hyperion leapt to his feet. "You were sleuthing without me. I thought we were partners?"

I sucked in my cheeks. "I didn't know I was going to find a body."

Hyperion paced. "Did he ask about me?"

"The body?"

"Detective Chase."

"Um," I said, "he did ask where you were."

"I knew it," Hyperion said. "He's totally into me. And we both drive Jeeps. It's a sign."

"Okay," I said, "but the body—"

"You should have brought me along," Hyperion said, "but no, you had to go it alone."

"I wasn't alone. I was with–"

"Your imaginary best friend." Hyperion folded his arms over his gray turtleneck. "Really, Abs, clinging to this illusion is getting a little sad."

"You can look him up–"

"Oh, I will." He rose. "I'll look up this dead wine merchant. But we'll have to keep my involvement in our investigation on the QT."

"I, uh…" I'd meant he should look up Razzzor. "Our investigation?"

The men looked at my partner. The duck did too.

Hyperion studied his manicure. "The last time I got involved in an investigation, I was practically arrested. It's been impossible for Tony to ask me out as long as I'm a suspect, or a witness, or whatever. We need to be smart about solving this crime."

In spite of everything, I couldn't help but admire Hyperion's boundless confidence. But I was already feeling guilty about playing detective. There was no reason Razzzor and I needed to dig ourselves in deeper.

Gramps frowned. "Abigail, you found the body."

"Yes?"

"And it's not the first time you've done something like that either," Tomas said.

"Well, no," I said.

"Doesn't that make you a prime suspect?" Gramps asked.

"I'm not a…" Oh, s^%$.

I totally was.

CHAPTER 3

It was a given I'd stick my nose in the murder. Razzzor wasn't going to let this go — he'd never trust the cops to get things right.

It was also a given Hyperion would get involved. Not only had he just finished binge watching a TV psychic show, but we'd solved murders before. We'd been pretty good at it.

Detective Chase probably wouldn't agree with that last bit.

The next evening, I sat on my heels and surveyed the tearoom's reach-in fridge. It was clean enough. Glancing over my shoulder, I made sure I was alone in the wide, industrial kitchen. I pulled my phone from my apron pocket and flipped to the photos I'd taken yesterday.

Acid rose in my throat.

Whitmore's body, sprawled on the tile floor. His desk, incredibly neat. Maybe that was what I'd thought so odd. Who kept their desk that tidy?

I studied a formation of boxes crowding the desk. There were three tiers stacked four boxes high and spread in a rough semi-circle. Winery logos decorated their cardboard sides.

A yawn cracked my jaw. I'd been up late last night researching Deva and the Wine Merchants. I hadn't learned much. But everybody blabbed to everyone about what they were doing online. Thanks to the internet, I'd learned Deva was going to be at a wine and cheese thing tonight.

I was going to be there too.

A soft noise at the open kitchen door made me turn. Hyperion lounged in the doorway. He looked like a male model in his button-up white shirt, open at the collar, and his skinny khaki slacks and loafers.

"When you're done," he said, "let's talk."

Hastily, I jammed my phone into my pocket. "How'd your class go?"

"I'm leaning a lot."

"Learning? I thought you were teaching the class."

"One needs to keep up," he said airily. "Continuing education keeps the brain sharp."

Hyperion was a true Tarot master. I wasn't sure what he had to learn at this point, but I stayed out of the Tarot side of the business.

"I'm done here." Glancing at the wall clock, I shut the door. I dropped my cleaning supplies in the plastic bucket. "Want some tea?" There was always time for a quick cup.

"Whatever you're having." He wandered into the hall.

Pulling off my apron, I walked into the front of the now-empty tearoom. Brushed-nickel canisters of tea lined the wooden shelves behind the counter.

Elderberry. I pulled down a canister – an elderberry and hawthorn berry blend.

Prying free the lid, I reached in for the spoon. A hot slash of pain bit my hand.

I jerked my hand from the canister. "Ow!" Puzzled, I peered inside.

A hawthorn twig stuck up from the mix of dried berries and rosehips.

I retrieved the thorny twig and laid it on the counter. "How did you get in there?" I was the one who mixed our tea blends. But I guess I hadn't been paying attention when I'd mixed this one. *Weird.*

I brewed the tea, arranged a white ceramic teapot and cups on a tray, and strolled into Hyperion's office.

If our tearoom's décor said "modern elegance," Hyperion's office was a gypsy caravan. Sheer, ivory fabric swagged the ceiling, obscuring the industrial pipes. On a low table, against one wall stood a makeshift altar of driftwood, crystals, and candles. Hyperion relaxed in a high-backed red velvet chair, a king awaiting his subject.

His massive tabby, Bastet, peered from his perch on an antique desk.

Negligently, Hyperion waved me to the matching chair opposite. A deck of Tarot cards sat neatly stacked on the round table.

I set down the tray, sat and poured my tea, adding the honey I'd brought. "Elderberry and hawthorn berries, with dried rose hips."

"We *could* both use the extra protection, I suppose."

"Protection?"

He glanced at the computer on his desk and shut the laptop. "Elderberry and hawthorn both correspond to protection. Magically, I mean."

I scowled and rubbed my hand. "It didn't protect me." That thorn had been sharp.

I poured him a cup.

"So... a postcard from your mother?" he asked. "I couldn't help overhearing, since I was totally eavesdropping."

I gave him a look.

"It's one of my superpowers," he said. "What do you expect? Well? Aren't you even the least bit curious what she said?"

"I know what she said. The only thing that changes on the postcards is the picture. Here's where I am now, spiritual growth amazing, wish you were here." They'd been coming since I was roughly three. I knew the drill.

Bastet dropped from his perch and rubbed against my leg.

"I'm sorry," Hyperion said quietly.

I wasn't. Postcards saved me from having to respond, since there was never a return address.

"So, each postcard is basically a kick in the gut," he said.

"Yeah. Thanks mom and dad."

"All right," he said briskly. "I suppose you've researched our victim, Whitmore Carson, too?"

I nodded, grateful for the change of subject. "I found articles about the wine shop in the local business pages. The Wine Merchants opened two years ago. I also found some social media stuff on Deva, who I saw go into the wine shop before us. Nothing on them pointed to murder. There was a bike messenger at the Wine Merchants that night too, but I haven't had time to figure out the messenger company yet. Anyway, Whitmore Carson had a business partner, Madge Badger."

"With a name like that she has to be the killer. Is the shop all hers now?"

"Or was she the one who introduced counterfeit wines to the shop?" I asked.

"If there are counterfeit wines. We have no proof of that."

Bastet hissed.

"Razzzor has proof." At least, I hoped he'd kept the wine bottle he'd found last week. We hadn't really had a chance to discuss that.

"Ah yes, your peculiar, phantasmic vapor—"

"You're still reading that Lovecraft word-of-the day calendar." I rose to leave. "Aren't you?"

He shuffled the Tarot deck. "It's expanded my vocabulary in such tumultuous, unutterable ways. Anyhoo, since Whitmore's social media sites were only about wine – the man was obsessed – I thought we'd do a Tarot reading."

"On Whitmore Carson?" My gaze slid to the clock Hyperion used to make sure his clients didn't overstay their readings. "I thought you said reading for people without their permission was unethical."

"Not in a murder investigation. Not when he's dead." He laid a card on the red velvet tablecloth and flipped it over. A woman handed a sword to a knight on a horse. "Justice. See? Whitmore wants justice. He's down with this reading."

"And now you're a medium too?" I sat again.

He shuddered. "Good Lord, no. I can't imagine anything creepier. Who wants to talk to the dead? They can't have anything new to say." He turned over another card.

The Devil.

In spite of myself, I shivered.

"Hm." Hyperion turned over a third card. "The seven of swords. It's obvious."

"Is it?" I asked, pretending cluelessness. Tarot was Hyperion's profession.

I knew more about the cards' meanings than I was willing to admit, but why steal his thunder?

"The devil represents being blind – or blinded – to something. And the seven of swords represents trickery and deceit. Obviously, Whitmore didn't know what was going on. He was tricked, blinded to the truth."

It was possible. Plausible even. But did it get us anywhere? "Okay, let's say Whitmore didn't know what was going on. He was fooled by the fake wine too—"

"Or by something else. We don't know this deception, whatever it was, was about counterfeit wine."

I checked my watch.

We both pushed back our chairs and stood.

I stared at my partner.

He stared back. "You're going to tonight's wine meetup," he said, accusingly.

"Well, yes. And before you say anything, I was going to tell you—"

"Too late. And I'm going too." He snagged a navy blazer off the back of his chair and slithered into it.

It wasn't like I could stop him. And wine socials weren't exactly my scene. I shrugged. "Fine."

"I know it's fine."

"Fine," I said.

"I'll drive. And don't say *fine* again."

"Okay."

He glared.

I grabbed up the tea things, hustled them into the kitchen sink, and we piled into Hyperion's green, Jeep Wrangler.

We drove north, to a chic wine bar in Santa Cruz.

A car pulled out in front of the shop, and Hyperion whipped the Jeep into the spot. "Told you," he said, smug. "The parking gods love me."

"Hm." They hated me. Not that I believed any existed. I preferred to look at the magical world like an anthropologist. It was interesting. The natives performed curious ceremonies. I was willing to observe and occasionally participate. But my New Age parents had cured me of any real interest in the occult.

When the people you're supposed to be able to count on come up short, you learn to treasure the people you *can* count on. I would never forget what my grandfather had done for me.

And I wouldn't forget Razzzor either. He'd once gotten me out of a very sticky and very unpleasant situation. My friend had also risked his own neck to do it. I wouldn't let him down now.

We emerged from the Jeep, and Hyperion straightened his lapels. He looked me over. "Good thing Beanblossom's is business casual. You don't look awful for someone who's been cleaning."

"Wow. Thank you for that heartfelt and totally backhanded compliment." I smoothed the front of my white, linen shirt dress.

We strolled into the bar. Men's heads turned at Hyperion's passage. That was the trouble hanging out with Hyperion – he sucked up the male attention wherever we went. I'd basically resigned myself to being a wallflower in his presence.

Ignoring the looks, my partner sauntered to the bar. "We're here for the Crush on You tasting."

The bartender looked him up and down and tugged on the collar of his white button-down. "You're early. Back room." He jerked his head toward an open doorway at the far end of the room.

We walked past walls lined with corks to a dimly lit, modern room painted near-black. High, black quartz tables and matching black wooden chairs dotted the room. Brushed-nickel pendant lamps hung from the ceiling.

Deva and a blond man stood chatting behind the bar. A tortoise-shell clip restrained the golden hair spilling down Deva's back. Her black cocktail dress skimmed her toned body. A sparkling gold pendant dangled around her throat. It was a bit like looking at a taller, slimmer, better dressed version of me.

It was also kind of unnerving.

The man she was speaking to turned toward us and his broad, Teutonic face split into a grin. "Our first guests! Getting in your tasting before the crowd? Smart."

"Normally," Hyperion said, "I prefer to make a later and more dramatic entrance. But I'll make an exception for good wine."

"Hi," I said, stretching my hand across the shiny black counter. "I'm Abigail."

He shook my hand, his grip firm but not unpleasant. "Zimmer. James Zimmer."

"And I'm Deva." She shook my hand, and I managed not to wince. The woman had a grip.

My partner beamed. "I'm Hyperion."

James blinked. "Hyperion? Wasn't he a sun god?"

"Thank you." Hyperion turned to me. "At last, someone who knows their Greek mythology."

"In my line of work," James said, "one needs to know all sorts of facts, plus the latest wine news."

"You're a...?" I asked.

"We're distributors," James said. "The least romantic part of the business, but we're a necessary cog in the wine industry machine."

"Distributors?" I said in my best "let's gossip" tone. "Then you must have heard about Whitmore Carson. What a shock."

"Whitmore?" Deva stilled. "What about him?"

"He was killed in his wine store," I said.

Deva swayed. The color drained from her face.

James grasped her elbow. "Deva? Are you all right?"

"I don't... Excuse me." Clutching her pendant between two fingers, she hurried from behind the bar and into a narrow hallway.

Guiltily, I scraped my teeth across my bottom lip. *Tactless.* But that was what I'd wanted, wasn't it? Reactions?

"Killed?" James dark brows slashed downward. "Are you sure? I saw Whitmore a couple weeks ago."

"Oh," Hyperion said, "he's definitely dead."

"I'm sorry," I said. "I didn't mean to upset her." Deva's distress had seemed genuine, genuine enough to twist my stomach. But *was* it real?

"She and Whitmore were... close." James glanced toward the empty hallway. "I don't like to pry into my employee's personal lives, but... well. What happened? Was it a robbery?"

"I don't know," I said, still looking toward the hallway where Deva had vanished. The local Sunday paper hadn't run the story, and I knew better than to call Detective Chase for the latest murder gossip.

"James, I brought that cheese you wanted." A slender woman with long blue-black hair clattered into the room on five-inch heels. Her red flower print dress whispered about her knees. It contrasted artfully with her worn denim jacket. She leaned over the sleek bar and kissed James's cheek, handed him a paper bag.

"Thanks, Layla." He motioned to us. "These are Hyperion and Abigail. This is my wife, Layla."

"Wife. Errand girl. Jill of all trades." She smiled and shook our hands. Her eyes widened in mock horror. "But where's the wine? You can't let people stand at a bar and not offer them wine."

James poured.

Layla turned to me. "So, Abigail. What's your story?"

Since I hadn't prepped a fake story, I settled for an abbreviated version of the truth. "I grew up in San Borromeo, did some work in Silicon Valley, and then I came home to open Beanblossom's Tea and Tarot."

"I'm the Tarot," Hyperion said modestly.

She pressed her hands together and raised them, prayerlike, to her lips. "Tea shop? Do you by any chance cater?"

"We do."

Layla grasped my hands. "I know it's awfully short notice, but my caterers came down with pink eye."

Yikes. "All of them?" I didn't even want to imagine pink eye in our tearoom.

"You know how contagious it is," she said. "And I've got an event on Saturday. Is there any chance you can step in? It's an outdoor event for fifty. Please, please, please?"

I didn't want to look too eager, but it might be a perfect opportunity for snooping. "I don't—"

"Yes," Hyperion said. "She means yes."

I shot him a look. "I was going to say I don't think we have any events planned for that day," I said. "But I'll check my calendar."

She scavenged through her chic red purse and handed me a card. "Please let me know as soon as you can."

"I'll call you tomorrow," I said.

James handed me a glass, half full of deep, red wine.

"Thank you," she said. "You're a lifesaver."

I hadn't agreed yet. Clearly, Hyperion wasn't the only one suffering an excess of confidence.

Layla looked around. "Where's Deva?"

"She, er, got some bad news," James said. "One of our customers, a man she was seeing, was killed."

Layla gasped. "Not Whitmore?"

"You knew him?" I asked.

"Barely. But poor Deva. And Beatrice – what must she be going through?"

"Beatrice?" I asked.

"Whitmore's ex-wife, Beatrice Carson." Layla touched her husband's sleeve. "Did Deva go home?"

James angled his head toward the narrow hallway, and the restroom sign above it.

"I'd better see how she's doing," Layla said. "Excuse me." She hurried off.

People trickled into the wine tasting, and James moved along the bar to schmooze. Layla returned. Deva did not. James's wife whisked behind the bar. She got busy pouring and talking up the wines, and our chance for interrogations were lost.

"You know very well you've got nothing going on Saturday," Hyperion hissed in my ear.

"It never pays to look easy."

"What idiot told you that? And why are you looking like your imaginary dog died? We have successfully infiltrated a wine cabal and scored new business for Beanblossom's."

I lifted a brow. "Cabal?"

"It could be." He winked over my left shoulder.

I turned to see a gorgeous red-haired man in an Armani suit leaning against the bar. "Go ahead." I sighed. "You will anyway."

"Hold this." Hyperion handed me his empty glass and wound toward the bar.

I stared glumly after him. I couldn't pretend ignorance about the mysterious blonde at the wine shop. I'd have to tell the police.

Worse, I'd have to tell Razzzor I'd done it.

CHAPTER 4

An insufferably smug Hyperion escorted me across the darkened sidewalk to his Jeep. He'd taken his sweet time getting the redhead's number, I thought sourly.

"We need to hunt the Badger." He unlocked my door and walked around to the other side of his car.

"Madge Badger? We could do that. Or we could just tell the police what we know. And what about the ex-wife, Beatrice?"

Hyperion paused, halfway in the car. "Tell Ton— the police. Right. The police. We should definitely do that. Why don't I do that? I know how busy you'll be tomorrow."

"You don't need to," I said innocently. "Tea and Tarot is closed on Mondays. I can go to the police station tomorrow. I know you've got your online classes."

He got inside the Jeep and shut the door. "Didn't you say you were going to spend Monday creating Tarot-themed tea blends?"

My eyes narrowed. I had no memory of that promise. "No." I buckled my seatbelt.

"I'm certain you did. We had a long conversation about the marketing opportunity you're missing. Tea and Tarot without Tarot tea? Think of all the sales you could make to my Tarot peeps."

"But–"

He started the Jeep. "Say no more. I'll brew up some ideas for you tonight, so you can work on them tomorrow. Pun intended." We pulled from the curb.

"What do you know about blending tea?" I asked. "No offense."

"I know that different herbs correspond with various magical properties. I'll give you the theme of each card – we'll stick with the Major Arcana, that's 22 cards. You can use herbs that correspond to the magical theme."

Twenty-two teas? That was a lot of recipes. "That–"

"Will tragically keep you busy all day. 'Uneasy lies the head that wears a crown,' and all that jazz. So, *I'll* go to the police station tomorrow. Now, now, you don't have to thank me. We're partners."

"Thanks, *partner*," I said.

"No problem," he said. "Besides, you don't want to look too desperate."

I *might look desperate? Pot. Kettle. Black.* "Desperate for what?"

"Desperate to clear your name," he finished.

"Hm." My phone rang in my purse, and I dug it free. Razzzor's name flashed on the screen. "It's Razzzor."

"So you *say.*"

I clapped the phone to my ear. "Hi, Razzzor. What's going on?"

"What were you doing at the wine tasting?"

"How–? Were you stalking Deva again? You've got to cut that out."

"I wasn't stalking Deva. I was stalking you."

"You can't be serious." I twisted in my seat. Two low headlights tailed behind us.

Damn. He was serious.

"Just kidding," he continued. "I planned on going to the wine tasting myself. But then I saw you and your friend go inside and thought I'd spare myself the torture. Was that Hyperion?"

I glanced across the seat at him. "Yes."

"He really does look like a male model. So, what happened?"

"Nothing happened. Deva got upset when she heard about Whitmore, went to the lady's room, and didn't come back. Her boss and his wife ended up running the tasting." I hesitated. "Razzzor, I think I have to tell the police about Deva. I've seen her now–"

"You can't."

"Why not?"

"Because you *can't.*"

"I *can't* withhold evidence."

"But there's a direct line from Deva to me," he said. "The cops will never believe I didn't recognize her. We used to date."

"Then you go to the police."

"You're a laugh riot," he said. "Look, she'll probably go to the police eventually on her own. Let's just give this a little more time."

"Time for what?"

"I've been learning all sorts of things online," he said darkly.

"Online? Tell me you didn't hack into the police department's computers."

"Why would I? You think *they* know anything? Look, all I want is one day. Is that too much to ask?"

It wasn't. Not for a friend who'd once risked jailtime for me. But what was he up to? Because Razzzor online and not gaming was... terrifying. "No," I said, grudging.

"You won't hold off?" His voice zinged up an octave.

"I mean, no, it's not too much to ask. We'll wait another day." I really hoped I wasn't going to regret this.

"Thanks."

"If you're not hacking anyone, what have you found online?"

"I never said I wasn't hacking *anyone*. Oh, and your friend's right brake light is out."

"Stop. Just stop." I looked over my shoulder. Behind us, Razzzor's Tesla turned a corner and zipped up a hill. "And you shouldn't talk and drive."

But he'd already hung up.

"What was that about waiting another day?" Hyperion asked.

"You can't go to the police station tomorrow."

"Why not?"

"Because... I was the one who saw Deva outside the wine store when that guy was killed. Now that I've met her in person, I can't pretend I don't know who she is. If I don't go to the police myself, it will look suspicious."

He slumped in his seat. "You're right. Oh, well. I had happy hour with the boys planned for tomorrow anyway. Knowing them, it will be a long hour."

"And I'll be too busy tomorrow creating tea recipes. We'll have to wait until at least Tuesday."

He straightened, and a corner of his mouth slanted upward. "Yes, *we* will."

*****

Hyperion did *not* send me a list of herbal symbolism for the Tarot teas. But serving Tarot teas wasn't a bad idea. Finding a list of herbs associated with different Tarot cards was easy. Crafting a decent tea out of them was a different story.

I rapped my pen on my dining room table and stared at my computer screen. Then I stared out the French doors at my herb garden.

It was another gorgeous California summer day. Monday morning sunlight streamed through the dogwood leaves. A sapphire Jay hopped onto my porch railing. Beanblossom's was closed for the day. I really should be outside taking advantage of California life.

But work first.

The first card in the deck, The Fool, was about optimism and taking chances. I wanted some good-mood herbs and pops of color for The Fool card.

I made notes about herbs that might work well together. Lemon balm was like an emotional cleanse – even its flavor was cheerful. Rose is supposed to soften the heart, and rose hips would provide color. Oat straw would work well with the lemon balm, and it was supposed to ease anxiety...

I caught myself staring at my computer again. Was Razzzor playing the fool?

And what about that bike messenger? Was he an innocent bystander?

I ran a web search for bike messenger firms in the area and found the logo the guy had been wearing.

I drummed my fingers on the blue tablecloth.

Last night's foray into private investigating had made things more complicated. But my instincts had been right. Razzzor had overcome his dread of crowds to play detective. That was big.

Yes, I'd been playing detective too, so I was a big fat hypocrite.

But.

Was this just about Razzzor's loathing of authority? Or was he in over his head with Deva?

My ex-boss was a genius at a lot of things. Relationships weren't one of them.

I typed Beatrice Carson's name into my browser. She owned a PR firm in San Borromeo. Her social media accounts were packed with glamour shots at swank parties. If she'd been mad at her ex-husband, it looked like she'd moved on.

My phone rang on the dining table. I snatched it up without checking the number.

"Hello?"

"Abigail?" a woman asked.

"Yes?" I said. I was *so* fed up with telemarketers.

"Hi," a bright voice said. "It's Susan."

I wracked my brains. "Susan who?"

"Susan Wilkinson," she said.

"Oh." *Uh, oh*. Susan was a local reporter. It was a good bet she wasn't calling to do a feature article on Beanblossom's. "Hi."

She laughed. "Don't sound so enthusiastic. I hear you discovered Whitmore Carson's body. What can you tell me?"

"I don't think I'm supposed to say anything."

"What about Razzzor? I hear he was there too. Can you get me an interview?"

"No," I said. "I'm not his executive assistant anymore." But my heart skipped an unpleasant beat. Dammit. How did she know all this?

"Are you dating?"

My face warmed. "No, we're friends."

"That's what they all say. Okay, what were you two doing at the Wine Merchants?"

"I like wine."

"Here's the thing. I heard that Razzzor's ex was dating Whitmore Carson. The murdered man. Who you both found."

"Are you sure that's a *who* and not a *whom*?"

"There's nothing less attractive than a pedant. Now about Deva Belvin, is it true she and Razzzor once dated?"

"Where'd you hear that?"

"I don't reveal my sources." She laughed. "Just kidding. It's going to be in the afternoon paper. Deva told me. I ran into her at the police station. She seems to think Razzzor killed the man. What do you think?"

Deva had ratted out *Razzzor?* I knew I should have gone to the station this morning. "I think it's ridiculous. Goodbye." I hung up.

How could I have been so stupid? How could Deva be so stupid? She'd dated Razzzor. Deva had to know he wasn't capable of murder.

I blew out my breath. In fairness, no she didn't. We learned unpleasant truths about people we'd thought we loved all the time.

On the plus side, Razzzor was right about Deva coming forward. On the minus side, if she'd fingered Razzzor to the press, she'd no doubt told the cops as well.

Rising, I scraped back my chair, and paced between the table and my living room couch. I had to do something.

The bike messenger. I knew what company he worked for. All I had to do was find out who'd delivered a message to the Wine Merchants that night.

Easy peasy.

*****

The messenger service worked out of a nondescript office tucked against the San Borromeo hillside. I circled the narrow streets, looking for parking, and ended up parked outside a wine bar only a block away.

Stepping from my car, I smoothed the front of my shirt. Out of the corner of my eyes, I saw a banana-colored surfboard swivel toward me. I ducked, narrowly avoiding getting smacked on the head. *Whew. Close one.* I sidestepped and promptly barked my shin on a brick planter.

The surfer, board on his head, ambled past. "Whoops. Careful."

Smothering a prodigious amount of curses (I may have read a few pages in Hyperion's word-of-the-day calendar too), I adjusted my briefcase-like purse. I hurried up the street and pushed open the dirty, glass door.

A bored-looking, purple-haired woman looked up and cracked her gum. "Can I help you?"

"I hope so. I ordered a delivery to be made to the Wine Merchants, here in San Borromeo, on Saturday. I don't know if you heard, but there was some, er, police action there. I just wanted to know if the delivery was made."

"Name?"

"Carson Whitmore."

"I meant your name."

"Oh. Abigail Beanblossom."

She peered at her computer. "I don't see any Abigail Beanblossoms."

"Are you sure? I paid the bill."

"Have you got your receipt?"

"No, I forgot it."

"Without your receipt, I can't help you."

I smiled. "But you must have some record of the location." I rattled off the address.

"Without your receipt, I can't help you."

My smile faltered. "What about searching by day?"

"Without your receipt—"

My head throbbed. "You can't help me." I started to turn toward the door. "What about the bike messenger? He was a young guy, brown hair—"

"Without your receipt—"

Gah! "Got it." Defeated, I left the office. Maybe Hyperion would know how to fake a receipt.

I wandered back to my hatchback.

"Abigail?" a familiar voice called, and I turned.

Gramps and Tomas ambled up the brick sidewalk in their rumpled jackets – Gramps was in his khaki and Tomas wore a local baseball team's orange and black.

"What are you doing here?" Gramps asked.

"Failing," I said.

"I find that hard to believe." Gramps sat on the edge of a brick planter filled with impatiens. "What's going on?"

I recounted my tale. "I just wanted to find out who the delivery guy was and what he saw," I finished.

"I can find out who made that delivery," Tomas said.

Gramps snorted. "How?"

"I once killed a man with a bottlecap." He huffed. "Do you really think I couldn't get information from a bureaucrat?"

"Bureaucrats are a lot tougher than enemy combatants," Gramps said.

"And I used to be a lawyer," Tomas said.

"Used to be?" Gramps asked. "I thought you were still paying your bar dues?"

"You know what I mean," Tomas said.

"I'll bet you can't get that information," Gramps said.

"I'll bet you manage my salsa stand at the next farmers' market that I can."

"And if I win, you manage my horseradish stall?"

"Deal."

The two men shook hands.

Tomas creaked down the street.

"What just happened?" I asked.

"Tomas is going to get the name of that delivery man or manage my stall at the next farmers' market."

"There's no way. The woman at the messenger company is going to be totally suspicious. I just asked her about him." And Tomas didn't have a receipt.

He was good, but even he couldn't fake one of those between here and the messenger office.

"Then I win." Gramps rubbed his beefy hands together, gleeful.

We made small talk and waited for Tomas. We'd just reached the what-do-you-want-for-next-week's-dinner stage, when a familiar voice hailed us.

"Abigail?" Hyperion strode up the walk in skinny khakis and a brick-red shirt, open at the collar. "Don't you think you're getting a teensy bit clingy? This is a boys-only happy hour. Where's Tomas?"

"Wait," I said. "You're doing happy hour with Tomas and my grandfather?"

"I *told* you we were. And shouldn't you be working on those tea recipes?"

"Actually, I do have an idea for—"

"Then why are you here?" he said.

"Ah. Um. Just, you know—"

"Got it!" Tomas ambled to us. "And the answer is, no one. And you're managing my salsa stall, Beanblossom."

"*No one* isn't an answer," Gramps said. "You didn't get the guy's name."

"It's no one," Tomas said, "because no one from that company had a delivery to that wine store. Ever."

"You said you'd find out who made the delivery," Gramps said. "And you didn't."

"Because no one made the delivery," Tomas said. "It's not my fault if Abigail was wrong."

"I wasn't!"

"Wait, wait, wait," Hyperion lifted one brown boat shoe and scratched his bare ankle. "Are you talking about the bicycle messenger from the wine shop murder?"

"No bicycle messenger from that shop delivered to the Wine Merchants," Tomas said.

"But I saw one," I said. "He was wearing their uniform, with their logo." Could he have stolen a uniform? But that spoke of premeditation. Who *was* this guy?

"You're investigating without me?" Hyperion sputtered.

"It's my day off."

"All right." He folded his arms, managing not to wrinkle his designer shirt. "There's only one answer."

"A fake uniform?" Or he really did work for the messenger company and was committing murder on his own time. Assuming Deva hadn't done it.

"You're working for me now on this case," Hyperion said. "It's obvious you're too involved. You're not thinking straight. You need someone with a clear head to take charge."

"Oh, do I?"

"And what we need," Hyperion continued, "is for you to conduct a stakeout."

Tomas rubbed his chin. "I see where you're going with this. The messengers will all have to return to base at some point. If Abigail can identify the man she saw, we can talk to him."

"You just don't want me at your happy hour," I said.

"I'm not running your salsa stand," Gramps said.

"You didn't kill anyone at that office with a bottlecap, did you?" Hyperion asked.

"Of course not," Tomas said. "I didn't have any."

CHAPTER 5

Since I'm such a lucky and persuasive person, I wound up watching the messenger service alone, sitting on the planter box. And not because I was taking orders from Hyperion. I was here because I didn't have anything better to do.

Besides, four people hanging around on a street corner would look weird.

An hour later, Hyperion strode down the sidewalk toward me. He carried a bottle wrapped in brown paper beneath one arm.

"A good supervisor checks in to see how their subordinate is doing on a new task," he said.

"You're not my supervisor. Where are Gramps and Tomas?"

"They said they had better things to do than cool their bums playing detective."

That was just depressing. Why did those two have an active social life tonight when I had bupkis?

I shifted on the bricks and nodded to the bottle. "Is that wine? I thought you were a tequila guy."

"I am a tequila guy, but our current mystery—"

"Current?" How many murders was he planning to investigate?

"—is wine themed," he continued. "Research was in order. While you were sitting around smelling the roses—"

"Impatiens," I said, testy. "And it's a stakeout, not sitting around."

"While you were smelling the random collection of flowers," he corrected, "I was gathering deep background knowledge on our victim and suspects at a wine bar."

"A wine bar? I thought you were going to introduce them to the wide world of tequila?"

"They have a great happy hour," he said defensively. "Do you want to know what we learned or not?"

"We?"

"Those two old guys are weirdly good at getting people to talk."

"Waitresses find them charming."

"So. Whitmore Carson was well liked in the San Borromeo wine community. His partner, Madge, was less so. Strong women are treated so unfairly in the business world."

I shifted on the planter. The bricks were cold. "Why wasn't she liked?"

"Strong personality. It was all vague. No tales of embezzlement, abduction, or occult rituals, which is disappointing, but that's life. Anyway, Deva is the distributor to our happy hour wine bar."

"She is?" Wow. Hyperion really was good at this. He and that detective might make a great pair.

He pulled out a bottle of Razzzor's wine.

I gaped, horrified. "Hyperion. That's…"

"Brilliant detecting?"

"Over a thousand dollars."

"It's okay. I charged it. Let's hope your imaginary friend pays me back before the bill comes due. Or should I take it back?"

"Let me call him." I pulled my phone from my bag.

"Hey, is that the messenger?" Hyperion pointed at a messenger entering the office across the street.

"No. Our suspect doesn't have a beard." I dialed Razzzor.

"Abigail, what's going on?" Razzzor asked.

"Hyperion bought a bottle of your wine from a local bar. Deva was the distributor. He thought you could test it and let us know if it's for real or not."

"It turns out I don't need to. I've recently deduced the fake labels are all dated 2015. The fakes also spell out the word *Saint* instead of using the abbreviation, *St.*"

"You *have* been investigating. Gimme." I took the bottle from Hyperion and studied the label. "It's a fake."

"You just want me to return it, instead of your imaginary friend reimbursing me." Hyperion snatched the bottle from my hands and clutched it to his chest.

"Hyperion will return the bottle," I said.

"No," Razzzor said, "don't do that. I don't want someone buying an expensive bottle of wine that's no good. I'll repay your friend. Er, does he take Bitcoin?"

"Do you take Bitcoin?" I asked Hyperion.

He rolled his eyes. "Cash only," he bellowed toward the phone.

"He'd prefer cash," I told Razzzor.

"Cash?" Razzzor paused. "Do people still use cash?"

"Yes," I said. "They do." *Sheesh.*

"I don't know, Abigail. This guy sounds a little off."

"It's not off. It's just cash."

"Fine," Razzzor grumbled. "I'll find some cash *somewhere* and bring it by your place later."

"Look." Hyperion nudged my shoulder. "Is that the guy?"

I glanced at the messenger entering the office. "That's a woman."

Hyperion squinted. "Are you sure?"

"It's not the guy."

"What guy?" Razzzor asked.

"We found the messenger company for that man who stopped by the Wine Merchants. Now we're trying to identify the messenger."

"You are? Abigail… Look, I appreciate you coming on the stakeout with me. But I didn't think anyone would get killed. You don't need to do any more."

"Don't worry," I said. "Hyperion's here."

"Didn't he once chain himself to a pier dressed like Oscar Wilde?" he asked doubtfully.

Changing the subject. "Have you talked to the police about Deva?"

Razzzor sighed. "Not yet."

"A reporter called. She told me Deva gave a statement to the police, and she mentioned you."

"That's a relief."

"You don't understand—"

"Oooh!" Hyperion grabbed my arm. "Is that him?"

I looked across the street, and my heart thumped. A tanned man with cropped brown hair and massive thighs emerged from the messenger's office pushing a bike. He looked to be in his mid-twenties. He was also roughly the size and shape of the man we'd seen at the Wine Merchants.

"It looks like him," I said. "Razzzor, I've got to go. Call me later." I hung up and dropped my phone in my bag.

This stupid stakeout had paid off. I stood and stepped into the street.

One of those bicycle party wagons full of drinkers swerved in front of me. My life flashed before my eyes. It was depressingly short.

Hyperion grabbed my elbow, yanking me onto the sidewalk.

A dozen girls in bathing suits jeered and peddled on.

"Don't drink and peddle!" Hyperion shook his fist at them.

I ordered my heart to return to its normal place in my chest and looked around. The bike messenger had vanished. "Where'd he go?"

Hyperion cursed. "Tourists."

"At least we know what time the messengers return to roost." I glanced at my watch.

"That's right," he said. "Think positive. And get moving on those Tarot teas you've been putting off all afternoon. I know delaying tactics when I see them."

I blew out my breath. It wasn't as if the bike messenger was going to return today, and I was all out of bad ideas. I might as well get back to the business that actually paid my rent.

"Want me to drop you at the tearoom?" he asked.

"No, thanks. I've got my car."

He nodded. "Then *sayonara*. And I'm part-Japanese, so that wasn't cultural appropriation." Hyperion strode down the street.

I returned to our tearoom. Beanblossom's had a bigger and more varied supply of herbs than my cupboard. I grew a lot in my garden, but those herbs were mainly for personal use. I'd had to outsource herbs for the tea blends we sold.

At the white front counter, I played with proportions and herbs for my "Fool" tea. The trick was the lavender. I loved its purple color and relaxing qualities. But too much, and it tasted like soap. I experimented with different blends until I was satisfied and poured the mix into a canister.

"One Tarot tea down. Twenty-one to go," I said to no one. Not that talking to myself was weird or anything. Since I was alone, who *else* was I going to talk to?

I drove home in misty twilight. We should probably come up with branded labels for the Tarot tea blends. Maybe I could find some stock Tarot images?

I parked in my driveway. Music roared from Brik's house, my hatchback shimmying to the beat.

A party on a Monday? I scowled at his modern, blue-painted two story. His driveway was filled with cars, as was the street. For a moment, I envied his elderly neighbors on the other side. They were partially deaf.

I should have brought some of that Fool tea home to improve my mood. But I did have some nice, calming chamomile in the garden.

Trudging into my bungalow, I kicked off my sandals and grabbed a pair of scissors. I took a deep, cleansing breath, which didn't do a damn bit of good. Then, I unlatched the French doors and walked outside, barefoot.

The redwood fence, covered in jasmine, only slightly muffled the music and laughter from next door. I walked down the garden path and tried to focus on the tanbark pressing into the soles of my feet. Solar lights illuminated the raised beds of herbs.

I paused and frowned at an empty spot between two small but lush bushes of white flowers. I looked left. Looked right.

I'd planted three chamomile plants. What had happened to the third?

I knelt, squinting in the dim light. Short stumps of evenly cut chamomile plant stuck woefully from the soil.

"Are you kidding me?" I shouted and didn't worry about my neighbors hearing. No one could hear me over the racket from Brik's house. I stood and swore some more.

Animals hadn't done this. The cuts were uniform, the stalks all clipped a neat one inch from the ground. Someone had stolen my chamomile.

I warred between anger and low-level anxiety. Stealing herbs wasn't exactly a violent crime. It was just super, super irritating.

And I couldn't imagine my neighbors stealing from me. They knew all they had to do was ask, and I'd give them what they needed.

But Brik had a random crew of guests flowing in and out of his house. One could have wandered into my yard by mistake and then decided to take advantage.

In fact, it was the only answer that made sense. They probably thought chamomile would make a nice cocktail garnish.

I returned inside, put on my sandals, and stormed to Brik's house. His door was open, as was his habit during his bacchanals.

I pushed through a throng of construction workers and barefoot women in business suits. A breeze flowed through the open doors at the rear of the house. I wound toward the wall of glass.

"Abigail! Abs! Abby, Abby, Abby!" Hyperion apparated at my elbow. "What are you doing here? Did you finish the Tarot tea?"

"Actually," I shouted, "yes. We now have Fool tea."

"Good job. Twenty-one more to go. Tequila?" He raised a shot glass.

"No thanks." I scanned the kitchen bar for chamomile but didn't see any traces of the herb. "Have you seen Brik?"

He motioned with the shot glass toward the backyard.

"Thanks." I made my way onto his new wood patio. Wide steps cascaded down to a concrete deck surrounded by planter boxes. It was chic and minimalist and went against everything I stood for. But I had to admit, it looked pretty cool.

People lounged in chairs beneath the pergola. Delicious smells wafted from the massive barbecue. I headed in that direction.

Brik turned and smiled warily. "Abigail. This is a surprise. Can I get you a burger?" He was dressed in jeans and a white t-shirt. It could have been painted on his well-built form.

I remembered my indignation and tried not to drool. "Someone was in my garden earlier."

He laid down the spatula, and his bronzed brow creased with concern. "Was anything stolen?"

"Yes. Chamomile."

His face screwed up in bemusement. Even looking puzzled he was sexy. I really hated that.

Really.

"You have... a plant thief?" he asked.

I tore my gaze from his bulging biceps. "An herb thief."

He rolled his eyes. "Oh, in that case—"

"The point," I said, "is they were definitely cut and not eaten, and... Have you seen anyone suspicious?"

He folded his arms. "You mean, has someone from my party raided your garden? Some of the bartenders can get a little overzealous. But no one's interested in your herbs."

My face warmed. "I'm not accusing anyone."

Okay, I kind of was.

I cleared my throat. "I'm only saying, someone's been in my yard. It's unnerving. That yard is my space."

He grimaced. "Sorry. I get it. Have you thought of installing cameras?"

"Who can afford that?"

"The price has come down. I can help you install them if you want."

"Thanks," I said. "I'll think about it."

"Look, I'll keep an eye out, and I'll let my guests know you've been having problems."

"I'd appreciate it."

In the grand scheme of things, a plant thief was small potatoes. There were worse things in the world. Like murder. But the theft seemed like an omen.

A bad one.

*****

I slept badly that night, bolting up like a prairie dog every time a squirrel ran across my roof.

The next morning, I got to the tearoom bleary eyed and in a foul mood. But I faked cheerfulness and hoped none of the staff noticed my fraud.

Tuesdays weren't super busy. Between our morning seatings, I called Layla Zimmer. The two of us discussed the menu for her tea party. We agreed on elderflower rhubarb fairy cakes. I was both excited and nervous, because the four tiers would be decorated with edible flowers. Done right, they looked as magical as they tasted. Plus, rhubarb was in season. I also had elderflowers in my garden and was looking forward to using them for the cordial.

But the fairy cakes were also kind of complicated. I hoped I wasn't biting off more than I could chew.

No sooner had I hung up, then the phone in my apron rang. I checked the number. *Razzzor.*

Breathlessly, I hurried into the kitchen and took the call.

"Hey, what's going on?" I asked.

"I had a long talk with Detective Chase this morning," he said. "I told them I'd recognized Deva outside the Wine Merchants. I also told them you didn't know anything about her."

That wasn't quite true. I hadn't known anything about her at the *time*. "Thanks."

Hyperion wandered into the kitchen and perused a tray of baked goods. He plucked a blueberry lavender scone from the tray and munched it thoughtfully. A crumb dropped to the front of his blue-and-white shirt and clung there.

"At any rate," Razzzor said. "you're out of it now."

"Not entirely." I rubbed at a spot on the linoleum floor with my toe. "I'm catering an event for Layla Zimmer this weekend."

Hyperion frowned.

"It just happened," I said and brushed the crumb from Hyperion's button-up shirt. "She needed a caterer, so I thought—"

"You'd take the opportunity to poke around," Razzzor finished. "Abigail, I can't come along to keep — to help. I wasn't invited. And I'm guessing caterers can't bring plus ones."

Only if he wanted to be part of the staff. And as much as I loved Razzzor, the thought of him serving tea and cake made me shudder.

"Look," I said. "It's no big deal. I'll do the job, keep my ears to the ground, and see what happens. Odds are, nothing will."

He laughed hollowly. "Where you're involved?" He paused. "Will Deva be there?"

"I don't know. I have the number of guests, but not their names."

"Okay. Be careful."

I crossed my fingers. "I'm always careful."

We said our goodbyes and hung up.

Hyperion threw the remains of his scone at me.

"Hey!" I caught it in one hand and took a bite. "Don't waste food."

"*I'm* going to cater? We're Tea and *Tarot*. What am I? Chopped liver?"

"She didn't ask about Tarot readings."

"Why would she have to? We were together when Layla asked if we could cater. Are you trying to protect me or something?"

"No, I'm trying to protect Razzzor. Deva pointed the finger straight at him. I can just imagine how his talk with Detective Chase went—"

"Whoa. He spoke to Tony? Did he say anything about me?"

"Why would Razzzor say anything about you?" I leaned against the kitchen's metal counter.

"Not Razzzor. Tony."

"The point is, Razzzor won't defend himself. He thinks anyone in government is out to get him, and he gets all stiff and weird. You should have seen him around the OSHA inspectors."

"Okay, I get that your imaginary friend is a loon. What I don't understand is why you're sticking your neck out for him."

"Because he's..." Heat rose to my cheeks. "He's a good guy. He did a lot for me. I owe him." But it was more than that. Razzzor and I were alike in a sick, sad, screwed-up childhood way. We got each other. "And besides, you're the one who wants to play junior detective."

"That's different. I'm a nosy optimist. I can't help myself. Causing trouble is a compulsion. What's your excuse?"

"It's only a tea party."

"Tell that to Alice and the Queen of Hearts. And you know what happened to her." He drew a finger across his neck.

"No one was beheaded in *Alice in Wonderland*. Except for some Jacks, I think."

"But the queen *tried*."

"There's no reason for anyone to consider me a threat or to come after me."

I jammed my hands in my apron pockets. So why *had* someone been lurking in my garden? Only to steal herbs? It seemed too coincidental a thief would show up after I'd gotten involved in another murder.

But why would a killer steal herbs, and draw attention to the fact he'd been lurking in my yard?

A Tarot reader named Sierra leaned into the kitchen. "Abigail? There's someone here looking for you."

"For me?" I straightened off the counter. "Who is it?"

"She says her name is Madge. And as an FYI, the lady's got a dark vibe. No offense if she's a friend of yours."

Hyperion and I glanced at each other.

"Madge Badger?" I asked.

She nodded.

"I'll be right there," I said. "Thanks."

Hyperion examined his manicure. "I'm sure there's a totally innocent reason a murdered man's business partner wants to see you."

I swallowed. "So am I."

CHAPTER 6

Hyperion and I strode into the tearoom. Teacups clinked on saucers. Tarot readers and clients murmured in low voices.

A tall, elegant woman with mid-length, honey-colored hair stood beside the hostess stand. She wore a linen jacket and matching slacks that managed not to have a single wrinkle. Around her neck hung a deep brown silk scarf.

"Hi," I said, extending my hand. "I'm Abigail Beanblossom. This is my business partner, Hyperion Night."

Madge shook our hands, her expression uncertain. "This is a private matter. Abigail, may we speak alone?"

"Why don't you take my office?" Hyperion asked, surprising me. "I'll show you the way," he said to Madge.

The three of us walked through the tearoom and to his small office. Twinkle lights blinked, framing its door.

He settled Madge in a red velvet chair, and then eased out the door, closing it behind him. It showed a suspicious amount of tact. But I guessed he figured I'd tell him everything anyway.

Or he'd bugged his own office.

She glanced at the cards on the round table.

"Hyperion's the Tarot side of the business." I sat across from her. "You're not allergic to cats, are you?" I tilted my head toward Bastet. The cat lay coiled on the altar and purred loudly.

"No," she said. "Cats are fine."

"What can I do for you?"

Bastet flicked his striped tail.

"I learned from a reporter that you found my partner's body – Whitmore Carson."

I scowled. Susan was such a blabbermouth. See if I ever trusted her with confidential information. "Your partner?" I said, pretending ignorance.

"At the Wine Merchants." She flushed. "He was actually more than a business partner."

More than? Since he'd been dating Deva, I hoped that meant Whitmore and Madge had just been good friends.

"I know I'm torturing myself and shouldn't," she said, "but can you tell me what you saw? What happened?"

"I'm sorry for your loss." My voice dropped, my insides knotting. "But I don't know what happened to Whitmore. A friend and I walked into the store, and there was no one behind the counter, so—"

"Why didn't you leave when you saw the shop was empty?"

"I– I'm not sure. Something seemed off. So we walked behind the counter, to the office, and that's when we saw... Whitmore."

Her breath hitched. "Did you try to revive him?"

"He was gone," I said. "We called nine-one-one, and then we waited with him. I'm sorry."

Madge blinked rapidly and stared at Bastet.

I'd been shocked and horrified when we'd found the body. But after that, I'd mainly been worried for Razzzor. Madge's grief changed that, and the awfulness of Whitmore's death hit me again.

"Did anything seem out of order?" she asked.

"Out of order? You mean, did it look like there'd been a struggle? No. The office looked okay." Then what was still bugging me about that scene?

Hyperion bustled into the room carrying a tea tray. "I thought you ladies would like refreshments. Is Earl Gray all right?"

"It's fine." Madge's smile trembled as she looked up at him. "Thank you."

He fussed about the table and backed from the room.

"You were saying?" I prompted. "About the office at the Wine Merchants?"

"Oh." She sipped her tea, keeping her head bent toward the cup. "The police moved all sorts of things. The petty cash was gone."

"A robbery?"

"That's what the police seem to think. But... the detectives took Whitmore's calendar."

Why confiscate his calendar if they were sure it had been a robbery gone bad?

She shook herself and set the cup on the red velvet tablecloth. "I don't know what they expect to find. I told them he never kept anything important at the shop." She smiled sadly. "We were all about the wine." But something in her tone struck a false note.

"Did he have any enemies?" I tugged on the hem of my blouse.

Her smile flattened. "His ex-wife. She hated him."

"Oh?"

"You know how it can be when relationships go bad," she said vaguely.

Not lately. I was in an epic relationship dry spell. "Do you know Deva Belvin?"

"The wine distributor? A bit."

"Is she your main distributor?"

Madge's brow furrowed. "She doesn't sell us wine at all. Why?"

That explained why Deva hadn't carried any when she'd walked into the

Wine Merchants. "Ah... I saw her leaving your wine shop right before we went inside that night. I believe she's given a statement to the police about her visit." Did Madge not know Whitmore and Deva had been seeing each other? But as a partner in the business, surely she'd know whether or not Deva was selling them wine.

"I don't know, but we haven't bought any wine from Zimmerland in years."

"Zimmerland?"

"The name of the distributor Deva works for. Their wine is excellent and expensive, but the deliveries were never that reliable."

She sipped tea, set the cup on the table. "Did he look...? Was it quick, do you think?"

I lowered my head, studying her. "I'm sure it was." But the only thing I was sure of was Madge had come here to get info. But what was she really after?

"That's what the police said. A blow to the head from behind. Whitmore didn't know what hit him."

Interesting. He must have trusted whoever had done it enough to turn his back on the person.

"He was hit with the bronze statue he kept on his desk," she offered, "of a woman in a vineyard. It seems... prophetic, somehow."

"Prophetic?"

She shook her head, her earrings swinging. "Nothing. I'm talking nonsense. But the police took the statue too. Whitmore didn't say anything to you when you found him?"

"No," I said. "Like I said, he was gone by the time we got to him."

She sank back against the chair. "Oh."

It was time to turn this around. "Was Whitmore, er, seeing anyone?"

"Yes, me. We were a couple."

Oh boy. "Did he have any appointments that evening?" I asked.

"Not that I know of. He..." Her brow furrowed.

"He what?"

She stood and grabbed her purse off the carpeted floor. "I've taken up enough of your time. How much do I owe you for the tea?"

"It's on the house," I said.

She hurried from the office.

I followed her through the tearoom and to the front door. She strode down the sidewalk and vanished around a corner.

"Interesting," Hyperion said at my ear, and I jumped. "She took off right after you confirmed he hadn't said anything to you. Think she was worried she hadn't quite killed him enough?"

"You were eavesdropping?" I let the door close.

"It *is* my office. Besides, you didn't think I'd leave you alone with a potential killer? She could be lying in wait to strangle you with that awful brown scarf."

"Thanks for planting that in my head."

He patted my arm. "I'm here for you."

Life in the tearoom continued without any murders. Hyperion huddled over his office computer. I buzzed from tearoom to kitchen, serving with the staff.

Hyperion was still in his office when I finished cleaning that night.

I turned off the lights in the now-empty tearoom and walked to his office, knocked on the door. The twinkle lights around the door blinked in a chaotic rhythm.

"Hyperion?"

The door popped open, and I sprang away.

He stuck his head through the gap. "Yes?"

"Are you teaching a class tonight?"

"On a Tuesday? No. I was just catching up on some internet stuff. Are you leaving?"

I hitched my bag over my shoulder. "Yes."

"All right. See you tomorrow." He shut the door in my face.

I stared for a long moment at the closed door. What was he doing in there? The twinkle lights winked.

Right. Didn't want, didn't need to know. I walked out the rear door, made sure it was shut. I rattled the doorknob before heading to my car. Twilight darkened the parking lot, and I lengthened my strides.

Hurriedly, I unlocked the Mazda and tossed my purse on the passenger seat.

"Hey," a man said behind me.

I whirled and bumped up against the car, still warm from the sun.

The bike messenger glared down at me. His dayglo uniform was blinding even in the parking lots yellow lights. "You've been following me and Deva."

"No," I said, heart hammering. "Honestly, I–"

"They told me you were asking about me at the shop. I saw you lurking outside."

"That wasn't me following you," I said. "I was *waiting* for you."

He stepped closer, and I pressed against the car. "Well, now I'm waiting for you. How does that feel?"

"Not so good," I admitted. And because fear sometimes made me mouth off, I said, "Especially since you had onions for lunch."

"You think you're funny?"

"I think onions aren't my friend. But since you're here, what did you see when you went into the Wine Merchants that night?"

"Stay out of my business, or I'll make you regret it."

"I already am."

His handsome face contorted. He raised a hand as if to poke me in the chest. "Don't–"

He flew backward and hit the pavement.

Hyperion frowned down at him. "Hasn't anyone told you it isn't nice to pick on women or the height-challenged? She's both. For shame."

My stare ping-ponged between Hyperion and the bike messenger. I hadn't seen... How had Hyperion *done* that?

"And BTW," Hyperion continued, "those bike shorts are not working for you. Though in fairness, they really don't work for anyone."

The bike messenger scrambled to his feet and snarled. "Stop following me." He strode into the twilight.

"How did you...?" I trailed off, hands shaking from the adrenaline dump.

"I followed you. Well, I wasn't going to leave you alone with a killer on your trail. I just had no idea he'd have such amazing thighs. Did you see them?"

"Yes. I mean, no. I mean, thank you. But how did you—?"

"Oh, just a little something I picked up in self-defense class." He brushed the sleeve of his blue-striped shirt. "It's easy when they're not looking."

"But–"

"Now let's not get shirty about the ethics of attacking from the rear. The best defense is a good offense."

I scanned the parking lot. The bike messenger was gone.

Which was when I realized I still didn't know the guy's name. My shoulders sagged.

"I know." Hyperion draped an arm around my shoulder. "Adrenaline releases are the pits. I'll follow you home."

Too rattled to argue, I got into my car and locked the doors. I waited for Hyperion to get inside his Jeep. We caravanned from the parking lot, up the hill, and to my yellow bungalow.

The street was blessedly silent. For once, Brik's house was party free.

Hyperion walked me inside. I followed him through the house as he commented on my discarded gaming controls, on the unmade bed, on the unwashed dishes that were giving me dirty looks.

When he was satisfied no one was lurking under my bed or in my pantry, he left.

I stood inside the open front door and waved while he drove down the street.

But a cold feeling slithered down my spine, as if I was being watched.

CHAPTER 7

I might have screwed the pooch by not getting the bike messenger's name. But he'd mentioned Deva. Maybe she knew the guy's name. I mean, how many bike messengers does a person know?

I found Zimmerland's phone number online and checked my watch. It was nearly seven. They were probably closed. But I dropped onto my couch and called anyway.

"Zimmerland Wines. This is Deva speaking." Laughter and soft voices murmured in the background.

Finally, things were going my way. That should have made me suspicious.

"Hi, Deva. This is Abigail Beanblossom. We met at the wine tasting the other night?"

"What?"

"Abigail Beanblossom? From the wine tasting?"

"Oh, you're not too late. We've just started. Come on down." She hung up.

Puzzled, I stared at my phone and shrugged.

I'd come on down.

Hurriedly, I changed into lightweight, sapphire slacks and a matching silk tank. I'm not a huge fashionista, but I've got my pride. And I figured cheap silk might be more wine-tasting-y than my current work attire. I looked up the address, got in my car and drove to Zimmerland.

The wine distributor looked more like a car dealership than a warehouse. The front was all big, glass windows sparkling with light. The building was new and modern and low-slung. Some creative gardener had formed the word *Zimmerland* out of succulents. They grew from a concrete sign roughly the size of a Buick.

The glass doors slid open automatically, and I walked inside. Men in jeans and white button-up shirts that seemed to glow with wealth mingled with women in cocktail dresses.

Feeling underdressed, I found my way to an up-lit bar made of greenish glass. Deva whizzed behind it, filling wine glasses.

I squeezed between two men who were probably billionaires, braced my elbows on the glass and caught her eye.

She walked up to me and smiled. "Haven't we met?"

"Yes, I'm Abigail. Abigail Beanblossom." *The one who sent you crying to the bathroom?*

The man on my right turned.

I blinked. "Razzzor?"

His thin brows shot upward. "Abby? Thank God."

Deva touched his hand. "I'll let you two catch up and be right back." She drifted to the other end of the bar.

"What are you doing here?" I hissed. *With the woman who narced you out to the cops?* And Razzzor hated crowds.

"I know." He tugged at his collar and grimaced. "It's not my usual scene."

"Do you even have a scene?" Is online gaming a scene?

"Coming here was the only way I could clear things up with Deva."

"And have you?" I asked cautiously.

"Sure. She's a good person."

"That was... quick," I said. "And suspiciously easy since she just accused you of murdering her boyfriend."

"She was upset."

"Razzzor, don't you think it's a little odd—"

Deva appeared with a bottle of red. "Are you drinking whites and reds, or one or the other?"

"Reds," I said.

"Then I'll start your tastings with the Sangiovese. It's lighter than you might expect." She poured me a glass and beamed at Razzzor.

Every alarm bell in my body blared. I liked Razzzor. He was an awesome guy, and super smart. My ex-boss wasn't bad looking either, in a boy-next-door kind of way. And was he using a tanning bed? Because his usual computer screen pallor was gone.

But the point is, he wasn't *that* charming. Not unless you accounted for the invisible dollar signs floating around his head. Why was Deva all smiles now?

"I take it you no longer think Razzzor killed your boyfriend, Whitmore?" I asked.

Razzzor glared.

Deva's mouth opened. Closed. "Oh," she said in a small voice. "You're *that* Abigail. Razzzor told me about you."

I guess I had been kind of abrupt. "Sorry. I'm just... surprised everything's okay now."

"I shouldn't have said that to the police," she said. "Of course Razzzor couldn't have killed anyone. It had to be Deacon."

"Deacon?" I pulled the wine glass closer.

"Deacon Alstatter. I went out with him once, and the guy won't leave me alone. He's been stalking me. Whitmore and I tried to keep it quiet that we were seeing each other, but somehow he found out."

I stiffened, my flesh pebbling. *Hell.* "He wouldn't happen to be a bike messenger, by any chance?"

"Yeah." She took a step backward, her knuckles whitening on the bottle. "How did you know?"

"Lucky guess," I muttered.

Razzzor shot me a look that could have fried a computer circuit.

"Excuse me," Deva said stiffly. "I have other guests." She stalked away.

"Nice going," Razzzor said.

"Because you were doing such a great job pumping her for information?"

He leered. "I wouldn't have minded pumping–"

"Razzzor. Her boyfriend was just murdered. Either you're a rebound, or she's a horrible person."

His face fell.

I felt like a rat.

"You're right," he said. "Sorry. I hate parties like this. I always end up saying or doing something stupid. But Deva and I are just friends."

A friend who'd fingered him to the cops. But there was no sense beating him over the head with that fact.

Yet.

"No, I'm sorry." I gulped the wine and grabbed a palate-cleansing cracker from a bowl. "I shouldn't be so grumpy. Her bike messenger's stalking me now. He surprised me behind the tearoom."

Razzzor's nostrils flared. "Did he hurt you? Are you okay? Why didn't you call?" He jammed the cuffs of his white shirt to his elbows.

"I'm fine. Hyperion showed up and scared him off." I stuffed the cracker into my mouth.

"I never should have brought you on that stakeout." He cursed softly. "It feels like it's happening all over again. I mean, stalkers…"

Unable to meet his eye, I looked down at the bar. "Yeah. There is a certain sense of déjà vu." But at least no one had been killed when I'd picked up my own angry little stalker all those years ago. The stalker Razzzor had helped me deal with when the police could not.

That experience had taught me many things I'd rather not have learned. For example: the first rule of Stalker Club? Don't talk about Stalker Club. If it gets back to the stalker, it only encourages him. I was surprised the police hadn't told Deva that.

I stared harder at the bar. No refill on the glass of wine materialized in front of me.

"What's wrong?" he asked.

"Nothing. I got what I came for – now we know who the wine messenger was. I'm headed home. Have a good night."

I moved through the crowd.

"Wait. You're leaving me? Here?" Razzzor hurried after me.

"You got here on your own."

"I don't like that this bike messenger knows who you are. Odds are, he's a killer. What if he followed you here?"

"On a bike? I think I would have noticed." I'd been checking my rearview mirror like it was a Serena Williams tennis match.

"Let me follow you home anyway. Anything to get out of here."

I stopped and looked up at him. "What about Deva? He's been stalking her too."

"I'll come back here after we get you home."

Of course he would. But his idea wasn't a bad one. And after my encounter in the parking lot earlier, and that feeling of being watched... "Thanks," I said. "I accept."

We walked out the glass doors and into the balmy night.

I paused beside a planter box filled with rosemary. Its scent twined around us.

"Razzzor, there's something I need to ask you."

He cocked his head.

"Did Deva tell you if she saw Whitmore when she stopped by that night?"

"She said she didn't see him and assumed he wasn't there, so she left."

"Did she check the office?" I asked.

"No."

"Okay, so she was close enough to Whitmore to drop by, and to be devastated by his death. But she wasn't close enough to check in the back office when he wasn't there? Doesn't that seem odd?"

His jaw jutted forward. "What are you saying?"

"I'm saying maybe she did discover his body, and left and said nothing. Or maybe..."

He frowned. "She killed him? No. No way."

"Why wouldn't she tell anyone he was dead?"

"Because she didn't see his body."

"We found it, and we didn't have a personal connection to him that would compel us to look."

"No, we were being nosy."

We strode past a red Tesla.

"What normal human being wouldn't call 9-1-1 when discovering someone bleeding on the floor?" I asked.

"She just didn't see him, okay?"

Razzzor stopped beside a blue Tesla that was not his own and blew out his breath. "Look, if she was the killer and wanted a better story, all she had to say was she went in, kissed him hello/goodbye, and ran off to her next appointment. But she didn't. She told the police, and she told me, that as far as she knew, no one was there."

"But the front door was unlocked. That didn't raise any red flags?"

Razzzor scowled. I knew that scowl. It was his stubborn, I-don't-want-to-hear-anymore-so-you-may-as-well-stop-talking scowl.

"I'm only saying, it looks bad."

He relaxed. "You're right. The police are probably asking themselves the same questions. I wonder if Deva has a lawyer? Maybe I should hire a private investigator. Do you know any?"

I clenched my jaw. That had not been where I was going. "My car's over there." I pointed to my Mazda, bringing down the tone of the parking lot amidst the Teslas and other luxury cars.

He walked me to my humble vehicle and gently closed the door after I got inside. I waited until he found his Tesla and drove up behind my spot, then backed out.

He followed me to my house, and I pulled into my tiny driveway. Razzzor parked on the street and met me at my car.

"You don't have to follow me to my door," I said.

His voice lowered. "This is a full-service gig." A warm breeze ruffled his hair, and something seemed to soften in his expression. He reached toward me. "Abigail—"

A door banged, and we started.

The high gate to my side yard creaked open.

The gate I was damn sure I'd locked.

CHAPTER 8

The gate drifted wide. Moonlight cast shadows in the passage between my house and the high, redwood fence.

"Did you leave that open?" Razzzor whispered.

"No." I rarely used that gate. Usually, I walked out my back doors when I was wandering around the garden. And I'd been paranoid when I'd left the house this evening. I'd rattled the gate, and it had been shut fast.

"All right," he said. "Stay here."

"No," I hissed.

He grimaced. "Fine. Then stay behind me." He crept into the darkened passage.

I tiptoed behind him like a cartoon villain. The scent of the jasmine trailing over the fence was heavy and sweet in the warm, night air.

"Duh, duh, duh, DUH, duhhhhhhhh, duh-duh-duh-duh," I whisper-sang. Sue me, I was nervous.

Razzzor glared over his shoulder. His glasses glinted in the full moon.

We passed my hose, on its coil against the wall, and the walkway opened up to the garden. Solar lights illuminated the tanbark paths. The dogwood leaves rustled. A leaf floated downward, landing on the table beneath the tree. The chairs surrounding it seemed eerily human in the cobwebby dark.

Razzzor's shoes crunched down the tanbark path.

I hung back and scanned the garden. A twisted vine hunched, gnomelike, against the fence. But I didn't see any movement, aside from Razzzor.

Beside the fence, he turned and shrugged.

Leaves exploded above him. A shadow catapulted over the fence and into my yard.

I gasped helpfully.

Razzzor leapt to one side and pivoted. In a motion I couldn't quite see, he sent the intruder skidding sideways.

The muscular figure stumbled against one of my raised planting beds.

My neighbor sprang to his feet. Brik lunged, lifting Razzzor off his feet and slamming him against the fence.

"Stop," I shouted, before Brik could pummel him into oblivion. "It's okay."

Brik stepped away, his broad chest heaving.

Razzzor sagged against the fence. He dropped his hands to his sides.

I released a long breath. *Whoa.*

"Who are you?" They asked simultaneously, pointing at each other.

"Razzzor," I said, heart thudding, "this is my neighbor, Brik. Brik, meet Razzzor. My uh..." Ex-boss? Gaming buddy? "...friend."

"I thought I heard someone sneaking around here." Brik crossed his arms, muscles bulging. He studied Razzzor through narrowed eyes.

"So did we," Razzzor said, stepping closer to me. "I mean, her gate was open."

Brik's brows slashed downward. "There *was* someone in here?"

"I don't know," I said. "Maybe. Or maybe the gate just blew open."

"Does it usually blow open?" Razzzor asked, accusing.

"You said someone was in your garden before," Brik said.

"What?" Razzzor turned to me. "You didn't tell me that."

"She keeps a lot to herself," Brik said.

"No kidding." Razzzor adjusted his glasses. "Why don't you have security cameras back here?"

I gripped my arms to keep from throttling them both. They'd been trying to give each other a beatdown a minute ago. Why were they ganging up on me? "Because I don't live in a police state?"

Brik shook his head. "Someone's been in here, and more than once. Exterior cameras just make sense."

"I can't afford a security system."

"They're not that expensive anymore," Razzzor said. "There are all sorts of do-it-yourself systems connected to wi-fi these days."

"I can help you install it," Brik said.

"So can I," Razzzor said.

The men glowered at each other.

"Thank you," I said. "I'm going inside and to bed. See you later." I walked up the porch steps and let myself in through the French doors.

When I turned to lock the glass doors, the men were still talking animatedly. Either they were going to kill each other or become besties. No longer caring, I yanked the curtains shut and went to bed.

*****

I studied our tearoom. It was Wednesday morning, and a smattering of old ladies had claimed white-clothed tables. But there were still a lot of empties.

Hyperion lounged against the white stone counter and yawned. "We need to do more marketing."

Maybe he was right. Online ads? Guest speakers? Free samples?

I straightened. *Free samples.*

"You're right." I strode into the kitchen, Hyperion trailing after me.

Rummaging in the kitchen, I found a hamper.

He watched me fill it with scones, sandwiches, and two coffee travelers filled with tea. I labeled the two containers – a mint and lemongrass blend and an English breakfast.

"Are you catering today?"

"Free samples," I said. "For local businesses. Your idea was genius."

"And the fact you're admitting it fills me with suspicion." He straightened off the door frame. "You're up to something."

I studied the hamper. "You have all sorts of good ideas. Tarot tea was a great idea."

"Which local businesses?"

Repressing a grin, I slid Beanblossom's Tea and Tarot brochures into the hamper. "There's a PR firm not too far–"

"You mean Whitmore's ex-wife, Beatrice Carson's company? I'm coming too."

"To help serve tea?" I asked innocently.

"For sample Tarot readings. Duh. No one can resist a free Tarot reading. I'll do quick, one-card draws." He made a gunslinging motion with his right hand, flicking an invisible Tarot card.

"They may not want their work disrupted."

"Good point. BRB." He hurried from the kitchen and returned a minute later with a fresh Tarot deck. He slid cards behind the wrapped scones. "People can do their own draws. And the cards are tax deductible as a marketing expense."

I checked my watch. "We've got to go now, before the lunch rush." Because in spite of the morning lull, there would be a lunch rush. This was a beach town, after all, and we could always count on the tourist trade.

He pulled a Tarot deck from the pocket of his blazer. "Have Tarot, will travel."

We loaded the hamper in the back of his Jeep and drove the ten blocks to the PR office. It was in a six-story building that looked like the FBI office in DC – grim and ugly. But when it came to office buildings, there weren't a whole lot of choices near the beach.

We found *Carson PR* on the sign board. "Third floor." I started toward the stairs.

Hyperion strode in the opposite direction. He stabbed the button for the elevator with one long finger. "Stairs? What are we? Savages?" he asked haughtily.

I shrugged and rode with him to the third floor. The elevator opened into a wide reception area in mid-century modern blues and oranges.

We strolled to the glass reception desk. Behind it, an elegant woman with gray streaks in her hair spoke to a younger, seated woman wearing a headset.

The woman in the headset looked up. "Can I help you?"

"I'm Abigail, from Beanblossom's Tea and Tarot. We're nearby, and I thought I'd bring by some treats for your office to say 'hello.'"

The older woman beside her smiled. "In other words, free samples. I like the way you think. I'm Beatrice Carson."

We shook hands. Beatrice wore a slim-fitting green suit that looked vintage 1950s. All that was missing was a pillbox hat and gloves.

"And I'm the Tarot side of the business," my partner said. "Hyperion Night."

Beatrice eyed his sleek gray trousers and collar-less white shirt. "If you're giving out free samples, I can do no less. Ellie, why don't you take that hamper into the break room and let the staff know we've got tea?"

"And Tarot," Hyperion caroled. "Cards are in the basket."

Beatrice's smile widened. "This way, please."

She ushered us into a spacious, modern office, and sat behind a desk with a smoked-glass top. Beatrice waved us into two chairs opposite. Windows overlooking the Pacific framed her, the blue of the ocean meeting the paler blue of the sky.

"Tell me more about your tearoom," she said.

"Tea and Tarot room," Hyperion said. "We almost didn't get it off the ground. Just as she was about to start the business, Abigail's ex decided he'd bounce and sue for spousal support."

Beatrice's expression hardened.

I frowned at his lie. If Beatrice learned I'd never been married, this was going to be a short relationship.

"The creep took her for nearly everything," Hyperion continued breathlessly, "but I'd been wanting to open a Tarot room. We realized that if we went in on it together, we could make it work. It turned out to be a genius combination. We've got Tarot readers available for readings at all hours. When the tearoom is closed, I hold classes there, and can serve Abigail's teas."

"Do you sell Tarot-themed teas?" she asked.

Hyperion shot me an I-told-you-so look. "They're in development."

"You've got a unique concept," she said. "You said your tearoom is nearby?"

"Only four blocks from the beach," I said.

"So you get the tourist trade." She nodded. "I'd imagine most of your tourists are local though, rather than out of state."

"Exactly," I said.

She drummed her long fingers on the desk. "We do a lot of B2C – that's business to consumer – work. Assisting with strategy, media relations, brand building, social media, and product launches. Have you thought of promo activities around the launch of your new Tarot-themed teas?"

No. I hadn't. When you're a crime-fighting small business owner, details sometimes fall through the cracks. "I've been more focused on development."

Hyperion patted my hand. "Abigail's still coming out of her shell after that brutal divorce."

Beatrice grimaced. "Believe me, I get it. After my divorce, it seemed like my success was weaponized against me. All my hard work, and I had to hand over half to my shiftless husband so he could..."

Her jaw clamped shut.

"He took her dog," Hyperion said.

Beatrice's eyes flashed. "What? If it makes you feel any better," she said hotly, "my ex took my best friend."

I winced. *Ouch.*

"As soon as the divorce was final," Beatrice continued, "she became his business partner." She put the word *business* in air quotes. "That mad badger claimed nothing was going on during our marriage and falling in love was just one of those things. But I don't–" Beatrice shook her head.

Mad badger? Madge Badger? And then they'd broken up and Whitmore started dating Deva? How had that gone over with Madge? And it sounded as if Beatrice didn't know Madge had been dumped for Deva. Which might explain how the police hadn't found out about Deva quickly. If neither Madge nor Beatrice knew... Had Whitmore and Deva been keeping things on the QT, or had Razzzor totally misread that situation? But James and Layla had seemed to know about the relationship.

Weird.

"He also got the house," Hyperion said. "Poor Abigail's living in a rental owned by her uncle."

Tomas was an honorary uncle, but in the cascade of lies Hyperion proceeded to spew, that detail was small beer.

Beatrice's fist clenched around a fancy-looking pen. "It's maddening. But living well really is the best revenge. And showing your ex that you're moving forward can be empowering."

She pulled a folder from a desk drawer. "Here's a bit about my firm. We'd be happy to draw up a sample promotional plan for your new Tarot teas, if you'd like."

I hesitated. There was no way I could afford her services, so I didn't want to waste her time. But she was a suspect, and this might give us another opportunity to talk. "I am curious," I said. "But I've got to warn you, our finances are pretty thin right now."

She grinned impishly and rose. "That's because you haven't worked with me yet. Good PR is an investment, not an expense."

Beatrice saw us to the door. We shook hands and left.

"OMG," Hyperion said when the elevator doors had closed. "Her ex and her best friend? She has to want them both dead."

"Except Madge Badger isn't dead." *Yet.* But a cold tentacle writhed in my gut.

The phone rang in my bag. I excavated it from the depths of my purse and answered.

"Abigail," Razzzor said.

"Hi, Razzzor." I shot Hyperion a look. Imaginary friend, my Aunt Fanny. "What's up?"

"Um. I've sort of been arrested."

CHAPTER 9

The outside of the San Borromeo PD was revoltingly charming. Spanish-tile roof. Adobe walls. Arched entrances. There was even a candy shop across the street. Under the circumstances, a bar might have been more appropriate.

Things fell apart a bit on the inside. The station's interior hadn't moved past its grim seventies-era update of laminate counters and ick-colored walls.

Hyperion scanned the station. "Did he say if Tony— if *Detective* Chase had been the one to arrest him?"

"No." I scowled. Could my partner at least *pretend* this expedition wasn't about ogling Detective Chase?

But at least Hyperion had come.

In my experience, most people run when times get unpleasant, or in my parents' case, when they got bored.

I dithered beside a row of plastic chairs.

I'd called Razzzor's lawyer but had no idea how long it would take to get Razzzor released. It wasn't as if the police were going to let us see him. And if he'd really been arrested, then he'd need to be arraigned first.

"Wait here." Hyperion strolled to a bullet-proof window. Bracing one elbow on the narrow ledge, he spoke to the desk sergeant.

I texted the lawyer: *Any news? We're at the station.*

A few minutes later, Hyperion returned, expression gleeful. "Detective Chase is here."

"Goodie. Did they say anything about Razzzor?"

"Who? Oh, your imaginary friend. I don't know. I didn't ask."

"Then why—?" My cell phone pinged, and I checked the message. My head waitress asking when I'd return.

A silver-haired man in a pinstripe suit strode past the desk sergeant.

I straightened. It was Razzzor's lawyer, Mr. Smith, of Smith, Smith, and Smith. I wasn't entirely sure which Smith he was, but it wasn't an issue that had ever mattered.

He stopped in front of me and frowned. "Ms. Beanblossom?"

"How's Razzzor?"

"He's asked me to tell you he's fine, and you don't have to stay."

"Is he going to be arraigned?" My stomach churned. "Was he really arrested?"

He raised a hand in a "stop" gesture. "He's being questioned. That's all I can say, aside from the fact your presence here is not helping."

Well, I didn't expect we'd exactly be helping, but...

"How?" Hyperion demanded. "Because our presence can't be hurting."

"Because Razzzor's covering—" Mr. Smith clamped his mouth shut. "Never mind."

"Covering?" I asked. "Covering for whom? Deva?" That idiot's suspicion of the cops was going to get him jail time if he wasn't careful.

The lawyer's brows lifted. "Deva? Who's Deva?"

"Razzzor thought she was pawning off fake wine with his vineyard's label," I said. "The wine distributor and his... ex-girlfriend?"

"Interesting. I understand Razzzor's dislike for cooperating with the authorities. It's not all bad. Frankly, I'm glad he's letting me do the talking. But I wish he'd tell me more about what's going on."

"Me too. But if he's not covering for Deva," I said, "then for whom?"

"For you, Ms. Beanblossom." The lawyer turned on his heels and strode back into the depths of the police station.

Open-mouthed, I stared after him. *For me?*

"Why would Razzzor cover for you?" Hyperion asked. "You didn't kill anyone."

"I know." Stunned, I wandered outside, to the police station's concrete steps. Razzzor was doing this for me? Why?

I gazed blankly at the candy store. Chocolate didn't seem like such a bad idea.

"We must solve the crime and save your mythical Razzzor, who seems to think you're guilty of something." Hyperion rubbed his chin. "What can he possibly think you've done? White collar crime? MURDER?" he bellowed.

People turned on the sidewalk to stare.

"Shut up," I hissed. "And he's not a myth. He has a lawyer."

He rolled his eyes. "Abigail, anyone can get a lawyer. *Rivers* have lawyers these days."

He was right about one thing; we had to help Razzzor. I had no idea what he thought he was covering for me about, but I needed to prove him wrong and get him out.

Something yellow flashed in my peripheral vision. Without turning my head, I widened my gaze.

My stomach spasmed. The bike messenger lounged in the entry of an upscale olive oil shop.

I turned to Hyperion. "We're being followed."

"The bike messenger in the olive oil shop?"

"He is the guy, right?"

"He's the guy," Hyperion said. "How do you want to play this?"

"I want to find out what Deacon knows."

"Deacon?"

"Deacon Alstatter," I said. "That's the bike messenger's name. He's stalking Deva."

"You were sleuthing without me again?"

"I was sure I mentioned it…"

"Well," he huffed, "you didn't."

"I'm sorry. I found Deva at a wine tasting. Razzzor was there too, which just goes to show you how desperate he is. He hates public events."

"I imagine it's tough being an imaginary friend in public."

"Will you stop?"

"All right," he said. "Let's split up. He'll follow you, and I'll surprise him."

"Deal. I'll walk toward the tearoom."

"Tea and Tarot room," he caroled and strolled in the opposite direction.

I turned and started down the gently sloping hill toward the tearoom.

The bike messenger emerged from the shadow of the olive oil shop. He trailed after Hyperion.

I froze, one foot raised. What the…? That wasn't the plan! Deacon was supposed to follow *me*. Why was he…? Cursing beneath my breath, I set my foot down, turned and followed the messenger.

Hyperion and the bike messenger strode briskly past tourist shops and up the hill.

Why follow Hyperion? Revenge for getting tossed in the parking lot? Or did he think Hyperion was somehow connected to Deva?

Hyperion paused outside a cigar shop. He studied his reflection in the window and straightened his collar. My partner nodded and walked on, up the crooked street.

The bike messenger followed.

So did I.

I pulled out my cell phone and snapped a picture of Deacon's back. Which wasn't super helpful, but I had to do something.

My breathing accelerated, and I wasn't sure if it was nerves or because we were walking uphill. Counter-surveillance might not have been the best idea. What if Deacon was really crazy? What if he had a knife?

Hyperion turned the corner into a brick alley.

Deacon hesitated, then followed.

I slid my purse off my shoulder and gripped the straps between one fist. My bag wasn't very heavy, but thanks to all the change in it, it wasn't nothing either. I turned the corner and stopped short.

Deacon lay flat on his back, his legs kicking in the air like an overturned beetle's.

Hyperion stood over him and brandished a garbage can lid.

My partner had hidden depths when it came to the martial arts.

"Why were you following me?" Hyperion asked.

"What's your connection to Deva?" Deacon countered. He scrambled to his feet.

Hyperion jabbed at him with the garbage can lid.

Deacon took a hasty step away.

I snapped another picture of him with my phone, catching his profile this time.

"Deva is a suspect in a murder investigation." Hyperion leaned slightly backward, lid extended.

"You mean the Carson guy?" Deacon brushed gravel off the seat of his bike pants.

"Who else?" I asked.

"Deva didn't kill him," he said.

"Did you?" My voice was higher than normal, and I cleared my throat.

"Are you videoing this?" Deacon asked.

"No." But it was a good idea. I switched to video. "You went inside the Wine Merchants after Deva left. Why?"

His jaw set. "I wanted wine."

"You didn't buy any," I said.

"No one was there." Deacon feinted toward Hyperion.

My partner made a quick, ineffectual jab with the garbage can lid. Deacon danced backward, out of reach.

Hyperion might know how to kung fu, but he had no chops when it came to garbage can defense.

"What exactly did you do when you went inside?" I asked.

"I walked to the counter," he said. "No one was there, so I rang the bell. No one came out, and I left."

"Why go inside at all?" I asked.

His tanned face spasmed. "I wanted to see him, that's all."

"Why?" Hyperion edged closer to me.

"None of your business," he said. "I told all this to the police. I don't need to talk to you. And what were you doing at the Wine Merchants?"

I started. He'd seen me there? "Someone's been selling counterfeit wine through that shop," I said.

"You think Deva did it? Stay away from her." He stepped forward.

Hyperion knocked him back with the lid. "Why were you following me?"

Deacon spat and strode down the other end of the alley.

"Lovely." Hyperion replaced the lid on the nearby garbage bin and brushed off his hands.

"Should we follow him?"

"Do you really want to?"

"It's not so much a question of *want* but *should*."

"I don't think he'll tell us more," he said, "and don't you have to get back to the tearoom?"

"Tea and Tarot room."

He clapped my shoulder. "And that is why we love you. You think of others. It's also why I'm going to your tea party this Saturday."

"What? How?"

"I called Layla Zimmer and told her Tarot readings were included in the fee. She jumped all over it," he said smugly. "No one can resist a free Tarot reading. No one."

CHAPTER 10

Hanging moss dripped from cypress trees. Grecian statues, faces worn and blurred by lichen, stood fretfully alongside mossy, brick paths. A low balustrade lined one of the paths, along the ocean cliff. The Zimmers' garden would be spooky as hell at Halloween. Today it was just... spooky.

I clipped a white cloth to the table and stood back, admiring the setup. Elegant roses in silver bowls. Glass apothecary jars filled with pastel macarons. Gold-embossed stemware.

And burning sage.

I sniffed and turned to glare at Hyperion. The Tarot reader muttered to himself and waved a smoldering bundle of dried leaves.

"What are you doing?" I asked. "The guests are about to arrive."

And we'd never had such a prestigious catering order. I didn't want to screw it up, even if it was a pretext for snooping. It was a near-perfect Saturday. The sun was shining. The birds were singing. And Razzzor was out of jail.

Razzzor was also avoiding me.

"I have it on good authority this place is haunted." Hyperion shuddered dramatically in his natty navy jacket.

"Who's authority?" I asked.

"Your grandfather's."

I snorted. Gramps was far too sensible to believe in ghosts. But I shivered a little in spite of the warm day and looked toward the cliff.

Waitresses from the tearoom wove through the tables, adjusting silverware and cloth napkins. The sky above the Pacific was mercury, the ocean the blue of drowning and dark waters.

I shook myself. Drowning? Where had *that* come from?

Next to Hyperion, I felt frumpy in my sensible shoes and Beanblossom's apron. He got to wear civilian clothes – in this case, skinny navy slacks and an immaculate, blue collarless shirt. Smoke curled around his sleek head.

"Can you sage somewhere else?" I asked.

"But I'll be working *here*."

I gave up. Hopefully, the skunky smell would dissipate by the time the party began.

A chill breeze touched the back of my neck. I shivered again and looked over my shoulder at the Moroccan arched folly and the Italian-style villa beyond. A faceless cupid stared at me from atop a trickling fountain. *Haunted?* Unlikely.

But I found myself stepping backward, scalp prickling, and unwilling to turn my back on the statue.

An uncanny shriek split the air.

Tarot cards shot from Hyperion's hands and scattered across the garden path.

"Stupid peacocks," he muttered and gathered up the cards.

I nodded agreement. They were gorgeous birds, but *yikes* were they loud. The Zimmers had at least three.

Layla strode down the path, her green stilettos clacking. "How's everything going? Where are the fairy cakes?"

"In the car," I said. "We didn't discuss when you wanted them brought out."

"They're so beautiful, I think they should be out now, don't you? The guests will start arriving any minute."

"Then I'll get them." I motioned to Brenda, one of our waitresses.

"I'll help," Layla said. "All I'm doing now is worrying. About this party," she added quickly.

We strolled down a path lined with statues of maidens in Greek robes. At the end of the path, the Pacific gleamed, a blue line.

"You've got nothing to worry about," I finally said. "Everything's prepped and ready." As long as the breeze carried away the scent of Hyperion's burnt sage.

"I know, but this is different for us. We usually do wine events. And I love wine, I really do. But it's gotten so the guests expect it. That's why James insisted on including champagne today. I hope that won't be a problem."

I wasn't sure how champagne would go with the tea, but it would work with the scones and fairy cake. "Champagne goes with everything," I said.

She threw back her head and laughed. "Don't let James hear you saying that." Layla paused. "On the other hand, he might agree."

"Where is James?" I asked. "I'd like to say hello."

"Oh, he'll make his grand entrance eventually."

I glanced at her, but her good-humored expression was unchanged.

"Enough about me," she said. "Tell me more about yourself. Do you have family in the area?"

"My grandfather," I said shortly. I didn't know where my parents were, and they'd made it clear they didn't care where I was. If they did, they would have sent Gramps something with a return address. I smiled, trying to shake off the foul mood that had descended. "What about you?"

"My parents are in Hong Kong. I've got a sister in New York, but here, it's just me and James."

We arrived at my car, parked beside a folly sheltering an ivy-covered statue.

"Dionysius," Layla said. "God of fun, wine, and the mysteries. In short, the perfect representative for my husband."

I cut another glance at her and opened the hatchback. "Has James got a mystery?"

"Only where he got his amazing palate from."

I removed a plastic cake container and handed one to Brenda.

"Can I peek?" Layla asked.

"The cakes are yours now." I unlatched the lid and carefully pulled it off.

Edible flowers, strawberries, and rice paper butterflies spilled across the top of the cake. Pink strawberry rhubarb curd dripped down the sides. I'd left bits of the elderflower cake bare, exposing tumbles of elderberry cream between the yellow layers.

Layla gasped. "It's more beautiful than I expected. It doesn't seem real. But we'll have to take the butterflies off to eat, and then what will they look like?"

"No, they're edible too."

"Amazing," she whispered. "It's a work of art."

"Thank you." I'd worked my butt off making those butterflies. I replaced the cover. Brenda, Layla and I walked carefully back to the tables, setting a cake on each one.

I took photos of the table settings. Guests began arriving, women in strappy summer dresses and men in neat slacks and shirts open at the collar.

The tea was ignored in favor of James's champagne, cooling in elegant silver buckets. Women wandered in and out of Hyperion's tent. I walked through the guests offering a tray of tiny sandwiches.

Deva chatted with a man with silvery hair and an ascot. Beatrice talked with Layla on the opposite side of the lawn.

I lowered my head to stare more covertly. Did Beatrice know Whitmore had dumped Madge for Deva? *Had* he dumped his business partner? Or had he been seeing both women at once?

I did a double-take. Madge, in a lipstick pink dress and lime green scarf, strolled through the gathering. She paused to speak to a trio of women. The women laughed in musical tones.

My shoulders tightened. Madge, Beatrice, and Deva – Whitmore's three paramours – in one place? Was Layla crazy? Or had she not known about their tangled history? And where was James?

I walked to our setup behind Hyperion's tent to refill my tray.

"Darling, you've got nothing to worry about." Hyperion's voice floated through the tent folds. "You've got the *World*."

I filled the tray with miniature almond, coconut, and pomegranate scones. Rounding the tent, I scanned for Madge. She was speaking intently to the silver-haired man with the ascot. His tanned face creased in a frown.

I made a beeline for her.

"No," Madge said sharply. "We didn't buy from Zimmerland." Her voice dropped, again inaudible.

I stopped, pretending to rearrange the canapes.

"Ms. Beanblossom. Fancy seeing you here," Detective Chase drawled from behind me.

Grimacing, I turned. "Detective Chase. Does this mean you don't suspect Razzzor?"

"Why would you think that?" He shoved back his cowboy hat with his thumb.

"Because you're here, and so are all the suspects." Except for James, who still hadn't made an appearance.

"Mm." He scanned the crowd then looked down at me. "You look like a woman who just learned she got up too late for the Black Friday sales."

"That's totally sexist." Though missing those sales would make me mad. It's not like I could afford full price.

"Sure is," he said. "What's got you bothered?"

"Did you know Whitmore left his wife for Madge? And then he started dating Deva? All three women are here."

"Are you expecting a cat fight?"

A peacock shrieked, and I flinched.

The detective wrinkled his nose. "Tell me that wasn't a peacock."

"The Zimmers have at least three. One's white. It's gorgeous."

"Birds are dirty animals, Ms. Beanblossom. Ever heard of bird flu?"

Breathless, Hyperion appeared beside him. "I have."

"Ah." The detective studied him for a moment. He put his hand on his hips and brushed back his suit jacket, exposing his badge. "You're both here."

"Beanblossom's Tea and Tarot catering, at your service." Hyperion bowed.

"How'd you finagle this gig?" Detective Chase asked.

I shifted my weight. "It was just... one of those things."

"Well, don't make a habit of it." He strode into the crowd.

"Of catering?" Hyperion asked. "Or snooping?"

"I'm pretty sure he meant the latter." I looked around for Madge, but she'd disappeared into the throng.

Hyperion snagged a mini-scone from my tray and popped it in his mouth. "Oh." He rolled his eyes. "These are yum. Are those red bits pomegranates?"

"To quote you: *duh*. Have you learned anything?"

"Aside from the fact Detective Chase is totally into me? Did you see that little move when he brushed back his jacket to show off his badge? Adorable."

Save me. Though odds were Hyperion was right. "Okay. I'm going to eavesdrop."

"Have fun." He whisked inside his tent.

I strolled through the gathering.

The silver-haired man in the ascot had cornered Deva. "Then where is it?"

he asked.

"Still in Burgundy, I'm afraid," she said. "The harvest was late. Weather is one thing we can't control."

"Oh, the French." The man scowled. "What's the ETA?"

I approached them. "Almond-coconut-pomegranate scone?"

Deva gave me a relieved smile. "That sounds wonderful. Thank you."

I handed her a napkin, and she took a scone.

"None for me." The elegant man waved me off. "Well?"

I backed away, but not far enough to miss the conversation.

Deva nibbled the corner of the scone and swallowed. "Two months."

"Two! Outrageous!"

"I hear you have pomegranate scones?" a woman said behind me.

I turned, smiling, and the fifty-something redhead took a napkin and scone.

"But how do you keep from smashing the seeds when you mix them into the dough?" the redhead asked.

"Very carefully," I joked and strained to eavesdrop on Deva.

But the redhead loudly peppered me with questions about the scones and Hyperion. It was like she was intentionally thwarting my detecting. Finally, she tucked my business card in her clutch and turned to go.

I bit back a curse. Deva and the man in the ascot had wandered off.

"Say, who's that man in the ascot?" I asked the redhead and pointed to the silver-haired man.

She turned. "Oh. That's Archer."

"Archer...?"

"Archer Simmons. Why?"

"Someone asked me to give him a message," I lied. "Thanks."

I turned and knocked the tray into Layla's midsection. I gasped, the tray wobbling. Scones skidded sideways and bumped to a halt against the tray's rim. I exhaled slowly, catastrophe averted.

"Abigail, you've got to help me," Layla whispered, her gaze darting.

I stiffened. "What's wrong? Do you want me to start cutting the elderflower cakes?"

"No, not that. There's a detective here. Can you get rid of him?"

"I don't think I can. I mean, he doesn't answer to me."

She clawed both hands through her hair. "I know, I know. I just can't... He's putting off our guests."

"Deva's a pretty smooth talker," I said. "Maybe she can distract him?"

"Deva?" She sniffed. "She's not as smooth as you think."

"Oh?"

"*I* know more about wine than she does. It's caused all sorts of problems, let me tell you." She glanced at the man Deva had been talking to earlier.

"What sort of problems?"

"It's nothing. James delegates too much authority. He doesn't understand that not everyone can do what he asks." She smiled. "But if that's the worst I can say about him, then I'm a lucky woman. James really is the most marvelous—"

"Taking my name in vain?" James, in a crisp white shirt and jeans, sidled up to her. He looped an arm around her waist, pulling her in for a quick kiss.

She giggled. "Have you been eavesdropping?"

"How else am I supposed to hear anything interesting?" he asked. "Abigail, this is wonderful. Thank you for pulling this together on such short notice. You've done an amazing job. And I hear we've got a Tarot reader as well?"

"My partner, Hyperion."

"The guests are raving. Maybe I need to have a Tarot-themed wine tasting?"

"You should talk to Hyperion," I said. "I'm sure he'll have all sorts of wine and Tarot pairing ideas."

"Brilliant idea. I will."

A scream echoed across the grounds, and I twitched.

Layla winced. "Those birds."

Dread weighted my chest. That was no peacock. I met James' startled gaze.

The woman screamed again.

James and I hurried toward the sound.

Hyperion popped out of the tent.

"Hold this." I handed my partner the tray.

Another scream, and James was running. I raced after him.

Detective Chase loped from the other side of the lawn toward the cliffside path. He vanished behind a wall of boxwood. We followed.

Deva stood, her hands to her mouth, looking over a low, white balustrade. Detective Chase reached her first, and Deva grabbed his arm.

James and I stumbled to a halt beside them.

I looked over the balustrade.

A woman in a pink dress lay motionless at the bottom of the cliff, waves crashing near her feet. A lime green scarf fluttered around her neck.

CHAPTER 11

Detective Chase walked away from the growing crowd and made a call. When he'd finished, the detective strode to an openmouthed James. "How do we get down there?"

Our host looked to the cliff, and his eyes widened. "It's not possible."

"There's a trail," Hyperion said. "This way."

"Show me." The detective and Hyperion jogged down the path and vanished behind a cypress tree.

"But it doesn't go to the bottom," James said to me. "Not all the way." He clutched his head. "This is awful. How could this happen?"

Aghast, I peered over the cliffside. Chase and Hyperion were nowhere in sight. The woman's body lay unmoving on the honey-colored rocks below. A green scarf fluttered around her neck.

Nausea spiraled up my throat. *Madge.* I stepped from the ledge and swallowed. Whitmore Carson and now his partner, Madge, were dead. Did someone have it out for their wine store?

I looked over my shoulder toward the party. The tables and Hyperion's tent were hidden behind a trimmed wall of boxwood.

Someone did this. I'd been right here – we all had been – and someone had killed Madge. And yes, I knew I was jumping to conclusions. She could have fallen. But what were the odds?

"What were you doing here?" I asked Deva.

Her teeth chattered. "I came to catch my breath and look at the ocean." She motioned toward the view of high cliffs and crashing waves and infinite blue.

Deva had struck me as an operator. Would she really leave a party with so many bigwigs to stare at an ocean she saw every day?

"What's happened?" Beatrice said at my elbow.

I glanced at the PR consultant. "It's Madge Badger," I said. "She's..." Unable to finish, I pointed to the balustrade.

Could Madge still be alive after that fall? My hands clenched. I hoped so. I really hoped so. We hadn't been friends, but we'd drunk tea together. I *knew* her.

Bracing my hands on the balustrade's white stone, I studied the cliff. It wasn't completely sheer, but it was probably an eighty-degree slope. Madge *could* have slid down the hill rather than fallen. She might be alive.

Tony and Hyperion appeared maybe thirty feet above her. They picked their way down the cliff. My grip tightened on the balustrade, cool and rough against my palms. *Be careful.*

Beatrice looked over the edge. She stared for a long time, then stepped back. "It must have been suicide. You couldn't accidentally fall – not with this railing."

Deva shot her a sharp look and strode away.

"The stupid woman," Beatrice murmured, and I didn't know if she was speaking about Madge or Deva. Both had dated her ex-husband.

"There is another alternative," I said in a low voice.

"That she was pushed?" Beatrice's eyes narrowed. "That, I could believe. But we'd be wrong to speculate. And I'm sure the police will reach their own conclusions."

Speculate. Speculate! "Who would want to hurt her?"

"Madge was a difficult woman. Two weeks ago, she came to me, furious. There was broken glass from a wine bottle in front of her tires. She didn't notice until she'd driven over it. She lost three tires."

"And she blamed you?"

"She always blamed me. But I didn't do it. I'd just returned from L.A. So, if I didn't do it, then who did?"

She looked down the path in the direction Deva had gone.

"You don't mean... Deva?" I whispered.

"Whitmore was a dog," she said in a low voice. "He dumped me for Madge, Madge for Deva... What if he'd gone back to Madge?"

"Could it have been an accident? The broken bottle, I mean."

She shrugged.

But Beatrice had just given herself a motive for killing both Whitmore and Madge. But maybe she figured she had nothing to lose? Maybe she thought it was a story everyone knew, so she might as well control the narrative.

I looked back over the cliff. Tony squatted beside Madge. Hyperion stood a few feet above them both. Tony looked up at Hyperion and shook his head. Hyperion briefly covered his face with his hand, nodded, and began his ascent.

A siren wailed in the distance.

"I'll meet the ambulance," James said to his wife. He hurried away.

Had they overheard my conversation with Beatrice?

Clutching the balustrade with both hands, I watched Hyperion climb upward. His foot slipped beneath him, and I gasped.

He grabbed a scraggly bush sticking from the cliff and lurched against its face. Stones and dirt bounced down the cliff to the waves below. Hyperion continued upward, and my breath released.

"The poor woman," the redhead who'd asked for my recipe said beside me.

"What an awful, awful thing."

"Terrible," I agreed. "Did you know her well?"

"We were in a networking group together. She doesn't have any family. That wine shop was her whole life. That and–" She checked herself and grimaced.

That and... Whitmore?

"This balustrade is too low. It's an invitation to sit or lean on it," the redhead continued. "She must have leaned out too far."

"We don't know what happened," Beatrice said sharply. "We shouldn't speculate."

"No, of course not," the redhead said.

"I need to talk to James." Beatrice strode down the brick path.

"Always working," the redhead said.

"You mean... James is a client of her PR firm?"

"I don't know. He could be. But Beatrice is a part owner in Zimmerland. Didn't you know?"

No, I hadn't.

"I doubt she's very involved in the business," she continued. "But it gives her bragging rights and access to all the best parties. And the wine, of course. Imagine her discount."

"What do you do?" I asked.

"Oh, I sing."

I looked over the cliff again.

Hyperion was gone, and my breath caught.

But Detective Chase was taking photos of Madge's body and not acting like Hyperion had just plunged into the ocean. So my partner had likely reached the main path and was making his way upward. I just wished I could see him.

"Hey," Hyperion said at my elbow, and I nearly jumped out of my sneakers. "Where are Layla and James?"

I blew out my breath. "James went back to meet emergency services, and Layla should be around here somewhere."

"Did I hear my name?" She extricated herself from a conversation with two older gentlemen and walked to us. "What do you need?"

"Detective Chase would like a list of everyone at the party," Hyperion said. "No one is supposed to leave."

"Is she...?"

"Yes," he said, voice taut.

Layla's face paled. "Oh, no. Abigail, I think we will need that tea after all."

"Right. I'll take care of it." I looked a question at Hyperion.

"I'm to stay here and show the cops the path we took down to the body," he said.

"How did you even know the path was there?" I asked.

"I snooped around while you were setting out your tea things."

Of course he had. I just wished I'd done the same – not that it would have prevented Madge's fall.

I nodded and made my way back to the lawn. A few partygoers remained, speaking in low voices.

Brenda hurried to me, her apron flapping. "What's going on? We heard someone fell."

"A woman was killed," I said to my staffer. "The police will be here soon. We're to serve tea to the guests."

We'd already arranged the tea service on four rolling trays. So, we waited.

Police and paramedics hurried past us toward the cliff with James. Guests trickled into the garden and spoke in hushed tones.

My staff and I walked amongst them with trays and offered tea. Most people accepted and continued their conversations, oblivious to my eavesdropping. But the partygoers didn't drop any nuggets of information that pointed to murder.

Tony Chase, staring at his hands and wrinkling his nose, hurried past.

"Detective Chase—"

"I'm out of hand sanitizer. You got any?"

"No, but—"

"I've got to wash up." He sped to the house.

"He has really got to get over his germophobia," I said beneath my breath.

Ten minutes later, the detective returned. "Everyone, may I have your attention?" Though he didn't speak loudly, the conversations faltered. Silence fell, the guests watching him.

"We'll try to make this as quick and painless as possible," he said. "Please have a seat at the tables. The officers and I will come and take your statements individually. Once that's done, you can leave. Thank you for your cooperation."

Muttering, the guests moved to the tables, spilling with flowers and food. My elderflower cakes hadn't even been cut yet. I doubted they'd get eaten. All that work, wasted.

I stared at my boring shoes. The food wasn't important. What had happened to Madge was important.

Heart leaden, I moved along the tables, refreshing teacups and passing out tiny sandwiches. Tony Chase and his officers worked through the guests. The crowd diminished until it was just me and my staff, Hyperion, and the Zimmers.

"You." Detective Chase pointed at me. "Let's talk." He strode into the Tarot tent, and I followed.

The detective sat on Hyperion's high-backed, red velvet chair. A tin lantern from Morocco hung from an iron holder beside him. It cast geometric glimmers of light across his chiseled face.

"Now," he drawled. "What exactly are you doing here?"

"Layla hired me – us – to cater this event," I said.

"When?"

"Last weekend."

"That seems like short notice."

I swallowed. "It was. Her other caterer had fallen through. When she learned I had a tearoom, she asked if we'd help out. I agreed."

"And you just happened to meet her?"

"There was a, um, wine tasting." Going hadn't been interfering in his investigation at all. I mean, it was open to the public. Why shouldn't I have gone?

"Did you go alone?"

"No?"

"Who were you with?"

"Razzzor?" I winced.

"You've been interfering in my investigation again."

Oh, boy. "I talked to Madge," I said quickly. "She dropped by Beanblossom's on Tuesday. A reporter had told her that I was one of the people who'd found the body."

"Why'd she want to speak to you?"

"I don't know," I said. "And she left in a hurry. We'd been discussing any appointments Whitmore might have had that evening he'd died. She said she didn't know of any. Then Madge seemed to think of something or realize something, and she left."

His jaw clenched. He looked away, toward the line of blue Pacific. "Ms. Beanblossom—"

"It's not my fault!" Deva's voice floated through the tent's thick folds.

We turned to look through the opening.

Hands on her hips, Deva faced Layla.

"I don't appreciate your tone," Layla said.

"I don't work for you." Deva stormed off.

Detective Chase rubbed his jaw. "Interesting."

Very.

CHAPTER 12

That night I lay in bed and stared at the ceiling. I couldn't get that fluttering green scarf out of my mind. Both owners of the store that had sold Razzzor's counterfeit wine were now dead. What did it mean? And what did it mean for Razzzor?

I hoped he'd been nowhere near San Borromeo during the party. But I didn't know. He was still dodging my calls. I'd left messages, sent texts, even looked for him on the gaming platform.

No Razzzor.

I rolled over and stared at my tiny water fountain. For the dozenth time, I reviewed the party in my mind. Layla Zimmer had been running back and forth between the house and the garden. She could have diverted for a quick meeting with Madge on the cliffside path.

Deva had found the body. But she could have been the one to push Madge over.

I pulled my sheets higher. And where had James been the whole time? Layla had said he'd wanted to make a grand entrance. If he had, it had been overshadowed by Madge's death.

And Beatrice... I hadn't been watching Whitmore's ex-wife.

Whitmore. Madge. Neither of them had any family. There was something depressing about that. At least I had Gramps and Tomas. My throat tightened. But they wouldn't be around forever. And then I'd be alone too.

And that was life.

At least I had my own business. I was independent. I'd built a life that allowed me to get by on my own, because there were few people I could count on.

I checked my alarm clock. It blinked eleven fifty-eight.

"Stupid insomnia." I slipped from my bed and shambled from my bedroom. Maybe a cup of chamomile tea would help.

Yawning, I reached for the living room light switch.

Something shifted on the other side of the French doors.

I froze, hand raised toward the switch. A figure prowled through my garden. The solar lights illuminated the bottom of a dark pair of trousers.

I raced toward the windows, banged my thigh on a dining room chair. The chair crashed to the floor. I stumbled, swearing, and trotted to the French doors, slapped the light switch.

Light flooded the garden.

The person was gone.

But *where* had he gone? Shaken, I turned and hurried to the front door. I grabbed my keys. They jangled as I ran outside, to my neighbor's. I pounded on Brik's door.

After way too long, he yanked it open. The top button of his jeans was undone, and he was bare chested.

I reminded myself that I was too freaked out to notice.

He raked his hand through his mane of blond hair. "Abigail? What's wrong?"

My teacup pajamas, for starters.

I tore my gaze from his taut abs. "Someone was in my yard." And so much for my independence. I'd run straight to my neighbor.

"Stay here." He strode past me and around the high fence that marked the boundary between our properties. I heard the gate rattle open and shut.

Breathing harder than a jog next door warranted, I sat on his top step. I watched the waning moon above the Eucalyptus trees.

My neck stiffened. Why hadn't I at least bought a motion sensitive lightbulb for the porch? They weren't that expensive. But I hadn't had time for the hardware store. And as convenient as online ordering is, I try to shop locally when I can. After all, I had a local business. Buying local was only fair. And why was my mind hamster-wheeling about lightbulbs, when–?

Brik strode around the corner of the fence. He shook his head. "Whoever he was, he's long gone. Was anything taken?"

"I don't know." I swallowed. "I saw him in the yard, turned on the light, and then came here."

"You turned on the light? Did you get a good look at him?"

Heat washed up my neck and face. "Um. No. I knocked over a chair, and I think he heard me. He was gone by the time I hit the light switch."

He rested his broad hand on my shoulder. "Hey," he said gently. "You weren't hurt. He didn't get inside. That's a win."

I nodded, mute.

"I'll be right back." He walked inside and emerged with a heavy-duty flashlight. "Let's see if there's been any attempt at a break in."

Pulse jittering, I followed him down the path between my house and the fence. The scent of jasmine was sweet in the warm, night air. He stopped beside my bedroom window and shined his light on the trim. "I don't see any damage. Do you?"

"Nope."

He did the same to my kitchen window, then walked into the garden and up the steps to the deck and the French doors. He shook his head. "I don't see anything wrong here either. Where did you see the guy?"

I turned and pointed. "Over there, by the lavender."

He walked ahead of me, scanning the ground with his flashlight. But if there were footprints, they were invisible in the loose tanbark.

Brik's flashlight beam moved across the base of the lavender.

I gasped and knelt beside the plant. A wide section had been clipped from the bush like a bad haircut. "He stole my lavender." I straightened. "This is ridiculous."

"Could it be a prankster?" Brik asked.

"There's nothing funny about stealing my herbs."

"It doesn't seem like the person has any intent to hurt you—"

I glared. "He broke into my yard."

"But he broke into your yard," he agreed. "Have you thought about those cameras?"

"I'm installing motion sensitive lights tomorrow. Or today." Because it had to be past midnight by now.

Brik walked me to my front door and checked inside the house. No one was hiding under the bed or in the closets. He rattled the windows, ensuring they were locked, and then left.

I didn't go to sleep.

*****

On an hour's sleep, I arrived at the tearoom early on a hectic Sunday morning. Hyperion looked harried too, his hair askew as he read cards at the tables.

I poured tea for a trio of elderly ladies and moved back toward the kitchen.

A Tarot reader named Sierra approached me and bit her lip. "I meant to give this to you yesterday, but I forgot it was in my pocket when I left. And I left before you got back from that catering thing." She handed me a creamy, white envelope made of thick paper. "It was the only mail."

"It doesn't look like a bill, so I'll take it," I joked, yawning. "Thanks." The envelope didn't have a return address. My name and the address of the tearoom was handwritten on its front in elegant script.

I walked behind the marble counter, pulled out a knife, and slit it open.

An oversized, black label fell onto the counter. Frowning, I turned it over. The note was short and written in silver pen:

Abigail–

It was such a pleasure meeting you. Thank you for the tea and conversation. This has been an awful time, but you cleared up an important issue for me. I hope we can meet up again soon.

Best,
Madge Badger

My chest tightened. *Madge.* I checked the envelope. It had been postmarked Friday. The note had made a speedy journey through the San Borromeo post office. And what was the important issue I'd cleared up?

I mulled over our conversation. She'd left looking like she'd had a revelation of some sort. But I didn't know what had triggered it. I swallowed bile. Had that revelation gotten her killed?

"Hey girl, everything all right?" Hyperion asked.

I looked up. My partner stood on the opposite side of the counter, a sympathetic expression on his face.

Wordlessly, I handed him the note.

He grimaced. "It must feel strange, getting a note from a dead woman."

"It feels..."

"What?"

It felt like a rebuke, but I shook my head. "You're right. It feels strange."

"I don't suppose there's any sense giving this to the police," he said. "It's just an ordinary thank you note."

"Yeah." I returned the label to the envelope. "She used these black labels at the wine store. They were hanging from the bottles in the same silver ink. I think they were tasting notes."

"That's smart branding, using them as thank you notes too. Think she got the idea from our PR consultant, Beatrice?"

"I don't think Beatrice was in the mood to help Madge with much of anything. She called her the Mad Badger."

He canted his head. "That's not necessarily an insult—"

"Who wouldn't be insulted by being called a mad badger?"

"—but in this case, I think you're right," he finished.

A waitress sped to his side. "Table three is interested in a fifteen-minute reading for the birthday girl." She nodded toward a quartet of middle-aged women.

"Ta. Duty calls." He rose from the stool and glided to the table.

I returned to work. And when the tearoom was closed and cleaned, I went to the home improvement store and bought motion-sensitive bulbs for all my porch lights.

I installed them that night.

CHAPTER 13

I didn't sleep long, and I didn't sleep well. But the tearoom was closed Mondays, so at least I got to sleep late. In an apron and pajamas, I baked mini tea cakes. I took two outside with a pot of English breakfast tea.

The air was slightly cool, morning fog hanging above the treetops. My garden was blessedly quiet, aside from the occasional scurry of a squirrel along the fence or call of a jay in the dogwood.

I ate the tea cake carefully. It was baked with a whole cherry inside, including the stem and pit. It simplified the recipe, but I couldn't serve them in the tearoom. Not without a better liability policy.

Stealthy footsteps padded behind me, and I stiffened.

I hadn't invited anyone over. And whoever it was hadn't shouted a greeting.

Casually, I picked up my cup of tea. Ripples disturbed the surface of the brown liquid.

The footsteps neared.

I leapt from my chair and flung the hot tea.

Razzzor leapt backwards. "Hey!" Tea splashed across his white t-shirt.

I breathed heavily. "What do you expect, sneaking up on me?"

It was a good thing I had a rotten throwing arm. I'd been aiming for his face.

"I wasn't sneaking." He peeled the shirt from his chest. "Ow."

I set down the cup, glad I hadn't thrown that and the saucer too. I liked that tea set.

He grabbed a tea cake and bit into it. "Augh!" He spit bits of cherry and tea cake onto the ground. "Are you trying to kill me? There's a pit."

"Which I would have warned you about if you'd given me the chance."

"I think I cracked a tooth."

"Good."

"Sheesh. Why are you so touchy?"

"You know what's a fun thing to do in the morning? Not sneak up on me." I blew out my breath. "Come inside. If we get water on that shirt now, it might not stain."

Grumbling, he followed me inside and into my tiny guest bathroom. "It's almost as if you don't want to see me," he said.

"Not want to...? Where have you been? I've been calling all week."

He tugged his shirt over his head, displaying a well-muscled torso.

Huh. Razzzor really had been working out.

He tossed me the shirt. "I've been avoiding you."

"At least you admit it." I ran water from the tap over the stain. Knowing Razzzor, this wasn't from a three-pack of shirts. It was expensive, like everything else he owned.

"I'm sorry, okay?" he said. "That cop kept asking me about you and about our relationship. My lawyer told me to put some distance between us."

"Well, that's just dumb." I squirted hand soap onto the stain and scrubbed at it. "We're friends, not co-conspirators."

"Yeah," he said glumly.

"Speaking of distance, where were you yesterday around eleven AM?"

"Biking. Why?"

The spot between my shoulders unclenched. "Good. There was another murder. Since you were nowhere near it, the cops will have to leave you alone."

His eyes widened. "Another? Were *you* near it?"

"I couldn't have done it. I have at least a dozen witnesses."

"Who was it?"

"Madge. Madge Badger."

His jaw sagged. "Whitmore's business partner? Where? How?"

"She was pushed – or fell – from the cliff at the Zimmers's house." I wrung out the cotton shirt. Wrinkled, but stain free.

His face turned gray. "The Zimmers's house. Here in San Borromeo."

My stomach quivered. *Uh oh.* "Where *exactly* were you biking?"

"In the hills," he said vaguely.

"Which hills?"

He gulped. "The San Borromeo hills."

"I thought you were supposed to steer clear of me. Why didn't you steer clear of me?" If he'd gone biking alone, he could still be a suspect. The cops would assume he could have biked to the Zimmers's house and killed Madge.

"I didn't expect to run into you biking–"

"You live in Silicon Valley. San Borromeo isn't exactly your backyard."

"I was worried, okay?"

I tossed the shirt at him, and it slapped wetly against his chest. "Worry more about yourself. Wait a minute – worried? Were you following me?"

"No. Being accused of stalking once was enough. I wanted to be near your tearoom in case something went down. But it's so crowded by the beach, I biked into the hills."

"I wasn't at the tearoom. I was catering a party for Layla Zimmer."

"Wait. You were there?" he asked. "You're a suspect?"

"No, like I said, I was in full view of everyone. I never went anywhere near that path until... after." But my insides wriggled. Had I been in full view of people the entire time?

He swore and pulled his shirt over his head. "Abigail–"

"The gig was good for the tearoom. Even Hyperion was there, reading cards."

"I can't believe this. Another murder. No wonder you freaked out when you heard me this morning."

"I freaked out because someone was in my garden again last night."

His jaw set. "That does it. I'm your new bodyguard."

"I don't think so."

He struck an action movie pose. "Hey, my sensei says I'm not bad. So. What are our plans for today?"

My plan had been to sit home and read a book. I couldn't imagine doing that with Razzzor hovering.

"I've got some marketing work that needs doing at the tearoom."

"Marketing? I'm great at marketing. I'll help."

He actually was a whiz at marketing, at least when it came to apps and other tech. And truth be told, I wasn't thrilled with the idea of being alone in an empty tearoom today.

Razzzor waited while I got dressed and grabbed my laptop and bag.

His Tesla smelled faintly of barbecue chips. Since that was most likely my fault, I didn't complain. Though I was a little surprised he hadn't had the car detailed since our stakeout.

He pulled from the curb. "Why kill Madge? Unless she knew something about the fake wine."

"These murders might have nothing to do with your wine." Casually, I felt beneath the seat and pulled out a crumpled bag of chips. I slipped the empty bag into my purse.

"I know it's not always about me," he said. "But this time, what are the odds it's not?"

We hashed over the crime and got nowhere. Razzzor was convinced a counterfeit wine scheme was behind it all. But I wasn't so sure. There were too many tangled relationships – Madge and Deva, Beatrice and Madge, Beatrice and Deva. The murders could easily have been a love triangle gone wrong.

"Or," I concluded, "there's a dastardly wine counterfeiting scheme worth killing over." I lowered my voice. "Dastards are everywhere."

Razzzor glowered. "Two people are dead and you're making jokes."

I sighed. "I'm not. I mean, I was, but I'm not making fun of their deaths. That was awful." I could sort of see killing someone in a fit of anger. It wasn't an excuse, but people snapped. But two murders...

I rubbed my hand on my thigh. At least one of the deaths had to have been premeditated.

We pulled into the parking lot behind the tearoom and stepped from the car. Fog hung over the low buildings. A crow pecked at something furry and flattened.

Razzzor made a face. "Who's in charge of this lot?"

"The birds." And they could have whatever was plastered to the pavement.

"It's a little dead." He glanced around the empty lot.

"Don't say dead. It's bad karma. And this is normal for Monday morning. The bank is the only business that gets any action at this hour." I nodded toward the rear of the bank, further down the lot.

He frowned. "Then why are you—"

A bang echoed across the lot. Razzzor staggered backward, one hand clapped to his shoulder. He dropped behind the Tesla.

Another bang and a ping. His side mirror cracked and fell to the pavement.

I realized I was still standing. My legs folded beneath me, and my knees hit the asphalt.

Someone was shooting. At us.

CHAPTER 14

Too stunned to move, I knelt beside the tire, my breath bottled in my chest. Somewhere on the other side of the Tesla, Razzzor groaned.

That jarred me into movement. I scrambled around the car.

Razzzor sat, wincing, against the front tire and gripped his upper arm. Blood seeped through his fingers.

Fear spiraled through me. "Razzzor. You're hurt." Oh, God. Razzzor had been shot.

"Yeah." He clenched his teeth. "No kidding."

I fumbled my phone from my purse and dialed 9-1-1. I'm not sure the dispatcher understood or believed me. I was so shrill and stumbling I'm not sure I would have understood. But she told me to keep under shelter and that the police were on their way.

I hung up, hands shaking. "How bad is it?" My voice was high and thin.

"I'm not letting go of my arm to check," Razzzor said.

"Do you want me to–?"

"No."

At least the blood loss hadn't dulled his mind. He knew I wouldn't know what I was doing. I really should learn first aid. Why hadn't I taken that class?

Wildly, I looked around the visible section of parking lot. We weren't well hidden, crouched behind Razzzor's car.

Fog hid the tops of the low buildings encircling the lot. Was the shooter on one of them? Was he repositioning for a better shot? I huddled closer to my friend.

"It'll be okay," he said. "Hey, remember that time that engineer you fired tried to blow up the office?"

"Yeah," I said, swallowing my fear. "Good times."

Razzzor hadn't had the heart to fire the lunatic, even after he'd been caught jamming the women's toilets with TP, flooding the restroom. I'd gotten stuck with the job, and then presto-blambo, bomb threat.

"Why are you bringing that up?" I asked.

"Shared danger — I don't know."

"Hey," I said, "the toilet bomber was a stalker too..." I trailed off. Stones and glass houses.

Years ago, I'd had my own cyber stalker. He'd deleted my college transcripts, ruined my credit score, and turned me into an online pariah. The police had tried to help, but the process had been achingly slow. Meanwhile, no one would hire me.

Except Razzzor.

He'd believed my crazy story. Later, he'd turned the tables on my cyber stalker and restored my online reputation. What he'd done had been illegal, if effective, but if Razzzor had gotten caught…

"Too?" he said. "I am not a stalker. I wasn't stalking Deva. I was staking out her wine-seller boyfriend for possible criminal activity."

"I meant the guy stalking Deva." And now, maybe stalking me. I couldn't believe this was happening twice.

I couldn't believe someone was shooting at us in sleepy San Borromeo.

Sirens wailed in the distance.

I cleared my throat. "Who do you think's shooting at us?"

Whoever it was had to be targeting Razzzor. I wasn't important enough to gun down.

"No one," he said, "I hope. I haven't heard anything for a while. Have you?"

"No. But I'm not sticking my head out to check."

"You've gotten awfully particular since you've stopped being my assistant."

"I wouldn't have taken a bullet for you even when you were paying my salary." And it had been a damned good salary.

A black-and-white screeched into the parking lot, followed by a maelstrom of cops and other emergency vehicles.

Things got chaotic at that point. Razzzor was whisked into an ambulance. I was questioned by Detective Chase. Uniformed officers searched the rooftops and alleys. But whoever had taken the two shots at us was gone.

Eventually, Detective Chase escorted me to the hospital emergency room. We watched Razzzor get stitches.

"It was just a scratch," Razzzor explained manfully.

Detective Chase grunted. He adjusted a paper mask over his nose and mouth with gloved hands. "So why would someone want to kill you, Mr. Razzzor?" he asked in a muffled drawl.

"It's just Razzzor," he said. "No mister."

"Whatever. Why are you on someone's hit list? Unless Ms. Beanblossom was the target?"

"No idea," Razzzor said.

I frowned. *No idea? Really?* What about the counterfeit wine angle? True, the police already knew about that, but it seemed worth a mention.

"I've made some enemies in my work though," Razzzor added helpfully.

"How many enemies?" the detective asked.

"I'll make a list. Or maybe Abigail–"

"No," I said. "I'm not drawing up an enemies list. This must have to do with Whitmore and Madge."

"We don't know that for sure," Razzzor said.

Dammit. He was still playing keep-away with the cops. "What about Deva?" I asked. "You suspected her of selling counterfeit wine to Whitmore. Now Whitmore and his partner are dead, and someone's tried to kill you. Deva was at the party when Madge was killed. And she was at the wine shop just before we found Whitmore."

He glared. "It wasn't Deva."

"Why not?" I asked.

"Because even if she was counterfeiting my wine, which she's not, it's small potatoes. It's not worth killing over to protect herself."

"Does she know that?" I asked.

"She's not crazy."

"Do you want to run this interview, Ms. Beanblossom?" the detective drawled. "Not that I mind. It's fascinating. I'm just starting to wonder what I'm doing in this germ factory. Besides, we inventoried the Wine Merchants. There was no counterfeit wine."

Razzzor blinked. "Are you sure?"

"You think just because I'm from Texas I don't know wine?"

"N-no," we stammered.

"Well," he said, "I don't. So we brought in an expert."

He asked Razzzor more questions I already knew the answers to and left, muttering about goggles and bacteria and eyeballs.

"Uncool, Abigail," Razzzor hissed. "You know we only tell cops the bare minimum. Besides, Deva wouldn't try to kill me."

"Right now, *I* want to kill you."

"Give a guy a break." His head dropped onto the thin hospital pillow. "I've been wounded."

"But did you die?" I snapped.

"No, but—"

"Then man up and face facts. That may have been a warning shot gone wrong, or it may have been attempted murder. And if it was the latter, whoever did this might try again. I'm calling Beech."

He paled. "I don't think we need to go that far."

"Tough." I dialed. Beech was a personal protection specialist Razzzor had used on more than one occasion. The guy was built like a Sequoia and his prices were Silicon Valley-high. But Razzzor could afford it. And I couldn't protect the idiot.

"Abs," a gravelly voice said. "What did he do now?"

"Someone shot him," I said. And why did Beech still have my number in his phone?

Mystery for another day.

I outlined the problem and told Beech where he could collect Razzzor. He promised to be here in an hour.

"An hour?" Razzzor said when I'd hung up. "I'm supposed to hang around here for an hour?"

"Yes," I said. "For all we know, you were followed to the hospital and there's a sniper outside." I twisted my necklace around one finger. What if whoever was targeting Razzzor *had* hired a sniper? With the money flying around Razzzor's world, it wasn't outside the realm of possibility.

I waited with Razzzor. I didn't trust him not to call for a cab and escape before Beech arrived. When the bodyguard finally did, I called an Uber for myself and returned to my tearoom.

Police officers still patrolled the parking lot behind our building. I let myself inside and locked the door behind me, leaning against its cool metal. Razzzor's life was over the top, but this was ridiculous.

"Hey, girl."

I yelped and high jumped about a mile.

Hyperion frowned and tugged on the collar of the gray turtleneck beneath his blazer.

His leashed tabby, Bastet, smirked.

"What's going on?" Hyperion asked. "There are cops all over the parking lot."

"Someone tried to kill Razzzor."

"Your imaginary friend? This reeks of a desperate cry for attention."

Bastet meowed in agreement.

"I'm serious." Clutching my oversized purse to my chest, I explained.

His jaw slackened. "You could have been killed. Are you all right?"

"I'm fine."

"What were you doing here on a Monday anyway?"

"I wanted to get out of the house. What are you doing here?"

He waved his hand negligently. "Oh, just some coursework for... You know—"

"No, I don't." I narrowed my eyes. "What exactly is this course you're taking?"

"Like I told you before, it's continuing education. And what I was about to say, was you know how it is. When you own your own business, you're always working." He hustled me into his cozy office, twinkle lights gleaming from the ceiling. Hyperion sat me at one of the high-backed, red velvet chairs. "Sit down. This time, *I'll* make the tea."

I let myself relax for a moment, then dug my laptop from my bag and booted up. How big of a crime *was* wine counterfeiting?

I surfed the internet and discovered one wine counterfeiter had gotten ten years for fraud. But he'd been selling fake wines worth a lot more than Razzzor's brand, defrauding clients of millions. Another fraudster got six years, but he'd also sold to big fish.

If Deva had been slapping Razzzor's label on other, cheaper wines, and doing it on a small scale, how much trouble would she be in?

Bastet sprang onto my lap. Absently, I petted the tabby.

Unless Deva was selling fake wine on a larger scale than Razzzor assumed. Wine counterfeiting was becoming a problem for high-end buyers. But we were talking wines that went for twenty or thirty grand. Razzzor's wines went for around a thousand, which still seemed bonkers to me. But for a fraudster to make any real money, at a thousand bucks a pop, she'd have to sell at quantity.

Since Deva worked for a distributor, *maybe* she could pull that off. But she hadn't been distributing to the Wine Merchants, and Razzzor had found a bottle there. Had she simply dropped one by as a gift for her good friend Whitmore? Was that why the cops hadn't found any other bad bottles at the Wine Merchants?

Or could the murders have nothing to do with wine fraud?

At a loss, I surfed for info on Razzzor's wine and found a review.

This comes from the producer's coolest estate from a site along the Russian River's Green Valley appellation. The wine is powerful, opulent and seductive, and uncannily reminiscent of a great Bordeaux. But make no mistake, this is a California wine. Immense, rich red fruits mask equally dense tannins which back up this wine, giving it both concentration and longevity.

I whistled. The wine had 98 points, and even I knew that was good.

Bastet slunk from my lap onto the table. He perched his furry butt on my laptop and purred.

"Move it or lose it, cat."

Bastet yawned. He knew I was all talk.

Hyperion glided into the room with an ivory cup on a saucer. "Our new Optimistic Fool tea. When are we going to get special labels made for our Tarot teas? And have you come up with any others?"

"You mean, in between my real job and getting shot at?"

He set the cup on the table and jammed his hands on his hips. "Really?"

I shrugged. "Sarcasm is only one of my many talents."

"But not time management? I thought you'd have the entire Major Arcana of tea knocked out by now."

"Ha. Good one." I sipped the tea. *Tasty.*

"Don't you think now is a good time to create more Tarot teas?"

I angled my head. That wasn't a bad idea. I was too rattled to do any real work. And there wasn't much I liked better than mixing herbs. "You're right. It's a perfect time."

"Good. I'll help."

I stared in surprise. "Since when do you work in the kitchen?"

"Since my favorite business partner was nearly killed."

"I'm your only business partner."

"Why quibble?"

I finished my tea, and we worked companionably in the kitchen. Hyperion made surprisingly good suggestions. By lunch we had two more Tarot teas – the Magician and the High Priestess.

Hyperion stretched. "I'm loving how productive we are. How shall we reward our hard work? Lunch? Booze?" He snapped his fingers. "I know. Both."

"Isn't it a little early?"

He raised his brows. "Please. Getting shot at must burn all sorts of calories."

"You must be right. For some reason, I'm feeling amazingly fit and alive."

We locked up and ambled across the parking lot to a wine bar that allowed pets.

Hyperion and I found seats at the long, black marble bar and ordered. Bastet coiled at his feet.

"Abigail? Hyperion?" Beatrice hurried to the bar. She looked a little like Katherine Hepburn in her vintage sapphire jacket with broad lapels. She wore matching wide-legged trousers. "Have you heard? Someone was shooting a gun in this parking lot!"

"Um, yeah. I did hear that," I said, wary. What was the PR consultant doing here?

"Isn't your tearoom right over there?" She nodded toward the back wall.

"Yes," I said.

"Lucky." She grinned. "Think of all the free publicity."

"I don't think a shooting is very good PR," I said stiffly.

"That's where you're wrong," she said. "No publicity is bad publicity. It's trite but true."

"Not if people think they're risking their life for a cup of tea," I said.

"We could try catering to the Goth crowd again," Hyperion suggested.

"No," I said. "No Goths. Goths are fine in principle, but all that black brings down the tone of the tearoom."

"You may have a point," he said. "But black does absorb negative energy."

"Oh," Beatrice said, "people will only worry if it was a random shooting. If someone was *targeted*, then everyone will think they're safe. It's all about blaming the victim. It's a denial mechanism. If someone was targeting X, then I, Y, am safe. It's delusional, but if we had to face reality every day, none of us would get through it. Now, the question is, who were they targeting? Was anyone hurt?"

"I don't know who they were targeting." I studied her. There was no way she'd just happened to show up here. True, her business was only blocks away, but this was too wild a coincidence. "And no one was badly hurt."

"Then you'll need to make something up," Beatrice said. "We can spin this, don't you worry."

"Is that why you're here?" Hyperion asked. "Trolling for business?"

She laughed. "Of course. Besides, when I realized where the shooting happened in relation to your tearoom, I had to check out the crime scene. But then I saw your tearoom was closed, so I came here for a drink. Half off wine before four o'clock? Now *that's* PR genius."

"It's funny," I lied, "but I tried calling you this morning. Your secretary said you were busy."

"I was on a call with India." Her brow wrinkled. "Monica didn't tell me you'd called."

"I didn't leave a message."

"Did you get a chance to look over our sample PR plan?"

"I did," I said guiltily. "It's great, but I don't think we can afford your services yet."

She smiled. "That's okay. You will. Just remember, when the press comes calling, and they will, the shooting wasn't random."

She strolled from the wine bar, her heels clicking on the tile floor.

The bartender set two glasses of wine in front of us.

"Does her visit strike you as a teensy bit suspicious?" Hyperion asked.

I sipped my Cabernet. "Since she didn't stay for the wine? Very."

CHAPTER 15

Hyperion leaned across the shiny black bar. He grabbed a cocktail napkin from its stack beside a bowl of mints, and sat back on his chair. "Let's review the suspects." He pulled a pen from the inside pocket of his gray blazer and clicked it.

"Deva," I said.

Bastet sprang into my lap.

"I'm loving the way you throw yourself into these cases," he said. "Really, I am. But do you think you maybe have a bit of a *thing* about Deva?"

"No. What's that supposed to mean?"

"I can't help but noticing that she looks a lot like you, only better. Might you be a teensy bit jealous?" He pinched two fingers together.

"This was so…" We *did* look a lot alike. *Coincidence.* "She was the first suspect we encountered. I'm going chronologically. Deva could have bashed Whitmore on the head and then left. And when Deacon went in right after her, Whitmore was already dead."

"Okay then," he said. "Deacon. Isn't he a bona fide stalker?"

"That's what Deva said. But she also accused Razzzor of stalking her, and he didn't."

"Can imaginary friends even stalk people?"

Lightly, Bastet bit my hand. I pet the cat.

Hyperion tapped his pen on his chin. "Anyhoo, it's possible Whitmore figured out Deva was selling him counterfeit wine. Maybe he confronted her, and she killed him."

I winced. "Actually, the police inventoried his store and couldn't find any fake wine."

"The police? You mean Tony?"

"He might have come by after the shooting," I admitted.

"And you didn't call me?" he said in an outraged tone.

"I was a little busy." I caught the eye of the waiter behind the bar, and he nodded.

"Some friend you are." Hyperion huffed. "But okay, I can see you might have had other things on your mind. I forgive you. This time. But that blows our counterfeit wine theory out of the water?"

Yeah. It did. It also made Razzzor look guilty – like he was using the fraudulent wine as an excuse to stake out her new boyfriend. "Razzzor believed it," I muttered, and I straightened. "Razzzor said he found a bottle of the fake wine there. He must still have it."

The waiter headed toward us.

"Let's keep it IRL," Hyperion said, "and get back to murder, shall we?"

The waiter made a smart 180 degree turn and walked away.

"Fine," I said, resigned to never seeing that waiter again. "Beatrice."

"Whitmore's ex who just happened to turn up here after you'd been shot at? That did seem a little too pat, but this is a small town. The news was probably all over the internet."

"Or she could have been the shooter and stuck around to see what happened next," I said.

"Exactamundo. Notice how she asked if anyone was hurt? Like she was trying to figure out if she'd managed to hit her target?"

"But that implies Razzzor was her target, because Beatrice could see I was okay. This has to be about the wine fraud."

"*Alleged* wine fraud."

"Thank you, Perry Mason," I said.

"Any time. What else?"

"If Deacon really is obsessed with Deva, then who knows who he'd hurt?"

He wrote the name on the cocktail napkin. "Including Madge? I didn't see Deacon at the Zimmers's party. Did you?"

"No. But if Razzzor was biking nearby, then the bike messenger could have been too. And that cliff trail is public access."

"But why kill Madge?"

I lifted my hands and dropped them into my lap. Bastet gave an outraged howl, and I quickly resumed petting the tabby. Pets were allowed, but not if they kicked up a fuss. "You see? It has to be connected to the wine shop."

"Or to jealousy. You said Madge had been dating Whitmore, and Deva took Madge's place dating Whitmore... I really wish I'd known him. He must have had charisma out the wazoo. Was Whitmore very good looking?"

"The only time I saw Whitmore, he was dead."

"We'll table that for now. Who else?"

"James and Layla Zimmer, I guess. It was their party, and Deva works for James."

"And again I ask, why kill Madge?"

"If Madge knew about the fake wine–"

He threw his pen on the bar, and it skittered over the edge. "Again, with the fake wine. Tony told you there wasn't any in that shop."

"But Razzzor said there was."

"And I'm supposed to take the word of your imaginary friend over a highly trained tall drink of water like Detective Chase?"

I slumped in my chair. "Yes."

"This is all he-said, imaginary-friend-said. We need facts."

"Then let's get them."

He propped his chin on his interlaced hands. "How?"

"Deva. She knows more than she's saying. Think you can get her to the tearoom?"

He sipped his red. "Watch me."

*****

Hyperion adjusted one of the red-velvet chairs in his office.

"How did you get Deva to agree to come here?" I asked from the doorway.

"I suggested we swap a Tarot reading for information on the murders."

My jaw sagged. "This was supposed to be covert."

He shot me a pitying look. "Honestly, how was I supposed to manage that? Deva may make poor dating choices, but she's not stupid. The way we've been lurking around the crime scenes has been totally suspicious."

"Razzzor is not a poor dating choice."

"I was referring to Whitmore. A man who dumps his wife for his business partner and then dumps his business partner for a wine distributor strikes me as a little flighty."

I looked around the office. "Where am I going to sit?"

"In the kitchen. This is a private reading."

"But—"

"You can hang around to ask her what kind of tea she wants. Do you have any of those scones or little sandwiches left?"

I folded my arms. "No."

"Can you make some?"

I glared.

"It'll loosen her up," he said.

A headache bloomed behind my eyeballs. "Fine. I'll make egg and cress sandwiches."

"Better ask first. She might have allergies."

Deva did have allergies. To cats. I escorted Bastet into the hallway after taking her order.

Hyperion pointedly closed the door on us.

The tabby sneezed.

"No kidding," I said. "This bites."

Bastet started to follow me into the kitchen. I shot the cat a warning look, and he sat in the dimly lit hall, a sour expression on his furry face.

"It's not my rules," I said. "It's the county's." But honestly, I wouldn't let the cat inside either.

I brewed Deva's turmeric golden milk tea, poured it over ice. Setting it on a tray along with a plate of four egg and cress sandwich triangles, I returned to knock on Hyperion's door.

"Come in," he sang out.

I opened the door with one hand and pushed it wider with my hip.

An uncut deck of cards lay on the table between them.

I sidled inside. "Here you go."

Deva wound her blond hair into a bun. Her highlights glinted beneath the twinkle lights. She wore a silky white tank and long, button-up camel-colored skirt. I was fairly certain it had not come out of a consignment shop.

"Oh, Abigail," Hyperion said, "be a dear and make me some of your iced masala chai, will you?"

My jaw clenched. "Certainly."

Bastet looked up smugly as I exited the room.

"It's for a good cause," I grumbled.

I made Hyperion's drink and returned to his office.

The deck still lay untouched between the two. If he planned on using Tarot to interrogate her, when was he going to start? Unless they really were hashing over the murders.

Deva's gaze flicked toward me, her hazel eyes indifferent.

"Thank you." He waved me away.

Grimacing, I did not slam the door on the way out. But I sure wanted to.

Thirty minutes later, his office door opened. "Enjoy the rest of your week."

"Thanks," Deva said. "That was... enlightening."

"I aim to please."

She turned to me. "Razzzor's a good guy, even if things didn't work out." She eyed me. "But I didn't mess with his wine. I can't believe he thought I would."

"Whatever. Ta!" Hyperion hustled her out the back door, closed it, and leaned against it. "Whew."

"So? What did she say?"

"She denied anything fishy was going on at the Wine Merchants, and was shocked, shocked to hear Razzzor's wine had been counterfeited," he said, doing his best *Casablanca* impression.

"And?"

"And she confirmed she's not a wine distributor for the Wine Merchants. Even if there was a fraudulent bottle in there, someone else must have sold it to them. Deva still has a thing for Razzzor, by the way."

"At least you admit he's real."

"I admit nothing. He could be a mass delusion for all I know."

"Anything else?"

He sniffed. "You know Tarot readings are confidential."

"Fine." I strode into the kitchen. "At least we know more than we did. I'll see you tomorrow."

I grabbed my purse from the long, metal table.

"What?" he asked. "No, *good job*, Hyperion?"

"You don't need my approval." Grinning, I strode out the rear door.

"What is your problem?" Deva shouted.

I scanned the parking lot. A fog had rolled in, turning the world sullen gray.

She stood beside a Tesla, her long curls quivering with indignation. "What is *wrong* with you?"

My stomach sank.

She was shouting at Razzzor.

CHAPTER 16

Razzzor raised one hand in a defensive gesture, his wounded arm limp at his side.

Late afternoon fog drifted over the rooftops, and a sharp stab of fear pierced my gut. But no one was aiming a gun at us. That sort of thing couldn't happen twice.

Could it?

"I came to see Abigail," Razzzor said. "She works here."

Deva's face contorted. "Bull."

"Hey, Razzzor," I called. "Right on time."

Deva pivoted on her low heels. "You– You were expecting him? Was he supposed to be listening in on my Tarot reading too?"

"I didn't listen in on your reading." Not that I hadn't tried. "And I thought you and Razzzor were okay?"

"So did I." She swore and strode away.

A car door slammed, and a sports car raced from the lot.

I folded my arms. "Well?"

"Honestly, I was coming to find you."

"You could have called."

"I did. You didn't answer. I got worried."

Frowning, I pulled my phone from my purse. *Whoops*. I'd turned off the sound. Heh heh.

"How's your arm?" I asked. "And where's Beech?"

"He was getting bossy, so I let him go."

"Razzzor—"

He reached for his shoulder and dropped his hand. "I'm fine. My arm's fine. And thanks for covering for me with Deva. And can we get out of this lot?"

I studied him. Jeans. Expensive white button-up. Eyes wide behind his wireframe glasses and moisture dotting his forehead. He looked like he was meeting with his first venture capital investor – terrified.

"Let's get a drink," I said.

He nodded. I led him to the wine bar.

The owner, Barry, stood beside the hostess podium. Tall, with an eighties 'stache and a receding hairline, he looked up in surprise at my return. "Where would you like to sit?"

"Outside?" I asked.

"Anywhere you want." Barry followed us to a table on the back patio, screened by wooden lattice.

"How's it going?" I asked the bar owner.

"Business is light. The shooting scared off the customers."

I nodded sympathetically. Who knew how it would affect my own customers? "Barry, this is my friend Razzzor. Razzzor – Barry."

Barry did a double take. "Razzzor? Wine Razzzor?"

Razzzor looked around, his expression panicky. "Yes."

The bar owner shook his hand. "Thanks for buying up all that bad wine."

"I didn't... Did I?" Razzzor looked to me.

"Hyperion bought nearly a case of your wine from me," Barry said. "He told me there was some question of it being fake, and he was buying it on your behalf. Was that wrong?"

"Um, no," I said. "And hopefully the wine is fine." But Hyperion hadn't mentioned the wine. He must have forgotten in the excitement of Razzzor getting shot.

"What's the tell?" Barry asked. "How can you know the wine's fake?"

Razzzor explained about the label.

Barry shook his head. "Good to know."

"Who sold you the wine?" I asked. "Do you remember?"

"Yeah." He braced his hands on his hips and looked at the floor. "It's hard to forget. I got it from the Wine Merchants. You heard what happened over there?"

"Yeah," I said. "Terrible."

Barry shook his head. "I don't know what's happening to this town. Too many people, I think. California's getting too crowded, and it's making everyone squirrely." He paused, and said in a lower voice, "Whitmore was a decent guy."

"Did you know him well?" Razzzor asked.

"I saw him at local business association meetings, that sort of thing. But his death was a blow. It's a small town. For something like that to happen…" He shook his head.

"I'd have figured you'd use a distributor instead of the Wine Merchants," I said.

"I do. Zimmerland Wines. But lately, there've been some guys from Menlo Park coming around – big money, good customers. They dropped in a couple weeks back asking about expensive wines, so I called Deva. But she was in Tahoe and couldn't help me out." An odd look crossed his face – doubt and guilt. "Anyway, the Menlo Park guys showed up here, and I didn't want to disappoint them. So I called Whitmore. He brought a case by thirty minutes later and gave me the wholesale price. Said he'd gotten a good deal on it. Now I guess we know why."

"And Deva?" I asked. "Was she really at Tahoe?"

"I guess so. Why?"

"It's just… You got a funny look on your face when you mentioned it."

"I heard she likes to gamble," Barry said in a low voice. "A lot. And she doesn't always win."

"No one always wins," Razzzor said defensively.

I sat back in my chair. "You think she has a gambling problem. What does she play?"

"High-stakes poker." Barry flipped his drying towel over one shoulder. "I've got a friend who plays. He recognized her when she stopped by once. He said she was into some scary people."

Razzzor's brows drew together.

"What sort of scary people?" I asked.

Barry shrugged. "No idea. But my friend doesn't scare easily. Anyway, thanks." He extended his hand to Razzzor, and the two men shook. "I appreciate you looking out for the customers. I'll be sure to buy more of your wine – and check the label." He took our orders and strode into the bar.

Razzzor hunched in his wicker chair. "I guess I really owe your partner now."

"I'll talk to him," I said.

"There's something we're not seeing," he said. "Deva wouldn't have done this."

"You can't still believe that."

"And just because she's a good poker player, doesn't mean she's a gambling addict."

"How do you know she's a good player? Barry said she lost."

Razzzor flushed. "Um. It was how we met."

"You were playing poker?" I asked, incredulous. Since when did he gamble?

"Some guys I know invited me to play. It was only the one time. Deva cleaned us out."

"If she owed money, that's a motive for her to counterfeit wine. Counterfeiting *your* wine was probably just a bonus."

His angular jaw jutted forward. "That's not fair. We only have that guy's word for it that she was in over her head."

"Oh, for—"

A waiter set our glasses of wine on the white tablecloth. I fumed while he fiddled with our individual mini-carafes.

The waiter glided away.

"Why would Barry lie?" I asked. "We need to find out if the wine Hyperion bought was counterfeited." I pulled out my phone and called.

"Tea, Tarot, and tingles," Hyperion sang.

"Please tell me that's not how you're answering our business line," I said.

"Of course not. You know how I answer our phone: Beanblossom's Tea and Tarot, where every day's a holiday."

I was never going to break him of that habit. "Barry told me you bought a case of Razzzor's wine?"

"He gave me the wholesaler price," he said. "But yeah. Your imaginary friend wasn't serious about paying me in Bitcoin, was he?"

"He'll pay you," I said.

"I'll take cash."

"So," I said, "where is it?"

"What?"

I smacked my forehead. He was doing this on purpose. "The wine."

"Oh," Hyperion said. "It's in the storage closet at Beanblossom's."

"Great. Razzzor and I are at the wine bar."

"Well, I'm not bringing it to you there. I can't. I'm at that taco truck everyone's been talking about."

"Seriously? Where is it?" I shook my head. *Unimportant.* But I did want to try those tacos.

"They're set up by the pier," Hyperion said. "Hey, thanks," he murmured to someone in the background. "So, is that it?" he asked me. "Because my fish tacos are getting cold."

"That's it. Talk to you later."

I hung up.

"Well?" Razzzor asked.

"Your wine's at Beanblossom's."

"Let's check it. If it's good, you can stop obsessing over Deva."

"Um, I'm not the one obsessing."

He gulped his wine. "I'll get the check." He scraped back his wicker chair and vanished into the bar.

Razzzor's case of wine wasn't going anywhere, so I sipped my wine more slowly.

When Razzzor returned, I reluctantly abandoned what was left, and we walked toward Beanblossom's. Razzzor's gaze darted nervously around the lot.

I caught myself hunching my shoulders. As if muscle tension could deflect a bullet.

I unlocked the door, and Razzzor hustled me inside.

I led him to the storage closet, aka the kitchen pantry. A box of Razzzor's wine sat on the floor beside a bin of flour.

Razzzor hefted the box and carried it into the kitchen, setting it on the long metal table in its center. He unfolded the top flaps and pulled out an ebony bottle, studying the label.

"Well?" I asked.

His shoulders slumped. "It's fake."

I pulled out another bottle and examined its label. It was fake too. "I'm sorry," I said.

"At least Deva had nothing to do with it."

"I guess not." But could Deva have sold the wine to the Wine Merchants unofficially? "Who distributes for your winery?"

"Zimmerland."

"Deva's company? What can you tell me about them?"

"Not much. I don't handle that part of the winery. But I know they work with high-end wine connoisseurs, selling wine at auction and stuff. Not my wine. At a thousand a bottle, mine is still considered lowbrow."

"Does Zimmerland know about the counterfeiting?"

"No," he said, grim, "and they should. Hold on." Hunched over his phone, he walked into the hallway.

I returned the wine to its case. I guessed we'd gotten our fingerprints all over the bottles, but so had half a dozen other people at this point. Should I call Detective Chase?

I smiled, shaking my head. Hyperion had bought the wine. I'd let him call Tony. My partner would love that.

Razzzor returned to the kitchen and shoved his glasses up his nose. "Okay. Zimmerland is having a VIP wine tasting party tomorrow. I'll talk to them then."

"Why not just call and tell them?"

"Because I don't have a direct relationship with them. My manager at the vineyard is the person who works with the distributor. And this is the sort of thing that needs to be discussed in person."

Razzzor at a wine tasting? True, VIP implied it would be small, but this seemed very un-Razzzor. "Don't you think a private meeting would be better?"

"Maybe, but... I got two tickets. I thought you could come with me?"

That sounded more like Razzzor. But I wasn't going to argue. If he hadn't invited me to the meeting, I would have been annoyed. "I'll come."

"Good, because I've sent them to you to hold."

CHAPTER 17

I propped my feet on my coffee table, slipped on my headset, and relaxed for the evening into some well-deserved zombie-Nazi killing in World War II Rome.

I blasted a Nazi, taking out an obelisk in the process. It tilted, achingly slowly, and crashed to the stone pavement, fragments scattering.

"Whoa," Razzzor said in my ear. "Did you have to take out a priceless Egyptian antiquity?" He shot a zombie crawling over the rubble.

"Yes." I adjusted my headset. "Yes, I did."

Three zombies emerged from a trattoria and staggered toward us.

"That obelisk was standing for thousands of years," he said.

"That obelisk was a bunch of pixels." I aimed and downed each zombie in turn. This was Razzzor's element. Online, through a headset, we could just be Razzzor and AbsOfSteele363.

He blew out his breath.

"What?" I asked.

"I don't think you're taking this seriously."

"Of course I'm not taking it seriously. That's the whole point of this game. They're zombie Nazis. Not only do they represent some of the worst of humanity, they're already dead. And they don't exist. There's no moral gray area, because there's no such thing as zombie Nazis."

Razzzor didn't respond.

"You weren't talking about the game, were you?" I asked.

"My psychiatrist says I should be more direct about telling people what I feel."

My thumb hovered over the controller. "Okay. What are you feeling?"

"I *feel* that you're not being fair to Deva. I saw the expression on your face when Barry mentioned the gambling."

"If she needs money, and she's mad at you, and she knows wine, and her boyfriend was selling fake bottles of yours... Well, *you're* the one who suspected she might be behind the wine counterfeiting." A zombie crawled out of a gelato shop. I blew its head off, splattering zombie brains across the stone wall.

"I know. I just... I thought she might be the real thing. You know?"

I set the controller in my lap, my insides twisting.

I knew. It might be better to have loved and lost than never to have loved at all, but it was also a major gut kick.

"I'm sorry," I said. "I had no idea things were that serious."

"I guess they weren't. Not for her, at least. We dated a month, and she ended things. She said I– it doesn't matter."

"She broke up with you?" I repeated, scrunching my forehead in thought. So much for revenge as a motive for faking Razzzor's wine. But if Deva needed money badly enough, maybe revenge didn't factor into it at all.

But if Deva needed money, all she had to do was ask Razzzor and he would have given her some.

He was that kind of guy.

"Did you two ever, um, talk about money?" I said cautiously.

"No. Why would we?"

Huh. I liked Deva better for not asking.

"I just feel like there's something else going on," Razzzor said. "Something we don't understand. And I'm not talking about the breakup. I'm talking about this wine business. Counterfeiting thousand-dollar wine isn't worth killing over."

I checked my watch. Eight o'clock.

"What's Deva's number?" I asked.

"What? Why?"

"It's time to talk to her directly. Clear the air."

"Do you think she'll talk to us?"

"I think I can get her to."

"Hold on. I'll get my phone." After a moment, he rattled off a string of numbers.

"Okay," I said, "hang on. I'll call her and get back to you. Watch for zombies."

"I've got your six."

I pulled off the headset, dropping it to my couch cushion, and called Deva.

"Hello?" she asked.

"Deva, this is Abigail Beanblossom."

"Oh." Her voice flattened.

I rubbed the seam of a blue throw pillow with my thumb. "Look, Razzzor and I stopped by the wine bar behind Tea and Tarot. They had a box of Razzzor's wine in stock. It was counterfeit."

She sucked in her breath. "All of it?"

"Every bottle. The owner told us he got it from Whitmore."

She cursed. "From Whitmore? But… why would he buy from Whitmore? I'm their distributor."

"Barry said you weren't available, and he was desperate. Where do you think Whitmore got that fake wine?"

"That's a good question."

There was a long silence.

"Maybe we should talk," she finally said.

Ha. "When?"

"Tomorrow afternoon. Come by my house. Razzzor knows where it is."

"Two o'clock?" I asked.

"That works." She hung up.

I refitted my headset. "Deva wants to talk. Tomorrow. Her house. Two o'clock."

"Seriously? I'll pick you up from the tearoom at one-thirty," he said eagerly.

"Deal."

"Clear the air… Thanks, Abs. You're the best."

"Um, *yeah.*" I just hoped our meeting went the way Razzzor wanted.

*****

Tuesday morning flew by at Beanblossom's Tea and Tarot. A family had booked the tearoom for their grandmother's ninetieth birthday. The old lady was as tart as a Granny Smith apple, cracking wise with staff and customers. Hyperion and his readers were kept busy reading for the guests, and six fairy cakes were devoured.

After the party departed and we'd cleaned up, Hyperion leaned into the kitchen.

"Ta. I'm off to tell Detective Chase about our amazing discovery."

I handed him an envelope bulging with cash. "For the wine you bought."

"From your imaginary friend?"

"And this afternoon, Razzzor and I are going to Deva's to talk to her about the wine." And I hoped Hyperion wouldn't ask to come along. Things might get awkward between Razzzor and Deva. I wasn't even sure *I* wanted to be there. But I doubted Deva would have agreed to the meeting without me as a buffer.

"Hm." Hyperion tapped his chin with the envelope. "So, you admit he's imaginary."

"He's not – Razzzor's real." Honestly, sometimes Hyperion could take a joke too far.

"Maybe. You do realize, a trip to Deva's might be considered interfering in a police investigation. But don't worry, I won't narc on you to the Texan detective." My partner disappeared around the corner, and the rear door slammed.

My staff could live without me for an hour. I finished helping them prep for the next serving, and I hurried out the rear door to the parking lot.

Razzzor leaned, arms crossed. against his Tesla. He straightened off it. "Ready?"

"Ha. I was born ready."

One corner of his mouth turned up in a lopsided grin.

We blasted into the Santa Cruz mountains. The Tesla raced past fern-laden slopes and damp redwood trees.

Razzzor cleared his throat. "So, what are you wearing to the thing tonight?"

"The wine tasting? Why? Are you afraid I'll let you down?"

"No," he said. "I'm afraid I'll let you down."

I shot him a surprised look. "Since when do you care about fashion?" His work wear was a faded band t-shirt and jeans.

"Things are different now."

"How?"

"It was different when we were building the company," he said wistfully. "I knew what I had to do, and I did it. Now..." He shrugged.

"You're bored," I said. For Razzzor, boredom led to frustration. Frustration led to doubt. Doubt led to obsessing about things he couldn't control. Like police investigations.

"I've been playing with some AI in my garage–"

"Razzzor, if you bring about the machine apocalypse, so help me–"

"Hey, I've seen *Terminator*. I wouldn't do anything dumb. The thing is, it's not the same as when you and I were creating."

"I wasn't creating. I was keeping everyone off your back so *you* could create."

"You were doing more than that."

The wind whipped my hair, and I clawed it behind my ear, bracing my elbow on the open window.

"Even if we were working together again," I said quietly. "It wouldn't be the same. It's never the same." Because you can't go back. Only forward.

He paused. "I know. I guess I'm a little jealous. You've got something cool with your Tea and Tarot room. Something unique and your own. You're in the building stage, the becoming, when everything's exciting, everything's a challenge."

When everything's terrifying. But he was right. There was something sparkly fun about a startup, once you got past the gut-burning fear of losing everything to a mistake. Hyperion and I had already made our share of those.

We drove in silence until we glided to a stop in front of a gated driveway.

I whistled and lowered my sunglasses. "Deva lives here?" I couldn't see much but plants and driveway past the iron gate. Judging from the Pacific-view location and size of the neighbors, Deva's place was swank.

"I told you she wasn't after my money."

"I never said she was." But I *had* thought it.

He reached for the squawk box. The spiked, iron gate swung open before he touched the yellow button.

"I guess we go in," Razzzor said.

I pressed deeper into the leather seat. "For someone who accused a man of stalking her, she's awfully quick to let us inside."

"We have an appointment." He drove into a circular driveway, its center island dotted with tropical plants. The Tesla slowed in front of a low, modern house.

"Wow. How much do wine distributors make?"

"She comes from a wealthy family." He parked behind a pickup truck filled with pool equipment, and we stepped out.

A tanned, blond man in beach shorts and a t-shirt swaggered around the corner of the white-painted house. "Oh, hey. You're not Deva."

"No," I said. "I'm Abigail. This is Razzzor."

"I thought you were Deva. That's why I let you in the gate." He nodded toward the Tesla. "It looked like the kind of car she'd drive. Her or one of her boyfriends."

"Her boyfriends?" I asked.

He laughed. "Oh, yeah. She's a real player. I'm Doug, by the way."

I cut a glance at Razzzor.

My friend shoved his hands into his pockets and looked glum.

"Nice to meet you," I said. "Hey, weird question: ever seen this guy?" I pulled up a picture of Whitmore Carson on my phone and showed it to him.

"Yeah, he was here a week or so ago," Doug said. "They had a huge fight. What, are you two detectives or something?"

"We think Deva may be in trouble," Razzzor said.

"In trouble?" Doug asked. "From that dude? Nah. She totally had him handled."

"What did they argue about?" I asked.

"Over another woman, if you can believe it. What was her name? Lilith? Delilah?"

"Layla?" I said.

The pool guy snapped his fingers. "Yeah. Layla, like the song. The dude kept asking, *Does Layla know? Does Layla know?*"

"Where is Deva?" Razzzor asked, looking around.

"Like I said, I thought you were her. I haven't seen her. It's no big deal. I don't need to see her to clean the pool. But she was going to pay me today." He winked. "Cash only, man."

"Have you considered e-currency?" Razzzor asked.

"Sure, if I want the Feds to track it. And I don't."

"Bitcoin is decentralized," Razzzor said.

I checked my watch. It was ten after two. "Maybe she got held up," I said. I dug my phone from my purse and called her. A phone rang faintly from somewhere inside the house, and I stiffened. The last time I'd followed the sound of a ringing phone, I'd found a body.

The call went to voicemail. I hung up.

My scalp prickled. So, she hadn't answered. It was nothing to hyperventilate about. She probably just hadn't heard the door. Maybe the pool guy hadn't even rung the bell.

"She must be inside." I walked to the door and pressed the bell.

The pool guy reached past me and turned the knob. The paneled door swung open. "Cool. Deva?" he shouted and walked inside.

Razzzor started after him.

I grabbed his sleeve. "We can't go in there."

"He just did. I can't leave her alone with a strange guy."

"Razzzor, no." I hissed and pressed the bell again.

"Deva?" the pool guy shouted from somewhere inside the house.

"You don't understand," I said, tasting something sour. "I heard her phone ring inside."

"We all heard it. She must be home."

"The last time I followed the sound of a ringing phone, something really bad happened."

"What happened?"

"Let the pool guy find Deva," I pleaded, "and she'll come to the door." I pressed the bell again.

"Seriously, what happened?"

"Nothing. It's not important. The point is, we're guests. We can't just go walking inside."

"Doug did."

"That's different," I said. "She owes him money."

"I'm not sure how that's different."

"He hasn't been accused of stalk—"

Doug streaked between us, knocking Razzzor into a banana plant.

"Hey!" I shouted.

Flipflops slapping on the pavement, the pool guy bolted across the driveway. He jumped into his truck. The pickup spat gravel and squealed toward the gate.

I gave Razzzor a hand up. He brushed tanbark off his jeans.

We looked through the open door at the contemporary black and white furniture.

I swallowed. "Deva?" I called and tiptoed inside, Razzzor breathing down my collar.

"You wait outside," Razzzor said. "I'll see what's up."

"No way. We stick together." I had a bad feeling, and whatever was inside, I didn't want him to find it alone.

We rounded a corner and walked through a living room filled with natural light and more white furniture.

"Deva?" he shouted, hurrying forward. "It's Razzzor and Abigail."

We turned another corner.

"Oh, no," I breathed.

Red wine stained a mod geometric rug. An empty glass lay beside a feminine, outstretched hand. Deva lay curled on her side, her eyes open and staring.

CHAPTER 18

Detective Chase pushed his cowboy hat higher on his head with his thumb. "So let me get this straight. You two thought it would be a *good* idea to come here. In spite of the fact that she was a suspect."

Arms limp at his sides, Razzzor didn't respond. He stared at the banana plant, a blank expression on his face. A Pacific breeze rustled the leaves. The tropical flowers in the driveway bent, bobbing.

"We thought..." I scraped my teeth across my bottom lip. "Razzzor and Deva were friends."

"*Were* being the operative word here," the detective said. "Ms. Belvin told us you were harassing her. That you couldn't get over the breakup."

Razzzor shook his head mutely.

"I was harassing her as much as Razzzor was," I said. "And I was with him today."

"You were with him this morning?"

"No, I mean–"

"All right. Enough of this." He nodded to a uniformed officer, and the man strode to our little group.

"Sir?"

"Take Mr. Razzzor to the station."

"What?" I said.

The officer grasped Razzzor's elbow and led him away.

My heart struggled to beat its way free as my chest contracted, squeezing. "Razzzor didn't do this."

"He sure seems to find a lot of dead bodies."

"But I was there too. I find dead bodies too." Oh. That didn't sound the way I'd intended.

"It's likely these murders are connected, but you couldn't have killed Ms. Badger. I had my eye on you at that party. We'll talk more later. You can go." He tipped his hat and strode away.

Frantic, I called Razzzor's lawyer and explained the situation.

He sighed. "Again? Thanks for the head's up. I'll go to the station now." He hesitated. "Don't worry, Abigail. I got this."

"I know." I gnawed my bottom lip. He had the best law firm in the Bay Area, mainly because he knew how to assemble a winning team. But when you've been dragged to the station under suspicion of murder... Who really had *that* under control? "Thanks."

We said goodbye and hung up. I stared at Razzzor's Tesla. I didn't have a ride. But I did have his phone, which started the car. He'd dropped it on the floor when we'd found Deva's body, and automatically, I'd picked it up.

I guess I was still used to picking up after Razzzor.

I texted the lawyer. RAZZZOR LEFT HIS CAR HERE. I'M TAKING IT TO THE TEAROOM.

After a moment he replied. DON'T SCRATCH IT.

I walked to the driver's side and got in, buckled up, started the ignition.

Knuckles white, I crept down Deva's circular drive. Razzzor wouldn't mind if I got a scratch on his car. But I didn't want to do that, not when he was undergoing a police grilling.

I drove at the pace of a very cautious snail and returned to the tearoom scratch-free. Pasting on a phony smile, I walked inside and got to work.

I received three texts from the lawyer that afternoon. They were all positive and told me not to worry.

Yeah. Sure. Right.

To take my mind off Razzzor, between seatings I walked down the street to the bundt store and bought a strawberry lemon cake. Full sized. Just for me.

I sat at the metal kitchen table and dug in.

Hyperion stuck his head through the open doorway and frowned. "Are you kidding me?"

"What?" I said through a mouthful of cake. "I'm on break."

He sidled inside and leaned against the door frame, arms crossed over his linen shirt. Somehow, he made it work over olive skinny pants. "Tell me you're not planning on eating the whole thing."

I pulled the cake closer. "I like big bundts."

"You're going to have a big bundt if you don't watch it. What's wrong?"

"Razzzor was taken in for questioning again. Deva's dead."

"Uh oh."

I told him what we'd found and swallowed another mouthful. "And of course Razzzor looks suspicious. Never mind that we found her together. He's got motive. The police think he has motive. But Razzzor wouldn't hurt a fly. It's not in him. And we're supposed to go to this Zimmerland VIP thing tonight, but I don't know if he'll be out."

"You're worried about your social life?"

"No, it was a chance to investigate." But it sounded kind of dumb when I said it out loud.

"Does your imaginary friend have a lawyer?"

"Of course. Calling his lawyer was the first thing I did." Especially since I had Razzzor's phone.

Hyperion nodded. "That's because you're practical. There's nothing more you can do for now." He hesitated. "But I suppose you'll try anyway, so chin up. We'll figure this out."

"Mrph," I said through a mouthful of bundt.

Feeling slightly sick, I waddled through the rest of the workday. It was a relief to finally close up, watch the staff filter out the front door, and get to cleaning.

I finished, grabbed my purse, and walked into the parking lot. The sun was lowering in the west, the blue sky darkening. I looked at my phone again, and the latest text from the lawyer: RAZZZOR OUT BUT IN MEETINGS. WILL TALK LATER.

I sagged against the tearoom's rough stucco wall. Thank God.

I looked at my Mazda. Looked at Razzzor's Tesla parked beside it. Looked at the text.

I didn't *need* to drive the Tesla home. But it would be awful if something happened to it in my parking lot. My Mazda had permission to be there and wasn't such a target for thieves.

I drove the Tesla home. Slowly.

Brik stood in his front yard, watering the lawn. My neighbor turned, the spray ricocheting off his pickup and onto his bare chest. He sputtered and jerked the hose away.

My phone pinged, and I parked and checked the messages. Razzzor's lawyer: R SAYS CAN'T MAKE PARTY TONIGHT. USE TIX. WANTS PHONE AND CAR BACK.

Relieved, I called the lawyer. The phone rang and went to voice mail. "I brought his car and phone home. He can pick it up whenever."

"A Tesla?" Brik strode across the concrete steppingstones to my driveway. "You have a Tesla?"

"It's Razzzor's."

Beads of water glistened on his muscular chest. Not that I noticed, because I had no business noticing. Razzzor was still in trouble, even if the police had let him go.

But.

Well, it was Brik.

My neighbor's blond brows sketched upward. "And he lets you drive it?"

"I'm a good driver," I huffed.

"It's a Tesla."

"It's just a car," I said loftily. "I don't see what the big deal is." Setting the pink bundt box on the hood, I texted Hyperion. WANT TO GO TO THE WINE THING WITH ME? I HAVE AN EXTRA TICKET.

I slammed the car door and walked to the house.

"It's a *Tesla*."

My phone pinged. *Hyperion.*
SORRY. BUSY 2NIGHT.
I cursed.
"Problem?" Brik asked.
"I've got to go to this VIP wine tasting tonight, and it's going to be weird going by myself." Normally, I don't mind doing things alone. But this was a VIP wine tasting, and I was about as close to a VIP as the Earth was to Neptune. Razzzor would have made good cover, and Hyperion's confidence took him everywhere.
"Sounds boring," Brik said.
"Tell me about it." I studied him. "Do you have a suit?"
"Why?"
"Never mind." Rich people didn't wear suits. In California, you got rich so you didn't have to wear suits. "Want to come with me tonight?"
"Like, on a date?"
My face heated. "No. It's an investigation."
"Oh boy."
"A woman was killed today. Her employers are hosting the event."
"Still? After their employee was killed?"
That was a good point. But I hadn't gotten any notification that the event had been canceled. Did the Zimmers even know Deva was dead? "I don't *think* it's been canceled."
"Like I said, sounds boring."
I shrugged. I wasn't going to beg. I'd just suck it up and go alone. "Okay." I grabbed my bundt and turned to my yellow bungalow.
"Unless..." Brik said.
I pivoted, one hand on the wooden railing. "Unless?"
"Unless I get to drive."
My brow furrowed. That was it? "Sure."
"Drive the Tesla."
"It's not my car," I said.
"I'm a good driver."
"It's Razzzor's Tesla."
"I don't see what the big deal is," he said. "It's just a car."
I blew out my breath. "Fine. We leave at six-thirty. It's a VIP event, so—"
"Put a shirt on." Brik grinned. "Got it." He ambled toward his house.
"A *nice* shirt," I called after him. Sheesh. What was it with men and Teslas?
I went inside and changed. Looking regretfully at what was left of the bundt cake, I rubbed my stomach. If the dress hadn't been high waisted, I wasn't sure it would have still fit. I took my time with my hair, debated different jewelry options, and stared at myself in the mirror.
The dress wasn't high waisted enough.
I pulled it over my head and tried on three more until I found one that didn't

make me look like Mrs. Claus.

The doorbell rang. Fiddling with my earring, I hurried to the front door and pulled it open.

Brik stood on the porch in a blue suit and a white shirt open at the collar. His hair was pulled back into a neat ponytail. He looked good enough to eat, even after all that bundt cake.

Brik flashed a weapons-grade smile, and my breath caught.

I was going out with a sun god.

Not that this was a date or anything.

He held out his hand.

My lips parted. He wanted to take my hand? I began to reach for him.

"Keys?" he asked.

I shook myself, cheeks burning. "Keys. Right. I mean, wrong. There are no keys. You need my phone – I mean Razzzor's phone. It's in my purse." I hurried to the dining room table and grabbed my clutch, realized the phone was in my other purse, and rummaged around inside. It wasn't there.

I frowned.

Ah.

I flipped open the lid of the pink pastry box and grabbed the phone from inside. "Got it." I unlocked the phone and tossed it to Brik.

He caught it one handed and rubbed his thumb over the screen. "Are those crumbs?"

"No. Why would crumbs be on Razzzor's phone?"

He eyed me. "I have no idea."

"We'd better get going." I hustled past him, then remembered I had to lock my door. He waited for me at the bottom of the steps.

We were off not quite like a rocket, since this was a residential street. But when we hit the freeway, I sank deep into the seat, my insides rearranging themselves.

"Eeep."

"The acceleration is amazing," Brik shouted over the roar of the wind.

We made it alive to the Zimmer's house, and I wobbled from the low car. Solar lights lit the driveway and the path to the door, which stood open. I hadn't been inside the Italianette manor during the tea party. Who wouldn't be curious?

Women in cocktail dresses and men in button-down shirts and jeans mingled in the high-ceilinged foyer. They flocked around upright wine barrels converted to tables. Heads turned toward us. The women's gazes lingered on Brik.

"I overdressed," Brik said in my ear.

"Trust me, that's not what anyone's thinking." At least, it wasn't what any of the women were thinking, and probably some of the men too. The suit hugged Brik in all the right places.

A man in a tuxedo stepped up to us. "Tickets?"

I showed him the tickets on my phone, and he nodded. "Welcome Ms. Beanblossom, Mr. Razzzor," he said loudly.

Now the men gave Brik a second, longer look.

Scratch that, one of the men had never stopped looking at Brik. He was good looking in a Hollywood sort of way. Hollywood hair. Hollywood smile. Hollywood tan. Hyperion would be sorry he missed this.

"Abigail?" Hyperion said behind me. "You came."

I turned, surprised. "What—?"

He air-kissed my cheeks. "You have bundt on your upper lip," he whispered.

Surreptitiously, I wiped off a crumb. "Why didn't you tell me you'd be here?" I hissed. He looked sleek as a seal in his charcoal suit.

"And ruin the surprise? Besides, it's sheer coincidence I'm here. I have zero interest in murder. So tawdry. So... *interfering* in police investigations."

"Did you and Tony have *the talk?*"

"I solemnly swore not to interfere in his investigation." He laughed. "But my fingers were crossed."

"How did you even get tickets?" I knew they hadn't been cheap.

"A friend."

Hyperion and Brik grasped hands.

"You clean up well," Hyperion said to my neighbor. "Let me show you to our hosts." Hyperion wedged himself between us, linked arms, and led us through the wine barrels.

James Zimmer waved. "Abigail, hello again." He smiled and shook my hand. "Where's Razzzor?"

"He had a last-minute meeting," I said. "He couldn't make it."

James shook his head. "These Silicon Valley guys. It's work, work, work. But that's how they make the big bucks." He shook Brik's hand. "I'm James Zimmer. Welcome to my home."

"Brik Jacobs." He looked around, taking in the flagstone floor, the ginormous chandelier, the wood-paneled walls. "Nice Travertine." Brik pointed at the stone floor.

"You've got a good eye. We imported it from Italy." James motioned around the foyer. "We remodeled the entire house, actually."

A slight tension gathered in my body. James was way too cheerful for someone whose employee was just murdered. Did he know?

A woman drifted past in a vintage fifties cocktail dress, her hair high on her head. From the back she looked like Beatrice.

"Whoever installed the floor did a good job," Brik said.

"Are you in the business?" James asked.

My neighbor nodded. "Contractor."

"Want a tour?" James asked, eyes twinkling.

"Yes," I said quickly.

James glanced at the gold watch on his wrist. "We've got fifteen minutes before we all repair to the wine cellar. Let's go."

"You mean this isn't the tasting?" I followed James up the curving staircase.

James laughed. "With this crew? They'd riot. This is just the warmup."

He led us into a sitting room. At least, I guessed that's what it was. A thick white carpet lined the huge room. An arched, floor-to-ceiling window looked over the gardens and toward the Pacific. A grand piano anchored one corner of the space.

"Was that Beatrice I saw downstairs?" I asked.

"Yes, she's here. I didn't realize you knew each other."

"We've met," I said. "I heard she's a part owner in Zimmerland."

"Part owner and VP of Marketing. We couldn't get by without her."

"I didn't realize she was so involved."

"She's even pitched in on deliveries, when the client was important enough." James winked. "But honestly, I don't begrudge her a little schmoozing. We've all got to make a living. She's expanded our business in ways you wouldn't believe."

No more small talk. I had to tell him about Deva. "James... there's something I think I need to tell you."

"You're a beer woman?"

"No. Have you heard about Deva?"

He frowned. "She was supposed to be here tonight, but she hasn't been answering her phone. Why?"

Hell. He didn't know. Did I have a right to tell him? And why hadn't the police talked to him yet? But I needed to say something. I drew a deep breath. "Deva—"

"James, I told you not to bring people up here until I was ready." Layla strolled into the room. She wore a black evening gown that draped so low over her back it barely covered her assets. She smiled at me and held out her hand. "James is always showing off. I told him to wait."

"Hi," I said.

"Abigail, it's so good to see you after that awful tea party. Not that any of that was your fault," she said quickly and unconvincingly.

"I'm still very sorry. And this is my, um, friend, Brik." I motioned to my neighbor.

"Tragic." Hyperion air kissed her cheek. "I still can't believe Madge is gone."

She smiled, wan, but she eyed Brik. "Are you here to collect the rest of your check? I may have to speak to the guards," she joked.

"Abigail manages the money side," Hyperion said. "I'm simply an enthusiastic oenophile."

"You were saying something about Deva?" James asked me. "Have you talked to her?"

"No." I squeezed my arms to my chest. "I mean, yes, but... She's dead."

James took a step backward, his face slackening. "What?"

Layla paled, her smile fading.

"I'm sorry," I said. "The police found her this morning."

"That's not possible," James said. "I spoke with her last night."

"In person?" I asked.

"No, on the phone. She was fine. I saw her yesterday morning. She came to the house. She was fine." James ran a shaky hand over his thick blond hair. "It can't be..." He swallowed jerkily. "How did she die?"

"I don't know," I said.

"But why didn't the police come to me?" he asked. "I'm her employer."

Layla laid a hand on his arm. "It's not always about us. Deva had a personal life. Parents. I'm sure they're notifying them first. The employer is last on their list, if we even merit notification. But..." She swallowed. "I assume her death wasn't natural. Not after Madge and Whitmore."

"How did you find out?" James asked me.

My shoulders curled inward. "Actually, the police discovered the body after... I did."

Hyperion lifted a brow but said nothing.

"She'd invited me over for... tea," I said.

Layla's smile was wintery. "That took some brass, inviting a teashop owner for tea."

"It was actually kind of nice," I said, then remembered I was lying.

"Was she worried about anything?" James asked. "Concerned?"

"Someone had been selling counterfeit wine ostensibly from Razzzor's winery," I said. "She was helping him figure out who."

James started. "Counterfeit wine? But Razzzor's wine only goes for a grand a bottle. No offense, but that doesn't make sense. Counterfeiters work with much higher priced labels, going for tens of thousands of dollars."

"It's a mystery," Hyperion said, and I shot him a look.

"Though the Wine Merchants did sell high-end wines," Layla mused. "Do you think Whitmore...?"

"If Whitmore and Madge were up to something," Hyperion said, "then who killed them? Who killed Deva?"

"This is awful." James clawed at his hair again. "If you'll excuse me?"

We murmured yeses, and James walked from the room.

"He and Deva were close," Layla said. "I'll be back." She hurried after her husband.

"Now," Hyperion said, "what have we learned?"

"Only that Deva was at the Zimmer's house yesterday morning," I said.

"You two gave more info than you got," Brik said.

He was right. But the night wasn't over, and we'd been left alone in this big house.

Snooping was mandatory.

Making my excuses, I ducked into an upstairs bathroom with a tub I could have done the backstroke in. There wasn't a single clue in the medicine cabinet or under the sink. I crept down the wide, carpeted hall and tried to look like I belonged there.

Gently, I tried a door.

Locked.

I moved on to a set of double doors and reached for the handle.

Voices floated from within – James and Layla.

Breath accelerating, I pressed my ear to the door, but it was one of those high-quality thick ones that muffled sound. Where was an empty water glass when you needed one?

"…blame yourself…" Layla was saying.

I flattened my ear tighter against the door and held my breath. Maybe if I didn't breathe, I could hear better.

"…can't believe it…" James said.

Someone cleared their throat behind me.

I leapt from the door.

Brik raised a brow. "Eavesdropping? Really?"

I smoothed the front of my dress. "Unsuccessfully," I whispered, "so it doesn't count."

"I don't think it works that way."

"You'd—"

Layla and James's voices grew louder. I looked around for a suit of armor to hide behind.

The doorknob rattled.

Brik picked me up, spun me to the other side of the hallway and set me down against the wall. "For once in your life," he said, "shut up."

Rude! "That's so—"

He kissed me.

Some people know how to kiss. I'm not sure I'm one of those people, but Brik was. Boy, was he. I felt myself melting in all sorts of ways.

Someone coughed.

Brik pulled away, looked over his shoulder. "Sorry," he said. "I didn't think anyone was here."

James and Layla stood inside the open doorway.

"Grab your joy where you can, my friend," James said sadly. He and Layla walked down the hall.

"And that's what you do when there's nowhere to hide." Brik stepped away from me.

"Eeep."

"What?"

"I said, I think I saw that move in an old film."

"Come on," he said. "Let's join the others."

Mind racing, I followed him downstairs. He was acting like the kiss was no big thing, just a ruse. And it wasn't a big thing. Brik had women in and out of his house all the time, so I wasn't exactly special. But he hadn't *had* to actually kiss me.

Back in the foyer, Brik and I made desultory conversation with a man who owned a university of some sort.

I was too busy replaying the kiss to pay much attention.

Hyperion stepped up to our small table. "I just met the most fascinating academic – some sort of prize winner in graphic design. He's right over there." He pointed toward a balding man with a goatee.

"Really?" the university man brightened. "Will you excuse me? I think I need to introduce myself." He wandered away.

"You can thank me for the rescue later," Hyperion said.

Layla walked into the foyer and smiled wanly. "Let's go downstairs to the cellar, shall we?" she asked.

Layla led us down another winding set of stairs to a stone wine cellar, and the temperature dropped. Racks of wine lined the walls. Wine barrels had been set up as tables here as well.

"I once got an offer to live in a wine cellar," Hyperion murmured to me. "But that's another story."

"That's nice." *Had* the kiss meant anything?

"Nice? It was a joke." He waggled his brows. "Or was it?"

I gnawed the inside of my cheek.

"What's wrong with you?" my partner asked. "Did you hit your head while you were snooping upstairs?"

My face heated. "Nothing happened upstairs," I whispered.

"Seriously? You and Brik alone, and nothing happened? What an abominable withered foulness, or in mundane terms: bummer."

"What are you two talking about?" Brik asked.

"Hyperion's spouting from his word of the day calendar again," I said.

"Those are useful vocabulary builders," Brik said.

"Not Hyperion's."

Waiters bearing bottles on silver trays filled our glasses. Layla led us through a tasting of French wines.

I glanced around the room for Beatrice, but she was gone.

"Keep in mind," Layla said, "this is the 2015. James went to Burgundy this year and sampled this vintage. He says it holds great promise. But you'll have to wait two years to try it, if you can get a bottle. I think this is going to be in high demand. Of course, you could lock in your bottles and buy futures." She winked.

Brik shifted, his sleeve brushing my arm, and I shivered.

"A friend of mine buys wine futures." Brik studied his glass, filled with ruby liquid. "I don't think he was spending as much as these go for though."

"How can you—" My voice cracked. "How can you tell?" I massaged my throat, and Hyperion eyed me.

"She hasn't mentioned price." Brik slid the tasting list toward me. "This is one of those, if-you-have-to-ask-you-can't-afford-it situations."

Like dating a neighbor. I definitely couldn't afford that. What would happen when we broke up? We'd have to pass each other on the street all the time. *Stop thinking about it.* The kiss meant nothing.

"Futures, schmutures. I'm a tequila man." Hyperion looked past me and grinned at the blond Mr. Hollywood I'd clocked earlier.

The man slouched, languid, beside a wine barrel and raised his glass to Hyperion. Did I know Hyperion's type or what?

"Excuse me," Hyperion said. "I've got detecting to do." He glided across the flagstones to the man.

"Is *detecting* his new euphemism for picking up guys?" Brik asked.

I sighed and sipped the wine. "Doubtless. What can you tell me about how futures work?"

"You buy the wine today, while it's still in the barrel. Then when it's ready, usually two years later, you get the wine."

"So, you're buying in advance?"

"Basically," Brik said. "It's kind of an investment. The price of the wine may go up when it's ready for bottling. Or it could go down."

"You know a lot about wine." *Ugh.* Did that sound like I was flirting?

He grinned. "Don't worry. I'm still a beer guy. But this is California. You can't help picking up a thing or two."

James walked into the room. "Apologies, friends. I just got some bad news. My friend and colleague, Deva, who many of you know, has passed away."

Murmurs of shock rippled around the stone cellar.

"I know." His voice choked up. "I don't have the details yet, but... I think we should raise a glass to Deva. A true lady who knew how to enjoy a good wine." He motioned to the waiters, who poured new glasses from dusty bottles of wine. "From my private vintage. This was one of Deva's favorites. A classic, 1974 Cabernet Sauvignon from her home in Napa."

The waiter poured our wines, and I readied mine for a toast. The other guests sniffed and swirled. James raised his glass. "To Deva."

"To Deva," we repeated.

I looked around for Hyperion. He and Mr. Hollywood had vanished.

So much for sleuthing. It seemed the detecting was up to me.

I touched Brik's sleeve. "I'm going to find the ladies' room."

"For real this time?"

"I didn't get a chance last time." Tossing my hair, I hurried away, Brik's gaze burning a hole beneath my neck.

I wandered toward the stairs and glanced over my shoulders. No one was looking.

Not even Brik. And I felt a squeeze of irrational disappointment that he hadn't followed. Why did Hyperion have all the fun?

I ducked down a hallway and stopped in front of a door, tried the knob. Locked.

Clutching my purse, I walked to another door. This one was unlocked. I slipped inside a dark room, fumbled for a light switch and flipped it on. Racks of dusty wine bottles stretched in front of me.

Wine bottles in the wine cellar. *Brilliant detecting, Abigail.* But I wandered deeper into the room. A piece of black paper on the floor caught my eye, and I picked it up.

It was a black label, like the kind Madge had sent me a note on. I turned it over. *This Margaux has the classic notes of ripe, dark berries, tobacco, truffles, violets and cassis. Pairs well with cheese, lamb and any roasted meat.*

What had I expected? A confession?

Absently, I pocketed the black label. I left the room, checked a few more locked doors, and returned to the party, none the wiser.

CHAPTER 19

I rejoined Brik in the wine cellar. "Have you seen Hyperion?" I asked breathlessly, and not because I'd been hurrying. I couldn't look at Brik without thinking of that stupid kiss.

He nodded toward the far corner of the room.

Hyperion and Mr. Hollywood stood chatting on opposite sides of a wine barrel table. My partner languidly motioned with his wine glass.

I frowned.

"Problem?" Brik asked.

"No." But the back of my neck prickled, like I was being watched. Had someone seen me sneaking around? I hadn't done anything wrong – unless you consider snooping through your host's house wrong. Okay, it was an ethical gray area, but desperate times, desperate measures.

Hyperion's friend ambled to another table.

"Excuse me," I said. "I need to talk to Hyperion."

Brik sipped his wine. "Go wild."

I strolled to Hyperion's table. "Did you find anything?" I asked in a low voice.

"An amazing bottle of champagne. And this phone number might have slipped into my pocket." He pulled a business card from his suit pocket.

"A witness?"

"A date, dummy."

Involuntarily, I glanced across the tables at Brik.

"Is something going on between you two?" Hyperion asked.

"No. No, I'm just worried. Three people associated with the Zimmers are dead."

"*Were* Madge and Whitmore associated with the Zimmers?"

"Whitmore was dating Deva, who's dead." But I gnawed my bottom lip. At the tea party, Madge had said Zimmerland *wasn't* their distributor. Had I misheard?

James strolled to our table cradling a black bottle of wine. "Your next tasting." He poured and rattled off tasting notes and dates and facts about Burgundy vintages.

Hyperion made a face. "What exactly is a Burgundy grape?"

James winked. "That's the trick. Burgundy is a place, not a grape. So a white from Burgundy is really a chardonnay, and a red is a pinot."

"Why don't they just say that?" Hyperion asked.

"History. The Californian winemakers were brilliant to label their wines by type of grape instead. It's much less confusing. Frankly, many California wines are just as good as the French. But Burgundy has history, cachet. And yes, marvelous wines."

"James," I said. "How long has Zimmerland been a distributor for the Wine Merchants?"

"Since never. Whitmore's got a cousin in the industry, and he uses him as a distributor. There was no way for us to break into that relationship." One corner of his mouth flickered upward. "Blood is thicker than wine. But believe me, Deva tried."

But the murders *had* to be connected to Razzzor's counterfeit wine. Or at least to wine.

"What's wrong?" James asked. "This is an excellent vintage."

"Abigail's not constipated," Hyperion said. "That's her puzzled face."

"Sorry," I said. "I can't stop thinking about these deaths. I'd thought Deva must have sold some wine to Whitmore and Madge. But you say she hadn't, and that jibes with something Madge said."

"It jibes?" James's thin brows lifted. "You needed verification?"

"No." Heat flushed from my chest to my hairline. "I mean. It's just…"

"Fiendish?" Hyperion asked. "Viperous? Full-tilt weirdness?"

I couldn't wait until December 31st, when his Lovecraft calendar ended. "Three people are dead."

"Yes." James looked at the bottle in his hands. "This is all too close. Their deaths must be connected."

"Have you any idea who or what that connection might be?" I asked.

"I'm the connection," he said simply. "What else could it be? Something's…" James gulped his wine. "Deva did mention… She said something about being stalked." James looked down. "But I didn't pay attention. I thought she was exaggerating. I should have though."

My pulse sped. "Did she say who was doing the stalking?"

"An ex," James said. "She didn't say more. I urged her to go to the police. I'm not sure if she did. If this ex knew about her relationship with Whitmore, if Madge saw something she shouldn't have…" His shoulders lifted, dropped.

Brik joined us at the table. "Is everything all right, Abigail?"

No, hell no. "It's fine," I said brightly.

My phone rang in my purse. Grateful for an excuse to look anywhere but at the three men studying me, I tugged it free. An unfamiliar number flashed on the screen.

"Hello?"

"It's me, Razzzor."

I turned away from the men. "Hey, we were just talking about you." I winced. I hoped we hadn't been talking about him. That would imply he was the stalker James had mentioned. "I've still got your phone, and your—"

"I've been arrested," he said.

"What?" I staggered backward and stepped on Brik's foot. He lifted me off. "Again?" I said, voice shrill.

"The last time was only for questioning. Can you call my lawyer? And my accountant. I think I'll need bail money this time. And a good PR firm. The timing is terrible. I'm right in the middle of a deal with a VC firm. If they find out—"

"I'll take care of it," I croaked.

He gusted a breath. "Thank you."

"No problem," I said automatically. *Arrested? For real?* "How are you doing?"

"Good point. Could you call my therapist too?"

"Yes," I ripped out, "but how are you doing?"

His laugh was uneven. "Not happy about jail. The way the detective was talking, I might have to spend the night. Ask the lawyer to bring cigarettes."

"You don't smoke."

"For currency."

"I don't think that works in..." I glanced at the men. They sipped their wine and pretended disinterest. "...where you are," I finished.

"Hey, currency always works."

"Fine, I'll tell him. Anything else?"

"I'm sorry about this, Abigail."

I swallowed. Razzzor had a sensible never-apologize-unless-you've-actually-done-something-wrong policy. It had kept him out of several lawsuits. "Sorry about what? You didn't do anything."

"For dragging you into this. I never thought it would get this out of hand."

"You didn't drag me into anything. I volunteered."

"Listen, I've got to go."

"Don't worry," I said. "I'll take care of—"

A dial tone as empty as my stomach sounded in my ear.

"What's wrong?" Brik asked.

I gripped the phone more tightly. "I need to leave. Sorry."

"So do I," Hyperion said. "Amazing wines, James. I'd like to talk to you about that 2012 Burgundy later. Ta."

He swaggered to the stone steps.

Brik and I made our apologies and followed.

"What's going on?" Hyperion hissed as we ascended the stairs.

"Razzzor's been arrested. Really arrested this time."

Brik frowned. "And this is your problem?"

"I've got to call the lawyer—"

"Wait, he used his one phone call to call you instead of a lawyer?" Brik asked.

"Of course. He knew I'd take care of everything. Plus, I have his phone with all his contacts."

Hyperion and Brik glanced at each other.

"But you don't work for him anymore, do you?" Brik said.

I lengthened my strides. "What does that have to do with anything?"

We emerged in the high-ceilinged foyer, empty aside from the wine barrels.

"I'm only wondering if you're seeing this Razzzor clearly," Brik said.

Hyperion made a circling motion near his left ear. "I think it's more of a mind's eye sort of thing."

Brik ran one hand up the back of his neck. "The guy's obviously a loner, and he's attached himself to you—"

"He's not a loner," I said hotly. "Okay, he is a loner, but he's also a genius. And he hasn't attached himself to me. I used to work for him. We became friends. I wouldn't have Beanblossom's if it hadn't been for him. I learned a ton from Razzzor."

Brik shook his head, and we walked into the warm night. Solar lights twinkled around the edges of the pavestone driveway.

"More importantly," I continued, "Razzzor's innocent. Whatever's going on must have something to do with that counterfeit wine."

"Or with love," Brik said. "You'd be surprised what people will do for love."

I cut him an uneasy glance. Had he bought into the Razzzor-as-stalker business? My mouth compressed. It didn't matter. Razzzor needed my help.

"So, call his lawyer," Hyperion said. "What else does your imaginary friend expect from you?"

"Razzzor's bigger than just a lawyer," I said. "He needs his accountant. His therapist. His PR guy—"

"PR?" Hyperion asked. "We should call Beatrice. Think of the possibilities for sleuthing."

"No. No way. What if she's the killer? She'll sink Razzzor."

"Fine." He folded his arms over his suit jacket. "But I'm ready for another madcap adventure. If we want to investigate, Whitmore's ex-wife would be an excellent source."

"He's not wrong," Brik said. "And neither are you." He opened the passenger door of the Tesla, and I slid in.

Hyperion gaped. "Hold the phone. When did you get a Tesla?"

"It's Razzzor's," I said, rolling down the window.

"And why is Brik driving it?"

"Because I can." Brik shut my door and walked to the driver's side.

"Since when do imaginary friends drive Teslas?" my partner asked.

We drove off, leaving Hyperion gaping in the driveway. I made phone calls for Razzzor as we whizzed down the mountainside to my modest and view-free yellow bungalow. But hey, it was a great bungalow, with an amazing garden. And a stalker in the front yard.

CHAPTER 20

The Tesla's headlights flashed across Deacon Alstatter, a bike helmet dangling from his fingers.

I stiffened.

"You know him?" Brik asked.

"He's Deva's stalker."

Brik hit the brake hard, and we lurched against our seatbelts. "What's he doing in your driveway?"

I realized I'd stopped breathing, and I inhaled sharply. "I don't know, but he's not exactly a fan."

Brik was out the door before I could unlatch my seatbelt. He moved like an angry shadow, quick and bristling with danger.

I lurched from the low sports car.

"...help you?" Brik's voice was low and deceptively pleasant.

Deacon leaned left, trying to see around Brik. "I'm here to see Abigail."

"You're a friend?" Brik's arms hung at his sides, his fingers curled.

"I don't think that's any of your business."

Brik's fists tightened. "Don't you?"

"What do you want, Deacon?" I asked to break the tension Deacon was too stupid to notice.

"You were there." The bike messenger's Adam's apple bobbed. "You found her."

My blood turned to ice. "Found her? You mean Deva?" How did Deacon know I'd been at Deva's? It hadn't been in the papers. The police weren't giving out that information.

"What did you see?" Deacon stepped toward me.

Brik slid left, blocking him.

"What are you talking about?" I snapped.

"Did you see her? What did she look like?" His eyes gleamed, feral, in the dim light of the streetlamps.

I recoiled, flesh crawling. What did she *look* like?

"That's enough," Brik said. "Get out of here."

Deacon raised his chin. "You can't make me. This is a public sidewalk."

Brik's hand shot out and fisted in Deacon's bike shirt. He lifted Deacon onto his toes. "Get out of here," he ground out and released his grip.

Deacon staggered backward. "What did she look like? What did you feel when you saw her?"

Sickened, I turned toward my house. I didn't want to deal with him. But I'd been the one turning over rocks in a murder. I couldn't be surprised by what I'd found beneath them.

"You're a part of it now," Deacon shouted.

There was a clatter.

I turned.

Deacon crouched on the ground, gasping.

Brik righted a garbage bin. "Go." His voice was hard and cold.

Deacon wheezed and staggered away.

I looked from Brik to the bike messenger's departing back. "What happened?"

"Forget it. Let's get you inside."

He walked me up the short flight of wooden steps to my porch and waited while I opened the door. Brik followed me into the bungalow. He prowled through the rooms, checking doors and windows.

I shifted from foot to foot by the front door.

Brik had been in my house before. The only reason he was here now was because he was a concerned neighbor. It had nothing to do with that kiss.

"Could this be the guy who was in your garden?" Brik asked.

"What? Oh. No. I don't think so. The thefts started before I'd even met him." But Deacon had been in the Wine Merchants the night of Whitmore's death and at the tearoom. Could he have tracked down my home address?

Brik's blue eyes seemed to crackle. "What's his story?"

My heart jumped, and I looked away. To cover my reaction, I pulled aside the curtains and glanced out the window. "I'm not sure."

I explained about seeing Deacon at the Wine Merchants, about how he'd followed Hyperion and me, about his obsession with Deva. "I don't know how he could have known I'd found Deva's body."

"Unless he'd been there," he said.

I exhaled slowly. "Yes. I didn't see him at Deva's though." But there'd been a lot of greenery around her house. He could have been hiding.

Had he killed Deva?

"What did he mean by *you're a part of it?*" Brik asked.

My stomach tensed. "I don't know." Stalkers are definitionally unbalanced. Had that been more insane rambling, or did Deacon actually know something?

"All right. I'll take the couch."

"Wait. What?"

"He's a stalker. Now he's stalking you. He could be creeping around the corner of your house right now. Tomorrow we're installing those video cameras. Tonight, I'm sleeping on your couch."

"That's, um, really... noble of you. But I'll be okay. I installed motion sensitive lightbulbs."

"Great." He pointed. "Now he'll be able to see what he's doing when he breaks through those French windows."

I folded my arms. "If this is your idea of a pep talk, it bites."

"I'm not trying to make you feel better. I'm trying to make you feel careful."

"Right now, I'm feeling annoyed." Because a big part of me wanted him to stay.

Just not on the couch.

But I couldn't tell him that. Dating a neighbor was a bad idea, and more importantly, I wasn't that kind of girl.

Dammit.

Plus, Deacon *had* freaked me out.

I wasn't about to admit that either.

I tried again, without enthusiasm. "You can't stay. The couch is too short for you."

"I'll sleep on the floor."

"I don't see much point in you staying if you're going to sleep."

"Are you going to get me a pillow or not?"

I got him the pillow and a pile of blankets, and I fled to my bedroom.

It took a long time to get to sleep that night, thinking of that kiss, imagining Deacon outside and Brik inside.

A really long time.

My neighbor left as soon as I got up, so at least I didn't have to impress him with my amazing breakfast skills. FYI, that's not sarcasm. I know my way around breakfast.

I pulled from my driveway when the sun was peeking over the eastern hills. It was impossible not to look at the lights shining through Brik's living room windows as I drove past.

I hurried through the day, glancing out the front windows for bike messengers.

The tearoom was crowded, and that was good. There was safety in crowds. Safety in the tarot readers moving through the tearoom, predicting fantastic futures. Safety in the warm scent of scones and herbal teas.

In spite of that, I was a little irked that Hyperion was AWOL. He didn't call, didn't write... And truth to tell, he didn't *have* to be there today. But it worried me. I left two messages which he didn't return.

At the end of the day, I sped through deep cleaning the reach-in fridge. I was determined to track him down at his house and make sure he was okay. I slammed shut the low refrigerator door.

"Hey, girl." Hyperion leaned in the kitchen doorway.

My muscles jerked, and I dropped the bottle of spray cleaner.

"Find any more bodies?" he asked.

Since I make an effort not to act like a crazy shrew, I didn't yell and ask him where he'd been. But it wasn't easy. "You're a laugh riot." I set the cleaner on the long, metal table. "I wasn't sure if you planned on showing up today."

"Had to." He yawned. "Got a class tonight."

"Mmph." I restocked the cold holding area with mini tarts and savories.

"I take it things with you and Brik did not end with a bang last night." He leered.

"Deacon Alstatter was lurking in my driveway when we got home. Brik spent the night to make sure he didn't return."

He straightened off the door. "Whoa. What happened? Tell me everything."

"Deacon was lurking, and—"

"Not about Deacon." He hurried inside and propped himself against the refrigerator. "About you and Brik."

"Like I said, he spent the night."

"And?"

"And nothing," I said. "He slept on the couch."

"Are you telling me that man spent the night in your house, and all you two did was *sleep*? What is *wrong* with you?"

"Not everything is about sex." I slammed shut the cold storage door.

"What *else* would it be about?" His eyes narrowed. "Wait a minute. Are you pulling my leg?"

Now he was just rubbing it in. "No."

"Because everyone knows good girls are just bad girls that don't get caught."

"I need to mop the floor."

"And?"

"You're in my way."

He stepped into the hallway. "No wonder you're grumpy. You're terrible at romance."

I *really* was.

He finally retreated to his office, and I got to finish cleaning. It wasn't my favorite part of owning a tearoom. But it was the most peaceful.

I doublechecked the kitchen, grabbed my purse, and walked to the rear, metal door.

Hyperion appeared at my side. "Where are you going?"

"Zimmerland Wines. They've got a store in Santa Cruz."

"I thought they were a distributor. Why do they have a store?"

"I'm not sure. But I went there for a wine tasting with Razzzor."

He arched a brow. "You and Razzzor?"

"Well, I didn't go *with* him," I corrected. "He was there though."

He patted my shoulder. "We'll leave your imaginary friend aside for now, shall we? I'm going with you."

"I thought you had a class."

"Had. Past tense. I held the class this afternoon, thanks to the magic of the internet."

"You were here this afternoon?" How had I missed that? I must have really been out of it.

"Mm. So, let's go. And no more arguing. This is for your own good. You're being stalked. It seems you've fallen afoul of a scabby, restless—"

"Lovecraft again?"

"He's so descriptive. Let's get a move on before all the good wine is taken."

He hustled me into the parking lot, and I locked the tearoom's metal door.

"Where's your car?" he asked. "Oh." He gazed at the Tesla. "I'll drive."

"No, I'll drive. It's Razzzor's car."

"You let Brik drive."

"He was blackmailing me."

"Intriguing. And you let him sleep on the couch?"

"Fine." I handed him Razzzor's phone. "You can drive." Anything to shut him up about my romantic incompetence.

Hyperion handled the car like a driver at Daytona, gliding in and out of traffic. We got to Santa Cruz in record time and parked outside Zimmerland.

We strolled up the walk.

"Looks like a car dealership," Hyperion said.

"Not on the inside."

"What's the goal here?"

"I want to learn more about wine futures," I said.

"Why? You can just look that information up online."

"It's an excuse. Zimmerland is selling futures, and I'm running out of suspects."

"Aside from creepy stalker guy?"

"Yeah." Could the murders have to do with love or insanity and not wine? "It doesn't matter. These people knew the victims. I want to learn more about Beatrice's role in the business. I need to talk to them," I said tightly and strode through the automatic doors.

Tonight the space was quiet and empty. We walked to the counter. After a moment or two, Layla Zimmer emerged from a back room. "Abigail, Hyperion... What can I do for you?"

I smiled. "I had to leave your tasting early and didn't get a chance to learn how the futures worked."

Her face brightened. "Ready for a lecture?"

"A lecture? I'm torn..." Hyperion propped his elbows on the counter, his head on his fists. "Okay. Yes."

Layla pulled a black leather folder from beneath the counter and opened it in front of us. She smiled. "Wine futures aren't new..."

The lecture wasn't as bad as it could have been. Brik had been right. Futures were a fancy way of paying in advance for a product with a price that might go up in the future.

She pushed a lock of blue-black hair off her forehead. "So, the question now, is which wines would you like to buy futures for?"

Hyperion rubbed his chin. "That is a toughie. I'll need to consult the cards." He reached for his pocket.

"But I'll need more time to decide," I said quickly.

"There's no hurry." Layla pushed the folder across the bar to me.

I studied the logo. "This looks like Beatrice's work."

"She's been an amazing marketing director. I don't know where she finds the time."

"It must keep her busy. What does she do?"

"Her focus is our auctions for private clients. Thanks to her, we're making a real name for ourselves. But at the end, it's all down to James. He's the one who works with the clients to help them grow or sell their collections. It's his expertise they rely on."

"Did Deva do that sort of work too?"

"No, she was a distributor only." She tapped the folder. "Keep it. Take your time. Now that that killer's been caught, we have all the time in the world."

My hand hovered over the leather binder. "Killer? You don't mean Razzzor?"

"Yes, he was arrested," she said. "It's ghastly, but... People can act so entitled, especially here."

My jaw hardened. *Entitled?* Layla lived in a freaking villa. "I've known Razzzor for years. He didn't kill anyone."

"How well do we really know people?" Layla asked sympathetically.

I bristled. "He didn't—"

Hyperion put a hand on my arm. "We do need to go. Ta!" He steered me from the shop.

I fumed. "Razzzor won't be in jail for long. He's got resources. Lawyers."

"Of course he won't," Hyperion said. "He's got you."

I stopped beside the Tesla. It was the nicest thing I'd heard all day, and it made me want to cry. "Thank you," I said.

He fiddled with Razzzor's phone and shrugged. "It's true. What next?"

"I need to buy security cameras for the house," I said briskly.

"Sounds intriguing. I'm in."

We drove to the massive home improvement store, and I bought a set of cameras. It was on sale but still a lot more than I'd planned to pay.

We walked through the parking lot to the Tesla, and Hyperion examined the box. "This looks complicated. Do you know how to install these?"

I exhaled heavily. "No." Brik had sort of said he would, but after that kiss, I didn't want to ask.

"I know a reliable handyman who might be able to help."

"A reliable handyman? That's like a unicorn in this town."

"Seriously. Let me ask him how much he'll charge to install it. In fact, I'll take the kit to him later, and he can look it over."

"Thanks," I said, suspicious. "That's nice of you. What's he look like?"

Hyperion winked. "You'll see."

I walked to the passenger side of the Tesla, and he frowned. "Did you do that?"

"Do what?" I reached for the handle.

"Stop!"

My hand froze beside the door.

"It's been boobytrapped," he whispered, eyes wide.

"What?" I walked around the car to him.

Hyperion pointed.

Colorful wires dangled from beneath his door, as if the Tesla had been disemboweled.

"What the hell?" Blood throbbed in my skull. "It wasn't like that before."

"No kidding." My partner rubbed his chin. "I'm no expert, but I don't think a Tesla is supposed to look like that."

I swore. Someone had sabotaged Razzzor's car.

CHAPTER 21

There is little more depressing than a Tesla on a flatbed tow truck.

Scratch that.

Last night's rideshare bill to San Borromeo was more depressing.

I studied the tearoom. We were between seatings, and sunlight slanted across the spotless white tablecloths. A waitress straightened the silverware at one table. A trio of card readers sat at another and discussed the latest Tarot gossip.

I lowered my brows. When everything seems to be ticking along, it's a sure sign life is about to go sideways.

Call it Abigail's Law.

Behind the white stone counter, Hyperion sniffed my latest Tarot tea creation. "Hermit tea. Nice. But we need special labels. Did you use the lemon verbena I recommended?"

"Yes." And I was kind of impressed he'd thought of it. Mixing herbal teas isn't as easy as it sounds. There's a lot of trial and error involved. My eyes narrowed, a suspicion darkening my mind.

He braced his elbows on the counter. "We have to put a stop to this. Last night's rideshare was like a bad dream. I thought we'd have to get out and walk the rest of the way home. And what if whoever sabotaged your car followed us?"

"*Razzzor's* car." I wasn't sure how he'd take the damage to his Tesla. Hopefully, I could fix it before he learned about it – not that I wanted him in jail a second longer. But the long arm of the law had its advantages.

The door swung open, and five women walked inside.

"Gotta go." I hurried to the hostess stand and beamed. "Welcome to Beanblossom's. Have you got reservations?"

Customers piled into the tearoom. I left Hyperion and the Tarot readers to fend for themselves. But Hyperion stuck close to me that day. He lingered in the tearoom giving readings and lounged beside the kitchen door while I cleaned after closing.

I closed the reach-in refrigerator and sat back on my heels, wiping my brow with the back of my wrist. "Done."

"Good," he said. "Cleaning is boring."

"You weren't doing any cleaning."

"Watching you clean is boring. The point is, we need more clues."

I stood, my knees crackling, and winced. "I did overhear Madge talking to a guy at Layla's tea party. His name was Archer Simmons, but I've got no idea how to find him."

Hyperion goggled. "Archer Simmons? *The* Archer Simmons? You can't tell me you don't know who he is?"

"I don't know who he is."

"He writes the society column for that big newspaper in San Francisco. The SF whatzit. You know."

"There are still society columns?"

"There are always society columns," he said. "His home's been featured in magazines. He lives here, in San Borromeo, in a massive house overlooking the ocean."

"You know him?"

"Are you kidding? I'm just a lowly Tarot reader and small business owner."

"So that's a *no*."

"I can't believe he was at the party and I didn't notice," he fretted.

"In fairness, you were busy inside that tent."

"No excuse. My gaydar should have been flashing. He must have written something about the murder at the tea party. How could he resist?" He whipped out his phone and scrolled through the screen. "Ha! Here it is. *Tea, Tarot, and Murder... James and Layla Zimmer presented an afternoon of Tea and Tarot, which was brought to a screaming halt by the tragic fall of Margaret Badger from their cliff path.*" He frowned, his fingertip brushing the screen.

"And?"

"And nothing," he sputtered, outraged. "It's a photo slide show after that."

"Any good pictures? Maybe they have clues."

"None of me. Stupid paper. These slide shows are a trick to get their websites more clicks. All they care about are online rankings. Where's the gossip? Where are the words? This is a travesty. I hate modern life."

"The food's pretty good though."

He nodded thoughtfully. "There is that. We need to talk to Archer. Call your grandfather."

The idea wasn't as daffy as it sounded. Gramps had lived here most of his life. He knew a lot of people. I called him and explained the situation.

"You want to interrogate Archer?" My grandfather's voice filled with doubt.

"Subtly interrogate," Hyperion shouted over my shoulder.

"Is that Hyperion? Will he be with you?"

I pressed a button on the phone and set it on the gleaming metal worktable. "You're on speaker now, and yes, he's here."

"In that case," Gramps said, "I'll call you back." He hung up.

Hyperion looked a question at me.

I shrugged. "If it was a no, he'd say so."

A few minutes later, Gramps called.

"Okay, you can go over there now," he said. "But don't make him wait. Archer's a little, er, eccentric."

"Don't worry, Mr. Beanblossom," Hyperion said. "Eccentrics adore me."

My grandfather gave us directions. We said goodbye and hung up.

"You heard the man," Hyperion said. "Let's not keep Archer waiting."

We took Hyperion's Jeep into the hills. The Jeep zipped around narrow curves. We zipped past high iron fences, colonial-style mansions, and expanses of groomed lawns. We'd entered the elite section of town. Every house had an ocean view, and sidewalks were *verboten*. They only encouraged the hoi polloi coming around.

Finally, we turned into a circular driveway. At its end was a mid-century modern house with massive windows. Clumps of browning, ornamental grasses dotted the front yard in a geometric pattern.

A swimming pool cut a swathe through a lush lawn. Three orange umbrellas shaded white-cushioned chaises. The house, low and white and smartly angular, formed an L, cradling the pool.

We parked and strolled up the concrete walk to the front door. Hyperion rang the bell.

Archer, in a gray suit and matching, shimmery ascot, opened the door. He glanced at me, and his gaze settled on Hyperion. "Ah, the Tarot reader from the party." He grabbed my partner's hand and tugged him inside. "I have *so* many questions."

Bemused, I followed them into a marble-floored living area with wood-paneled walls.

"Sit, sit." Archer motioned us to the gray couch and matching chaise lounges. He dropped into one of the chaises, crossing his feet at the ankles.

Hyperion and I sat across from him on the sofa.

Archer's eyes twinkled. "I'd hoped to get a reading from you, then poor Madge popped over the cliff. Tragic. Utterly tragic. Of course, I've got a pretty good idea what's in store for my future, but I was curious, you understand?"

Hyperion nodded. "Tarot can be a remarkable tool for self-development. The cards depict archetypes from our universal unconscious. They allow us to tap directly into our subconscious and superconscious knowledge."

"That's what *I* said." Archer leaned forward. "Tea and Tarot. Layla was brilliant to think of the alliteration, which is, between the three of us, very un-Layla-like."

"We actually own the Tea and Tarot room in San Borromeo," I said.

"That explains where Layla got the idea," Archer said. "I knew it couldn't be her own. Too original."

"You know the Zimmers well?" I asked.

He examined his manicure. "How well does one really know anyone?"

I waited.

"There *was* Layla's unfortunate youthful trauma," he eventually continued. "She was one of those pudgy girls. The other girls treated her horribly. You know how awful children can be. Then there's her marriage – was it for love or money? James and Layla make an excellent power couple, but women can be so mercenary.

"And James – so mysterious! Sweeping in from the exotic east and dropping buckets of money on our tiny little town. But what a palate that man has. *Some* people think less of him because his family owns a chain of East German supermarkets. Utter snobs. Why *couldn't* a grocer or an auto mechanic know how to enjoy a decent glass of Burgundy, I say?

"Now Hyperion, how did you become a Tarot reader? Did you always know there was something different about you?"

"Since birth," Hyperion said promptly. "My tiny hands would fist, and I'd break into the most astounding howls whenever my father got the idea of investing in cryogenics or some other hair-brained scheme. My mother says I repeatedly saved the family from hardship and ruin. Now they're happily building a pension from the scientific research institute they work at. It's very top secret, very hush hush." Hyperion pressed his finger to the side of his nose.

"And how do they feel about your career?"

"I'm a tremendous disappointment. They hoped I'd use my powers for good rather than predicting romances and career changes. But what I do *is* good. It gives people direction and hope."

Archer stretched his legs out on the chaise. "Exactly. We're a lot alike. We both bring happiness. So what if it's for entertainment purposes only? What's wrong with entertainment in this tragic world?"

"Not a damn thing," Hyperion said.

"Scones make people happy," I said, trying to get back into the conversation. It wasn't the wittiest repartee, but our host took it in stride.

"Oh, yes. Your elderflower rhubarb cakes were gorgeous *and* delectable. I confess I took one home when no one was looking, but they would have gone to waste. It was a noble thing I did. And I must have your card." He nodded to the window overlooking the pool. "As you can see, I've got ample room for entertaining."

I cleared my throat. "Actually, we wanted to ask you about Madge. I saw the two of you talking before she, er, fell."

"I heard she was pushed," he said, "but of course, I couldn't put that into my column, such as it is. Can you believe what they've done to it? The media is infested with philistines. Now these online papers are all photos and barely any text. I can't decide if it's all about the clicks, or if they think people can't read anymore. I told my editor I'd add extra paragraph breaks to make my columns more scannable." He put the last word in air quotes. "But no, she insists on no more than 150 words. What can I possibly say in 150 words?"

Clearly, not a lot. Archer seemed more the conversational-novel type. Now I just needed to steer him to the point. "It was frustrating for us too. Hyperion and I were busy working, and we'd hoped to learn more about what happened from your article. What did Madge say to you at the party?"

"I don't think they were her last words, if that's what you're looking for," Archer said. "She must have talked to other people after me. And they frankly weren't very interesting. Is it difficult becoming a Tarot reader?"

"You have no idea," Hyperion said.

I clawed my hands through my hair. "Do you remember what Madge said?"

"Madge?" Archer studied the white-painted ceiling. "She was going on and on about the shipping date of some of the wine futures I'd bought. They're shipping late, which is frustrating, but it's wine, darling. Grapes. Nature. A living thing. And like an elegant woman, it takes its sweet time getting to you."

"Why?" I asked.

He blinked. "The harvest in France, my dear. It's late. Weather." His hands fluttered toward the ceiling. "But I don't know why *she* was so frustrated. It isn't like she'd bought wine futures from Zimmerland. They were out of her league," he whispered behind one hand.

"How so?" Hyperion asked.

"The most expensive bottle Madge and Whitmore sold wasn't more than a thousand dollars – a trifle, a bagatelle. The finest Burgundies Zimmerland sells can go for much more than that. Oh, Whitmore talked a big game about vertical expansion and catering to the Silicon Valley crowd, but—"

The phone rang in my purse, and Hyperion frowned.

"Sorry." Embarrassed, I fumbled my phone, about to turn it off, when I saw the lawyer's name on the screen. "Excuse me, I've got to take this."

Archer pointed to the open glass door to the swimming pool.

I rose and walked outside. "Mr. Smith?"

"Abigail, I'm free," Razzzor said.

My shoulders dropped. "Free? That's wonderful. What happened?"

"A witness saw me biking the morning of Madge's death. I couldn't possibly have gotten there in time to kill her. Not that I would have. But the point is, I have an alibi. And speaking of my bike, I'm getting a little tired of it. When can I get my Tesla back? And my phone."

"Your Tesla?" My mouth puckered.

"Why are you saying *Tesla* like you've never heard the word before?"

"I know it. Your Tesla…"

"Yes. My Tesla. The electric sports car coveted by all lovers of electric sports cars."

The Tesla. Oh, boy. "Um, about that…"

CHAPTER 22

Dazed, I returned inside Archer's house and stopped short.

My grandfather and Tomas lounged on the couch I'd just abandoned.

Archer braced his elbows on his knees. "Now, let's talk murder suspects."

"What?" I asked.

"It's obvious why you came here." Archer winked at Hyperion. "I *am* a reporter after all. You have quite a track record helping the San Borromeo PD. That wasn't in the papers, that was me calling in favors. FYI, not everyone in the department looks favorably on amateur detectives."

"By not everyone, you mean nobody?" Tomas asked.

Archer laughed. "Right in one. I looked those two up as soon as you called, Frank. Of course, I can't publish anything I suspect about Madge's death. I'd get slapped with a massive libel suit. But it won't hurt to be ahead of the game when the real killer is caught."

"How do you know Razzzor isn't the real killer?" I asked.

"His lawyer just called to tell you he was free, didn't he?" Tomas asked.

How had he known? "That was Razzzor, actually, but—"

"How'd he take the news about his car?" Gramps asked.

"Not well." Apparently there was a long waiting list for repairs. Razzzor's car might be out of commission for months.

"I never felt the need to drive a fancy car," Gramps said.

Archer laughed. "That's because you're an accountant."

Hyperion snapped his fingers. "Suspects?"

This was wrong for so many reasons. But everyone was watching me expectantly. "James and Layla Zimmer. They own the wine distributor where Deva worked. They could have been behind the counterfeit wine—"

Hyperion pulled his Tarot deck from his suit pocket. "I thought the police said they found evidence Deva was behind the fakes." He riffled through the cards and laid out the Emperor and Empress on the low table.

"They found her fingerprints on the labels for Razzzor's fake wine, but the evidence could have been planted," I said.

Hyperion raised a brow. "And someone killed Deva to frame her?"

"Or because she knew too much?" Tomas asked.

"Too much about what?" Archer asked. "Who else?"

"Deacon the stalker," I said.

"Hm." Hyperion flipped through the cards. He drew the Knight of Cups, slapping the card upside down on the white-stone table.

"Motive?" Tomas asked.

"Deacon was obsessed with Deva, who was dating Whitmore," I said. "He could have killed Madge because she knew too much."

"And now he's obsessed with you," Hyperion said.

Tomas frowned. "You didn't tell us that." He reached into the pocket of his baggy trousers and pulled out a bottlecap.

"Someone's bothering you?" Gramps asked. "I don't like this, Abigail."

Uneasy, I eyed Tomas, spinning the bottlecap between his knuckles. I'd seen what he could do with those. "We don't know he's the one who cut the wires in Razzzor's car," I said.

"But it's the sort of thing a crazed stalker would do," Archer said.

I tore my gaze from Tomas. "Finally, Beatrice Carson, PR consultant, Whitmore's ex, and enemy of Madge Badger. She's involved in Zimmerland wines too, as a marketing director. Motive: jealousy. Insanity. Both."

Hyperion slapped another card on the coffee table. "I'm giving her the Queen of Wands, reversed. She's dynamic, attracts attention, but we're not certain of her motives."

"Thanks," I said dryly, "the visual aids help."

"Sarcasm is not appreciated," Hyperion said.

"It's not one of your better qualities, Abigail," Gramps said.

"So, who had the opportunity to commit the murders?" Tomas asked.

"Deacon entered the Wine Merchants before we discovered Whitmore's body," I said. "He could have snuck onto that cliffside path behind James and Layla's house to kill Madge. And he could have gotten into Deva's house too."

"But do we know where he was when Deva and Madge died?" Archer asked.

"No," I admitted. I had a lot of ideas, but few facts. "We know Layla, James, and Beatrice were at the tea party when Madge died."

"Basically, anyone could have killed Madge," Tomas said.

Hyperion sighed. "We're supposed to be eliminating suspects. This isn't getting us anywhere."

"What we need are timelines," I said. "Who actually had an opportunity to murder Deva, Whitmore, and Madge?"

Archer snorted. "Good luck getting a straight answer from that crew. Their defenses will be up." He examined his fingernails. "But a society reporter, working on a story about something completely different – there are events going on all the time, you understand – a reporter *could* make some calls and find out where they were."

That was a terrible idea.

"That's a great idea," Gramps said. "No one will think twice about you asking around. You're always sticking your nose in."

The three older men laughed.

"How do you three know each other?" I asked cautiously.

Archer waved a negligent hand. "Your grandfather's done my taxes for years. He's always telling me to spend less money. It's excellent advice, which you youngsters should definitely heed since I won't. And Tomas helped me out of a sticky legal situation once."

"It's a small town," Tomas said. "We old-timers all know each other."

"Did you hear Barney O'Dell died last week?" Archer asked.

Gramps and Tomas nodded, somber.

"We're all vanishing," Archer said. "Who will remember Barney now he's gone? He doesn't have any family."

"We will," Gramps said.

Archer shot him a pitying look. "And how long will we be around to remember?" He stood. "But enough with the sturm und drang. Make yourselves comfortable. The bar is over there." He nodded to a cabinet of polished white stone against a wood-paneled wall. Archer strode from the room.

Creakily, Tomas rose from the sofa. "If memory serves, Archer's got good taste in booze."

"Does he have tequila?" Hyperion asked.

Tomas raised a bottle.

"Yum," Hyperion said. "I'm in."

"Does anyone think this could bite us in the butts?" I asked. Archer might be an old friend, but he was still a reporter.

Tomas rattled ice into a tumbler. "You can bet Archer will try to run a story on this little caper, but not until it's safe, legally speaking. Archer didn't get where he is today by running stories before their time."

"Got any red wine?" Gramps asked. "A glass a day is good for you."

I paced the room while the men chatted like everything was normal. But it wasn't normal. And I wasn't thrilled everyone I cared about was jumping into a murder investigation on my behalf. I'd only gotten into it on Razzzor's behalf.

After ten minutes, Archer returned. "I've solved the crime. Your stalker did it."

"The others all have alibis?" I asked, incredulous.

"James said he was home with Layla the night Whitmore was killed, so that lets them both out. And Beatrice was at a client dinner in Santa Cruz. Assuming the killer of Whitmore was also the killer of poor Madge and Deva, your stalker is the only one left."

If the alibis checked out. "Thanks. You've been a big help."

His eyes twinkled. "I'm always helpful. And you've got some quid-pro-quo in your future."

"You're right," I said. "I owe you."

"I was talking to Hyperion," he said.

*****

"I should have guessed Sundays would be your busiest time." Beatrice Carlton braced one elbow on my hostess stand and ran her hand along the thigh, smoothing her vintage red suit.

I pushed a wisp of hair from my face. "Have you got a reservation?"

"I'm not here for tea, though of course I'd love a cup. I'm here to bring you this." She handed me a slim folder. On its front was printed: *Beanblossom's Tea and Tarot.*

"Oh." I grimaced. "Thanks." Had we agreed she'd draft a PR plan for me? I couldn't remember. But we'd been so busy today, I was having trouble remembering my own name.

"And we need to talk about Razzzor."

"Unfortunately, you're right. This really isn't a great time."

The tearoom had reached "genteel roar" volumes. Silverware clinked on cups and plates. The murmurs of conversations swelled the room.

Gramps and Tomas sat at the counter in matching, rumpled *SF Giants* jackets. Sierra, who was quickly becoming one of my favorite Tarot card readers, was giving Tomas a reading. The two men roared with laughter.

"Unfortunately," Beatrice said, "under the circumstances, I don't think there is such a thing as a good time. Razzzor is meeting with his investors tomorrow."

I shook my head. "I've missed a step. How are you involved with this?"

"Razzzor didn't tell you?" She arched a brow. "He hired me to manage his PR through this crisis."

I stared, my chest tightening. He'd hired a murder suspect for his PR? "Crisis? But he's out of jail."

"But he was *in* jail, a suspect in multiple homicides. Investors tend to shy away from that sort of thing. I've managed to keep it out of the papers – don't ask how – but the news is too juicy to quash any longer. Tomorrow, the papers will be full of stories about Razzzor being unfairly hounded by incompetent local cops, which is better than stories about Razzzor being a killer, but..."

"Investors won't like it," I finished. "What do you need from me?"

"The more I know, the better I can spin. Have you got twenty minutes?"

I looked around the full tearoom. Waitresses bustled past, pouring tea and serving tiny sandwiches. Our next seating would be in two hours. The staff could handle things without me for now.

Gramps caught my eye, and I nodded.

I spoke to one of the waitresses, then led Beatrice to Hyperion's office. He didn't mind when I used it, as long as I didn't touch any of the crystals on his altar.

"How can I help?" Motioning her into a high-backed chair, I sat in the matching chair opposite, putting the round table between us.

"Tell me about Razzzor's relationship with Deva."

I tilted my head. "Wouldn't that be better coming from Razzzor?"

"He hasn't been particularly forthcoming, but he did say I could talk to you. So, I'm talking to you."

"I can't really help you there." I spread my hands. "I didn't know he was dating her until he told me he suspected Deva had been counterfeiting his wine."

"The fact that she was counterfeiting his wine could help or hurt him. It gives him a motive, but it also makes her look like a criminal."

"Are we sure she was?"

She looked up from her notebook, her eyes narrowing. "You think Deva wasn't?"

"Well, who killed her? It wasn't Razzzor. Was she counterfeiting the wine on her own? Or was she doing it with someone at Zimmerland?" Or was something else going on, something that involved the woman seated across from me? Because these seemed like odd questions for a PR consultant to be asking. I smiled harder.

"Be careful. There's no evidence James knew anything about that wine. If you say that to the wrong person, it's slander."

"I'm saying it to you, because I understand you work for Zimmerland as well."

She set down her pen. "Yes. Zimmerland's marketing is part of my portfolio."

"And you're an owner, aren't you?"

"In a small way. At any rate, the police are satisfied Deva was responsible for Razzzor's counterfeit wine. No doubt she was selling it through Whitmore's shop. He always had pretensions to grandeur."

"You said there was no evidence James knew anything about the wine counterfeiting," I said pleasantly. "How can you be sure?"

She sat back in the throne-like chair and crossed her arms. "I talked to James, and to the police. Of course, they looked at him as a suspect, but if they had anything, they'd arrest the man."

Or the cops wouldn't tell a PR consultant – and part owner in Zimmerland – about their investigation. I couldn't believe they'd told her as much as they had. But had they? Or was Beatrice lying?

"Now tell me about you and Razzzor," she said. "Are you dating?"

The muscles in my neck seemed to twang. "No."

"Would you date him? Having a solid girlfriend would be a huge help."

"No."

"I've offended you."

I tried on another smile. "A little. I get what you're saying, but Razzzor and I are good friends. Too good to pretend to date."

She pushed me for more details on Razzzor. But I could tell her heart wasn't in it, and I saw her to Beanblossom's front door exactly twenty minutes later. At least she hadn't lied about how much time she'd needed. But she'd been lying about her reasons for coming here – or at least omitting some key facts.

I watched her walk down the sidewalk.

"Trouble?" Gramps came to stand beside the hostess station.

Tomas stood behind him. "Need a lawyer?"

"That was Beatrice Carson," I said.

"The PR consultant?" Tomas asked. "The one married to Whitmore?"

"Not anymore," I said. "They're divorced." Do you become a widow when your divorced husband died?

"What did she want?" Gramps asked.

"She said she was working for Razzzor and needed info to protect him. But I think she was playing detective." I'd done it enough myself to recognize the behavior.

"Suspicious," Tomas said.

Gramps grunted in agreement.

"Want us to follow her?" Tomas asked.

"No," I said. *Lord, no.* "She's probably just returning to her office. It would be a waste of your time."

Tomas nodded. "No problem-o." He checked his watch. "Yikes. I've got to meet Maricela."

"Your granddaughter?" Gramps said. "I haven't seen her in ages. How is she?"

"Come along and see for yourself. She's back from Harvard for a visit."

"Will you be okay here on your own?" Gramps asked me.

"Of course. Go." I kissed his bristly cheek.

Tomas hugged me goodbye, and I watched the two elderly men wander down the street.

And I'm sure it was a complete coincidence that they happened to amble in the same direction Beatrice had taken.

CHAPTER 23

"You interviewed a suspect without me?" Hyperion pressed a hand to his navy blazer.

I sat on my heels in front of the reach-in fridge, cleaning cloth in my hand. "I told you, Beatrice dropped by the tearoom without an appointment."

And Gramps and Tomas had never returned. I glanced at my phone on the kitchen's metal table. Had they followed her? They were both terrible with cell phones. The fact neither was answering likely didn't mean anything.

Or they were in dire trouble, and Tomas was without his bottlecaps.

I glanced toward the empty hallway behind my partner.

"Besides," I continued. "It's not my fault you weren't there."

"I have a big class assignment due."

I studied him carefully. "What *is* this class?"

"Oh," he said, "you know, continuing education."

"Do Tarot readers need that?"

He drew himself up. "One should always keep learning. Once you stop, brain rot sets in." At his feet, Bastet meowed an agreement. "The brain is like a shark. When you stop swimming it dies."

Bastet tilted his head, looking less happy with that analogy.

My cell phone rang on the long table in the center of the kitchen. "Could you see who that is?" I asked.

He picked up the phone and glanced at the screen. "Unknown. A local area code. Probably a telemarketer."

I stood and extended my hand.

"Your funeral." He handed me the phone.

"Beanblossom's Tea and Tarot," I said.

"I'm calling for Abigail," a feminine voice said stiffly.

"That's me. Is this Layla Zimmer?" I glanced at Hyperion.

"Put it on speaker," he mouthed.

I clicked the speaker button. "You've been harassing our customers," Layla said. "I want it to stop."

My stomach tightened. She couldn't mean Archer, could she? Hyperion and I glanced at each other.

I rubbed my sweaty palms on my apron. "Layla, I–"

"I'm talking to a lawyer tomorrow about getting a restraining order, or a cease and desist, or maybe even suing you for slander. Possibly all three."

My legs wobbled. "For what? Layla, I–"

She hung up.

What? What had I done?

"She's bluffing." Hyperion rubbed the back of his neck.

I paced the kitchen. "What if she's not?" We couldn't afford a lawsuit. Actually, there wasn't a whole lot we could afford. "You don't think Archer complained–"

"No," Hyperion said swiftly. "He's definitely not the type to narc." He paused. "He might be the type to follow up by asking for comments though."

"Oh, damn."

"Archer didn't strike me as the stupid type. He wouldn't have thrown us under the bus." He checked his elegant watch and jumped. "I'm going to be late for my online class."

"Are you teaching this one, or is this part of your continuing education?"

"Teaching. Ta." He bustled from the kitchen and into his office.

Bastet trailed behind him, striped tail high.

I tried not to think of lawsuits as I put the finishing touches on cleaning the kitchen. But that's like not thinking of an elephant once someone's told you not to. Impossible.

I called Tomas. To my relief, he answered.

"Abigail?" Voices and laughter flowed through the background.

I sagged against the counter. So he wasn't hot on the trail of Beatrice. From the sound of it, the return of his granddaughter had turned into a party.

"Is something wrong?" he asked.

"Maybe." I told him about Layla's call.

"Lawsuit?" he said. "Where is this coming from?"

"I'm not sure. I mean, Beatrice was here earlier, but she came to me, and we…" *Oh.* "I might have mentioned someone at Zimmerland wines could have been behind the murders. But she was asking my opinion about Razzzor, and…" And my conversation with her made less and less sense the further it was in the rearview mirror. "And she is a part owner of Zimmerland," I finished.

"I knew that woman was up to no good. I could tell the minute she walked into Beanblossom's."

I massaged the back of my neck. "Are we at risk?"

He was slow to answer. "For a restraining order? That depends on the judge. But a restraining order shouldn't hurt you – not as long as you follow it." But his voice was laced with doubt.

My stomach wormed. "What aren't you telling me?"

"I need to do some research into slander law," he said. "I'm not really up on it."

"But?"

"Well, if you accuse someone of a crime, that's slander."

I swayed, my mouth going dry. Had I accused anyone of actually committing murder? I didn't think I had. But maybe I had.

"Don't panic," he said. "This lady's probably just blowing off steam. If her lawyer's got her best interests at heart, he'll tell her you're not worth the trouble."

That's us. Not worth any trouble. No trouble at all.

"You call me if you get served," he said. "You hear?"

"I hear. Thanks. I'm sure it won't come to anything," I lied. A lawsuit. I couldn't lose Beanblossom's. Beanblossom's was my livelihood. My security.

"And you've got liability insurance," he reminded me. "You're covered."

"Right. Right. I'm covered." I hoped. Please let me be covered. I was a big believer in insurance, but insurance didn't cover everything.

I raced home and dug my insurance paperwork from my desk. I was covered for business and personal liability. I *should* be okay.

Right?

I paced in front of the gaming console and wished I could talk this over with Razzzor. He always had a good head when it came to business matters. It was stupid to panic. So far, all I'd gotten was a threat. This wasn't a lawsuit.

Yet.

Stop thinking about it.

To distract myself, I baked mini cherry and almond tea cakes. And since they were mini, I ate about half.

Then I baked almond scones for Brik, since they were his favorite. And a batch of cinnamon chip scones for Gramps. I'd already started mixing the latter when I realized I didn't have enough milk. I stared into my fridge. Vanilla coffee creamer. That was milkish.

I stirred in creamer and baked the scones. After they'd cooled, I tried one. Wow. Wow, it was delicious. I could never use coffee creamer in scones at my tearoom – not for my Californian, organically-inclined customers. But the vanilla hit was amazing.

Finally, at midnight, I had to admit to myself that the baking wasn't calming me down.

Full and slightly sick, I waddled to the French windows.

My aproned reflection was a blur in the reflective glass. The garden's solar lights laid a trail of starbursts across my torso. If I believed in omens – and I didn't, I really didn't – they looked menacing on my wavering body. Like wounds.

But omens were Hyperion's purview, not mine, and–

A dark figure slipped past my dogwood tree.

I hissed an indrawn breath and grasped the back of a chair, my heart banging.

Slowly, I edged sideways, hiding behind the curtains. I peered around them. It was impossible to see the darkened garden clearly with my living room lights on. But I stared hard anyway.

A shadow moved like liquid between the raised beds.

My hands clenched. I might not have any control over whether Layla sued me, or whether the insurance company would cover it, or the fact that my artificially flavored scones tasted totally better than anything I could serve in my tearoom. But dammit, I was sick and tired of that prowler.

I yanked the handle of the French door. The window rattled in the frame, and heat flushed from my chest to my scalp. The door was locked.

The shadow froze, then darted toward the corner of the house.

I swore and raced for the front door. A light brightened behind me. I flipped the deadbolt and shot onto the low, wooden landing. Footsteps pounded toward me. The deck light blinked on overhead.

Unthinking, I shrieked a tearoom battle cry and leapt over the banister, realized how stupid that was midair, and landed hard, facing the street.

A body plowed into me from behind. I ricocheted at an angle and stumbled into the redwood fence.

The cascade of jasmine padded my fall but didn't break it. Pain shot up my elbow and through my skull. I grunted and rolled from the dirt bed and onto the brick walk.

Footsteps raced down the road.

I stared at the porch light and sucked in lungfuls of air, breathing through the pain. *Stupid, stupid, stupid.* I could have been killed. Forget about the intruder, I could have broken my neck with that stunt.

The porch light blinked out, and the stars came into focus. I breathed more slowly and the pain eased.

The porch light flashed on, and I flinched away.

Brik leaned over me, the light haloing his golden hair. "You okay?"

Oh, good. Now my humiliation was public too. "Unhhh..."

"Because you don't look okay." He squatted beside me. "What happened?"

I sat up, because staying down was just getting weird. "Someone was in my garden."

"Did you catch them on video?"

The video cameras. I closed my eyes. I hadn't installed them. "No," I ground out.

"Don't tell me they weren't armed."

"Something like that." I clambered to my feet, and pain screamed up my wrists. I gasped, clutching my arm. "I haven't actually set them up yet."

"Abigail, the cameras are useless if they're in a box."

"Yes," I said testily. "I get that. I haven't had time."

"I'll install them," he said. "Tonight. After you call the police. Let me see your hand."

I clutched my wrist to my chest. "I, um, don't have them."

"You don't have hands?"

"Cameras. I don't have the cameras."

"I thought you bought them."

"I did, but Hyperion's got them."

"Why does he have them?"

"It's a long story."

"Are you going to let me see your hand or not?"

Gritting my teeth, I extended my arm.

His touch was gentle, and in spite of the pain tensing my muscles, I found myself relaxing.

"I don't think you've got a sprain and nothing's broken. Call the cops. I'll check out your backyard and see if he did any damage."

Since I don't like being told what to do, even by someone who looks like a Viking moviestar, I walked ahead of him into the garden. The solar lights did a good job of illuminating the tanbark paths but little else.

Brik pulled a mini flashlight from a loop on his belt and flashed it on.

"That was coming prepared," I said.

He shrugged. "Flashlights can make good defensive weapons, if you know how to use them."

Setting aside the question of why Brik needed a defensive weapon when he came to my house, I let him take the lead. He scanned the garden for signs of destruction. There were none.

"Where did you see him?" Brik asked.

"I first saw him by the dogwood tree, and then he was moving toward the house."

We walked to the dogwood, and he squatted beside the redwood fence. "It looks like he came over here, through the Hendersons' yard." His flashlight beam illuminated half a dusty footprint.

The Hendersons were an elderly couple, and they were out of town this week. Sneaking through that way would have been easy – scaling a six-foot redwood fence, less so.

I took a photo of the print with my phone, then called Detective Chase.

Just because calling the cops hadn't been my idea, didn't mean it was a bad one. I was done with taking chances.

Mostly.

CHAPTER 24

"Trouble?" Detective Chase asked.

"Someone was in my yard. Again." Phone to my ear, I paced the deck and glared at the porch light. It worked fine if I was on the porch, but it's motion sensor didn't extend to the back of the yard. My intruder had avoided tripping it by the simple expedient of staying off my porch.

Brik lithely scaled my redwood fence and dropped into my neighbor's backyard.

"Did they get into your house?" the detective asked.

"No, just the yard." I told him what happened.

"Okay, I'll send a uniform over to check for prints, but don't get your hopes up."

My gaze flicked to the night sky. "Heaven forbid."

"I got a call from Layla Zimmer today."

"Oh?" I asked warily.

"She told me you were harassing her customers. *She* called it harassing. I call it interfering in an investigation."

I winced. "Ah..."

"Yeah. Fortunately for you, the case is closed, so there's nothing to interfere with."

I stopped in my tracks. "It is?"

"Deva's prints were found on the back of your friend's faked wine labels. And the only way they could get on the back—"

"Is if she'd put the labels on the bottles herself," I finished. "But who killed Deva?"

"Suicide. Poisoned wine."

"That's awfully neat."

"Suspiciously so," he agreed.

"But the case is closed."

"That's what my captain tells me," he said, his voice neutral. "Funny thing, we didn't find any empty bottles at her house. Just a few unused labels for Razzzor's wine."

"I... guess she could have run out."

"I don't like guessing."

"But the case is closed."

"Yup," he drawled.

"Well, thanks," I said, puzzled.

He hung up, and I stared at the phone for a moment. Detective Chase had been weirdly forthcoming. It was almost as if he *wanted* me to interfere some more.

I clicked on my phone's photo album and examined the pictures I'd taken in the Wine Merchants.

Stealthy footsteps padded along the side of the house. My muscles tensed. I backed toward the French doors.

"Abigail." Razzzor rounded the corner of my house.

"What are you doing here?" I hissed. "It's past midnight."

"Is it?"

"And why haven't you been answering my calls? You're not still mad about your Tesla, are you?"

"Of course not." He raked a hand through his hair. "I'm sorry. It's been... Deva. You know?" His voice choked with emotion.

Chest tightening, I looked away. I'd accused him of worrying about a car when someone he'd loved had been murdered. I was a jerk.

"I know." I set my phone on the porch table and awkwardly grasped his hand. "But the bad times are the times you should be with people who care about you. Not avoid them."

He shot me a wry look. "You're a fine one to talk."

"That's why we made such a great team."

"Made?" His expression softened. "Abigail, we could–"

Brik hurtled over the fence and landed beneath the dogwood tree.

Razzzor stiffened and stepped in front of me.

"It's okay," I said. "It's Brik. The intruder came back."

"What?" Razzzor said. "Why didn't you say something?"

Brik strode to the porch and climbed the steps. "Nothing on your neighbor's side of the fence. Hey, Razzzor. Sorry about your car. I hear there's a huge waiting list for repairs."

Razzzor's face fell. "Yeah. In the grand scheme of things, it doesn't matter though. What happened here?"

"Abigail didn't install security cameras."

"Yeah, she's got this thing for privacy."

"I don't entirely blame her, but with all that's going on..."

"She needs to take action," Razzzor said.

"Hello?" I pointed at my chest. "I'm right here. *Right* here."

"The thing is," Razzzor said, "security cameras tell you someone's been around. But at night, or from the wrong angle or distance, you can't really see who it was."

"You're the tech guy," Brik said. "What's the answer? More cameras? Better cameras?"

"I don't think Abigail can afford a professional security system."

"No," I said tartly, "Abigail can't."

"We need to catch this guy," Razzzor said.

Brik rubbed his chin. "You're thinking of a trap."

Annoyed, I jammed my phone in my apron pocket. "Is there a reason you stopped by, Razzzor?"

"What? Oh. My lawyer said our best move now is to stop investigating."

"Mr. Smith hasn't talked to the police lately," I said.

"Why?" Razzzor asked.

"They've closed the case."

Razzzor gawked at me. "That's... But..."

"That's good news," Brik said. "Since you're not in jail, you must be in the clear."

"They know who killed Deva?" Razzzor asked.

"They think it was suicide."

"What? No way."

"They found her prints on the back of one of your wine labels," I said gently.

He shook his head. "Well, but... that's different."

"It's motive," I said. "It proves she was behind the wine counterfeiting."

"If she did it, it was only to get at me. She wouldn't kill someone over it or commit suicide. She wasn't depressed. She wasn't desperate. Deva was a force of nature."

Deva had a gambling problem. I gnawed my bottom lip. "The thing is, Detective Chase didn't sound convinced either."

"There you go," Razzzor said.

"But the case is still closed," I said uncertainly.

"Then we've got to get it reopened," Razzzor said. "Maybe Beatrice can help."

I blinked. "Hold up. You *did* hire her?" I'd thought she was lying to wheedle info out of me.

"I've been having trouble with my old PR firm. My lawyer recommended her for crisis management. She should have no trouble getting the press on the local PD's case over this."

"But that's..." Why was I arguing? Razzzor wasn't trying to play private detective anymore. He wasn't a suspect. He was safe. "That's a great idea." But a warning siren sounded in my brain.

"Now all we need to do is catch the jerk who's invading your space." Razzzor rubbed his hands together and turned to Brik. "I saw this gizmo in the movies. I bet you could build it."

I snorted. "Oh, for Pete's—"

"Gizmo?" Brik asked.

"I'm going to bed," I stomped across the porch to the front doors.

Razzzor and Brik ambled down the steps, animatedly discussing whatever harebrained scheme Razzzor had come up with.

"Be safe," Razzzor tossed over his shoulder.

"Nah," I said, "I'm going to be reckless."

The men laughed and turned the corner.

I shook my head and went inside, and I managed not to slam the doors. Deva hadn't killed herself, and Detective Chase knew it. Beatrice was a suspect. Asking her for help was madness.

Also, my wrist ached. How was I supposed to serve tea with an achy wrist?

One corner of my mouth lifted in a grim smile. And how were the cops supposed to come after me for interfering in an investigation, when there was no more investigation?

CHAPTER 25

I guess I hadn't been sleeping well. Because when the doorbell rang, I jerked sideways and nearly fell out of bed.

Grumbling, since Monday was my day off and this was way too early, I stumbled to the front door in my t-shirt and pajama shorts and yanked it open.

A perky blonde smiled down at me and handed me a legal-sized envelope. "You've been served. Have a great day!" She turned and jogged down the steps and to a waiting Honda Civic.

I stared at the envelope, my insides plunging. *Served.* It was happening. I was being served, and Layla had only threatened me with a lawsuit on Sunday. How had she gotten a lawyer so fast?

I tore open the envelope, nausea spiraling through my gut and up my throat. Layla and James Zimmer were suing me for slander.

I shut the door and crawled onto the nearby couch. Last night's conviction fled in the face of grim legal reality. How had I gotten myself into this mess?

I groaned and buried my face in a blue throw pillow.

The doorbell rang again, and I lifted my head.

Layla couldn't be suing me twice, could she?

I rolled off the blue-gray couch and cracked open the door like there might be a live bomb behind it.

Hyperion bustled past me. "I don't smell baking. Where's breakfast?"

I slammed the door and sat on the arm of the couch. "What are you doing here? It's Monday."

"I know. Beanblossom's is closed, and I'm starving. Why are you still in your pajamas?" He eyed them critically. "Honestly, Abigail, your night attire standards are slipping."

"It was a bad night."

"What's wrong?"

I handed him the summons, and his eyebrows shot to this hairline.

"Yikes," he said. "That's no fun. Good thing you've got liability insurance."

"How do you know I have liability insurance?"

He shot me a look. "Because you're an insurance-to-the-hilt type of gal. Have you called them?"

"Layla and James?"

"No, your insurance company."

"Not yet."

"I don't see why you're drawing out the suspense. Call the company."

I eyed his empty hands. "Did you bring my security cameras?"

"Um, no. Was I supposed to bring them today? We're not going to have time to install them with all our investigating."

I groaned and fell backward over the arm of the couch, my legs dangling. A throw pillow whumped to the floor. "Hyperion, it's investigating that got us sued."

"Hm. I'm not named on this lawsuit."

I shot him a death stare. "How *I* got myself into this."

"Well, I'm *not* named." He shrugged and ambled into the kitchen. Plates rattled, and a cupboard door thunked closed.

Razzzor.

Beatrice.

Lawsuit.

"Screw it." I stood up and walked into my bedroom. This case wasn't over, and I had a bad-to-the-bone feeling hiring Beatrice was a mistake.

I located my phone on my nightstand and called Razzzor's lawyer.

"Good morning, Abigail. Don't tell me you've broken down and are going back to work for Razzzor?"

"No. I have not fallen on my head and lost my mind. How are you holding up… Fred?" I winced. But I couldn't call him Mr. Smith. I just hoped I'd got his first name right.

"I love my job. Razzzor has paid for two of my children to go to college, and the third is applying to Stanford. What can I do for you?"

Relaxing, I sat on my unmade bed. "I was calling about Beatrice Carson. Razzzor told me you hired her?"

"Yes. Razzzor and I both agreed we needed someone for crisis management, but we'd had complaints with his old PR firm. Then Beatrice called on Friday, and she had excellent references. Razzzor said he knew her, so it seemed like kismet."

"Wait. *She* called *you?*"

"Yes, why?"

The microwave in the kitchen dinged.

"Do you have many PR firms calling to offer their services?" I stared blindly at the mini fountain on my dresser. The water splashed a cheery staccato. I reached over and switched it off.

"We've got all sorts of companies calling to offer their services. Normally, my receptionist holds them at bay. But Beatrice managed to wrangle her way past Meghan. She really is good."

To get past Meghan the desk dragon, she'd have to be.

"My razor-sharp legal mind tells me that you've got some concerns about Beatrice's firm," he said.

"What? Oh. No. I just want to do some checking. Thanks."

"No problem. You don't want to hang up your apron and come manage me, do you?"

I laughed. "No, thanks."

He sighed. "I had to give it a shot. Talk to you later."

We said our fare-thee-wells and hung up.

So, Beatrice had offered her services. *How convenient.*

Hyperion wandered into my bedroom carrying a small plate and eating a scone. "OMG, this scone. There's something different about it. It's more vanilla-y or something. Is this a new recipe, and when are you bringing it to the tearoom?"

I set the phone on my nightstand and stood. "I can't bring it to the tearoom."

"Why not?"

"Lack of wholesome ingredients."

"You're kidding, right?"

"Nope. I ran out of milk, so I used vanilla coffee creamer."

He studied the scone. Looked at me. "I'm torn." He shrugged and took another bite. "But I never bought into that body-is-a-temple business."

"Beatrice finagled her way into being Razzzor's PR consultant."

"That simply could be crass commercialism. Or it could be Beatrice wanting to be on the inside, knowing what he knows."

I ran my hand through my hair, tugging loose several strands. "That's what I'm worried about. I'm calling my imaginary friend."

I dialed Razzzor.

"Abigail?" he asked cautiously.

"Did you know Beatrice called your lawyer to offer her crisis management services? Fred didn't find her. She found him. Last Friday."

"She... What? Friday?"

"As in four days ago. She's up to something."

"I guess that's fair," he said, "since I only hired Beatrice so I could keep an eye on her."

Nonplussed, I pulled a pillow to my chest. *Razzzor* had an ulterior motive? And he'd always seemed so innocent. "I thought you'd given up on investigating these murders?" I sputtered.

"I had. But... then her name came up, and I thought, why not? Keep your friends close and enemies closer, right?"

I expected that sort of thing from Hyperion, but from Razzzor? Had the earth's magnetic poles reversed? "Have you learned anything?"

"Not yet."

But I was willing to bet Beatrice had learned lots. After all, you need to know all about a crisis to manage it. "We need to talk to Beatrice."

"Sure. I can be in San Borromeo in forty minutes."

"I'll call and set an appointment. See you in forty."

We said our goodbyes, and I hung up.

"Want to tackle a PR consultant?" I asked Hyperion.

"Er, can't. Got a class. Rain check?"

"Sure," I said uncertainly. Wow. He was taking these classes seriously.

"I'm just going to make a doggie bag, so I don't starve. Don't tell Bastet." He sidled from my bedroom.

I called Beatrice. After some wrangling with her receptionist, I was put through to the lady herself.

"This is Abigail Beanblossom. We need to talk."

CHAPTER 26

I settled into the leather chair and laced my fingers over my stomach. Beside me, Razzzor shifted, writhing in his seat. I smiled at Beatrice.

She looked between Razzzor and me. In the window behind her stretched a line of blue Pacific. "You said you had some pertinent and private information?"

"Yes," I said, "but first, I'm curious why you contacted Razzzor's lawyer last Friday."

She touched her graying hair. "Sometimes, the personal touch is the best way to find new clients."

Tension spread through my body. "That's good," I said. "I was afraid it was because you're a murder suspect too and wanted to keep an eye on the investigation."

Razzzor coughed, his face reddening.

Beatrice's expression remained maddeningly bland.

"Murder suspect?" On the opposite side of the desk, she leaned back in her executive chair. "My understanding is that the case was closed." She smiled at Razzzor. "Fortunately, we were able to keep your name out of the papers."

"Yeah," he said, "th–"

"You were at the party when Madge was killed," I said. "And you have no alibi for the deaths of Whitmore and Deva."

"No alibi?" She arched a brow. "I was on a call with a client in India at the time of Deva's death."

I didn't buy it. I don't care how great she was at PR, my accusation should have seriously pissed her off. "Can you prove that?"

"Easily." She leaned forward and tapped on a computer keyboard. Beatrice swiveled the monitor to face us. A video of men and women in business suits and saris surrounding a conference table flashed on the screen. In the corner was a smaller video of Beatrice. "I keep a record of all my conference calls for Emmie to transcribe." She tapped the top of the monitor with a pen. "As you can see, the video is timestamped, both India and California time."

I folded my arms. "Anyone can fake a timestamp."

Razzzor cleared his throat. "Um, it's actually not that easy."

I clawed a strand of hair out of my face. "But it can be done," I said, losing confidence.

"Mmm..." Razzzor shot me a pitying look.

"When you divorced Whitmore because he was cheating with Madge," I said, "you had to pay him palimony. You practically funded his wine shop."

"It's true my palimony payments are over now that he's dead. But they were irritating, not enraging. If I didn't kill Whitmore when he was cheating on me, I would hardly have killed him now, years after the fact."

I crossed my legs, my stomach hardening. "You hated Madge and Whitmore."

She shrugged. "I felt bad for Madge. Whitmore dumped her for Deva, and unlike me, Madge was stuck working with her ex. Besides, the police have closed the case. They're convinced Deva killed Whitmore and Madge."

"That's not entirely true," I said. I was going to be right about *something* today if it killed me.

Her eyes widened slightly. "Excuse me?"

"I spoke with someone at the San Borromeo PD. He told me the case is closed, but it's not solved."

"Who told you that?"

"I can't say," I said. "But Razzzor and I wouldn't be here if we didn't have good reason to be worried."

"Well, I hope you're convinced I had nothing to do with it."

"The evidence of that video is pretty clear," Razzzor said.

She drummed her fingers on the desk. "Then you may not be out of the woods, Razzzor."

"No," he said. "I never believed Deva killed anyone."

"I think it's time you told us what you know about Whitmore, Madge and Deva," I said. "After all, you are working for Razzzor."

"Hm. I suppose it can't hurt if you have a fuller picture of events." She pushed her chair from the desk and swiveled it to face the ocean window. "Whitmore and Madge went to school together. A part of me always knew there was something between them, though I told myself I was imagining it. *Just good friends*, he'd always say. But that's so rarely true between members of the opposite sex, isn't it?"

The leather cushion on Razzzor's chair squeaked beneath him, and his flush deepened.

She rose and walked to a bookshelf and pulled out a worn-looking orange yearbook. "Whitmore's senior year. Don't ask me why I have this." She handed me the book.

I flipped through the pages. Yup, there was Whitmore, in pimples and glasses. And Madge, looking daring in big hair. And... I frowned over a pudgy young girl. "Is this Layla?"

She smiled. "Layla Francis, now Layla Zimmer. Poor girl."

"Why poor girl?" Razzzor asked.

"Madge and Whitmore bullied her horribly."

My head jerked upward. Layla had said she'd "barely" known Whitmore. But they'd gone to high school together, and had had a long, and apparently painful, history.

"Whitmore told me as an adult he felt awful for it," Beatrice continued. "He apologized to her years later. Do you know what she said?"

We shook our heads.

"She told him the bullying toughened her up," Beatrice said.

Remembered hurt spiraled through my gut. As a kid, I'd dealt with my share of mean girls. I'd made an easy target, with my AWOL parents and hand-me-down clothes twenty-years behind the times. I hated bullies.

"But it was the *way* Layla said it," Beatrice continued.

"What do you mean?" I asked.

"She was lying. She never really forgave them."

"Are you suggesting *Layla* killed Madge and Whitmore?" I raised my brows. "After all these years? But why kill Deva?"

"Layla worked with her husband, and Deva worked with them both. Maybe she saw or heard something she shouldn't have."

"I suppose it's possible," Razzzor said.

Beatrice smiled. "Anything's possible. Don't worry. As long as the police have other suspects to put in the papers, you'll be fine. I'll make sure of it."

"I don't want you throwing other suspects to the media," Razzzor said. "That wouldn't be fair. Layla could be innocent."

"I suppose," Beatrice said, her tone neutral.

"Don't give the bullying story to the media," Razzzor said flatly.

She spread her hands. "It's a mistake, but you're the client."

We left her office and dithered on the brick sidewalk in front of a taqueria.

"Do you think Layla could be responsible?" Razzzor asked.

I studied my sandals. None of this had played out like I'd expected. "I don't know."

And I had no idea how I could find out without digging myself into more legal trouble. I hadn't been hit with the threatened restraining order yet. But I could only assume it was still working its way through the system.

"People can carry grudges," he said.

I knew that better than most. I still couldn't forgive my parents for abandoning me. But since they'd never asked for forgiveness, I figured I was off the hook.

He checked the clock on his phone. "Listen, I've got another meeting in San Jose I've got to get to. Are you okay?"

"I'm fine. Take care." I kissed him lightly on the cheek and walked to my car. When I turned grabbed its door handle, Razzzor was staring after me. I waved, got inside, and drove home.

I might not be able to talk to Layla and her pals directly, but there was always cyber stalking. I booted up my computer and searched for her name.

Layla was all over social media, mostly with a wine glass in her hand. I did find her quoted in a newspaper article about Zimmerland Wines. She'd talked about the benefits of wine futures. Maybe she was more involved in the business than I'd thought.

I gnawed my bottom lip. But did any of this matter? *Could* this have been an old high school grudge that had gotten out of control?

I frowned over a photo of Layla and Archer, then I called the older man.

"Hello?"

"Hi, Archer. It's Abigail Beanblossom."

"Frank's granddaughter! Have you cracked the case? Have you got a juicy story for me?"

"Not yet. You said you bought wine futures from Zimmerland?"

He snorted. "Like any investment, it was a risk. One that did not pay off this year, to my woe."

"What do you mean?"

"One buys the wine before it exists, so one doesn't know if it's going to be any good or not. And honestly, French wines are *so* overrated. Give me a good California pinot any day of the week."

"And you were disappointed in the wine you received?"

"When I *finally* received it. It was months late. I got it yesterday and couldn't wait to try it, and when I did...? Meh."

Could Archer have received a fake wine? My excitement grew. If that was true, Layla and James were fraudsters, and the wine could be real evidence.

But were they killers?

"Archer, I need that bottle." And I had a feeling he was going to make me pay for it.

CHAPTER 27

"You can't have the bottle," Archer said.

My stomach bulleted downward. "Did you throw it out?" Would he let me dig through his garbage? And how far was I willing to go for Razzzor?

"No, I have not thrown it out. I want to keep the label for my collection."

"Then what—?"

"You can't have it without Hyperion," Archer said.

I grimaced at the phone on my kitchen counter. I'd put it on speaker while I arranged scones in a basket. Afternoon sun streamed through my kitchen window. "But... why?"

"I want my Tarot cards read."

Now? "What about a reading IOU?"

"No, I need my cards read today. You have no idea how stressful it's been."

"I'll ask Hyperion."

"You do that." He hung up.

Archer knew how to drive a bargain. But I needed to see that wine bottle, so I called Hyperion.

"Abs! I was just about to call you. How was your adventure with Beatrice? Is she the killer?"

"Apparently not," I mumbled. "She's got a rock-solid alibi." And I'd been so sure she was guilty. Fresh doubt slithered into my mind. I'd been wrong about Beatrice. Was I right about Archer's wine?

"Archer did tell you everyone had alibis except for that stalker."

"Yeah, yeah, yeah." But that's only what people had *told* Archer. They could have lied. "And, um, speaking of Archer. He got a bottle of wine from Zimmerland that's suspicious." I winced.

"He said that?"

"No, he said it wasn't as good as he'd hoped for. But I think it's suspicious."

"But Layla and James couldn't have killed anyone," he said.

"They gave each other alibis. They could have been lying."

"I adore your skeptical mind."

At least he hadn't called it seething, effusive, or corpulent (three of this week's calendar words). "Anyway, Archer said I could get the bottle, but only if you came along and gave him a Tarot reading."

"When?"

"Um, today."

"I'm a little busy today with my class."

"Oh, come on. This is murder. You love solving murders."

"That *is* true. But this spell has to be worked at a certain time of day."

I ground my teeth. "Is this spell absolutely necessary?"

"It is to my grade in this class."

"Okay, but how will the teacher know that you cast your spell at a particular time? This is a homework thing, right? How will your teacher know when you did it?"

"Are you suggesting I cheat?" he asked in an outraged voice.

"Ye-es? I mean, you'd be cheating for a good cause."

"Fine," he huffed. "But only to show Tony that he can rely on us for support."

We discussed schedules. I called Archer and we set a time, then I called Hyperion back.

An hour later, I pulled behind Hyperion's Jeep into Archer's circular driveway.

Hyperion lounged against his car. "You're right on time."

"I'm always on time." I hefted the basket out of my hatchback. "And I brought scones."

We walked to his front door, and Hyperion rang the bell.

After a minute or two, Archer opened it. He wore a spiffy navy-blue suit and blue-and-gold striped ascot. "Hyperion, Abigail, how nice to see you both. Come in, come in."

We followed him into his living room, with its fog-colored marble floors and bare wood paneling. He dropped onto the gray couch and motioned us to sit. I glanced toward the wall of windows facing his pool, and chose a soft, mid-century modern chair. Hyperion sat beside me.

I set the basket on the low table. "I brought scones."

He smoothed his silvery hair. "How delightful. Would you be so good as to make us tea? I'd prefer to have a *private* reading."

"Sure," I said uncertainly. "Your kitchen is...?"

"That way." He pointed. "You can't miss it."

I rose and carried the basket through wide hallways and past walls of glass. In the kitchen, I stopped short, blinking. It looked like something out of the space age, ginormous and decorator-house clean.

I wanted to live in this kitchen.

But where did he keep his tea? Not under the counter. That would be weird.

I glided across the marble floor to a wall with ovens – plural. Feeling foolish, I touched one of the wood panels. It sprang open, revealing a tall cupboard filled with dried goods.

I touched more panels. Finally, I found the tea things. I boiled water, set out a tray for the scones, and futzed about, giving Hyperion time to do his reading.

When I thought enough time had passed, I carried the tray into the living room.

Hyperion and Archer leaned back in their seats. Tarot cards lay spread on the coffee table before them.

"Ah, Abigail, you found everything I see," Archer said.

"Yes." I set the tray on the table. "How did the reading go?"

"Alas, we don't always get what we want." Archer shot Hyperion an inscrutable look. "But the reading was excellent."

The older man tried a scone. "This is delightful, Abigail. But I knew it would be. I ate my fill at that fateful tea party. Poor Madge. Have you learned anything more?"

"The police have officially closed the case," Hyperion said.

"Then they think Deva was the killer?" Archer rubbed his hands together. "What a story. Lust, wine and money."

"That might not be the whole story though," I said.

"Ah, more skullduggery. Tell me more." He leaned forward, elbows on his knees, chin on his fists.

"We're still investigating," Hyperion said. "Don't write that article yet."

"I'm curious about that wine you got from James," I said.

Archer grinned. "You believe it was counterfeit, don't you?"

"It had crossed my mind."

He leaned sideways and plucked a bottle from behind the arm of the couch. "I'm sorry to disappoint you, my dear, but this was the real deal."

"How can you be sure?" I shook my head and studied the bottle of Duvrosone Bordeaux. "You said it was disappointing."

"True, but I'd know their wine anywhere." He pulled out another bottle. "This was from five years ago. Go ahead. Compare the two."

I took the two bottles, both empty. They weighed the same, looked the same. I scrutinized the labels. Same paper. Same color ink. Same font.

Archer shrugged. "That's the thing about futures. You're making a bet, an investment. And not every gamble pays off."

"Could this be a real bottle with fake wine in it?" I asked.

"Sweetheart, if you have a new real bottle, with the real wine, why fill it with the fake stuff?"

"Yeah." Chagrined, I stared at the logo on the bottle. Where had I gone wrong? "I guess that wouldn't make much sense."

"The Burgundy wasn't all I'd hoped for," Archer said. "Disappointing, as it was from the Margaux region, which is normally excellent. But the only thing really wrong with this wine was how long it took to receive it. James has an amazing palate, but his business sense is sorely lacking. I hear some people *still* haven't received their bottles. Oh, James was very apologetic to me. He brought the case over himself." He sighed. "I suppose when one demands wine of this caliber, one must make allowances."

Unwilling to let go of my theory, I studied the bottles. There was something familiar about that logo.

"What's wrong?" Hyperion asked.

"It's this logo. Is this wine sold in stores?"

Archer barked a laugh. "You won't find this at the local grocer's, that's for certain."

"Would it have been at the Wine Merchants?" I asked.

"Unlikely. They were a respectable wine store, but this is a little out of their range, I'd think."

I thought back to my time inside the Wine Merchants. The racks of wine bottles, black labels dangling off their necks. Walking into the office. The stacks of boxes. Whitmore, lying on the floor...

I straightened. "Oh my God." The pieces of my murder puzzle were fitting together. But... No, that didn't make sense either. Did it?

"Abigail?" Hyperion snapped his fingers in front of my nose. "Earth, to Abigail."

"Sorry, it's just... You did get the real wine," I said.

"I already told you that," Archer said.

"Thank you." I jumped to my feet and pumped his hand. "You've been a big help."

"I have?"

"He has?"

I tugged Hyperion's sleeve. "Let's go. We've got a call to make."

"To whom?" Hyperion asked.

"Such grammar," Archer murmured.

"Forget the grammar," I said. "How's your French?"

CHAPTER 28

It is a truth universally acknowledged that when one wants peace and quiet, one is damn well not going to get it.

Bastet and my grandfather's duck, Peking, communed on one of my lounge chairs beneath the stars. Brik flipped burgers on the grill. Gramps and Tomas debated the ins and outs of barbecued peaches with Hyperion.

I stuck my finger in one ear and pressed the phone tighter to my head.

"Duvrosone, bonjour."

"Um, bonjour," I said in my best high school French. "C'est Abigail Beanblossom à l'appareil."

Smoke from the barbecue drifted toward the redwood fence, covered in thick jasmine.

"Oui?"

In broken French, I tried to ask when this year's wine shipment had gone out.

A flurry of irate French blasted from the receiver. My neck stiffened. The man hung up.

"Well?" Hyperion asked.

"He hung up." What a jerk. My French wasn't that bad. I mean, at least I'd been trying.

"But what did he say?" Hyperion asked.

"He was talking too fast for me to understand."

Brik checked his watch.

Gramps shook his head. "That's why I stick with California wine. It's just as good."

"You drink two-buck Chuck," Tomas said. "What do you know about good wine?"

"I know a glass of red a day is good for you," my grandfather said.

"That's true," Hyperion agreed, prying the phone from my hand. "Chocolate too, but only the dark stuff."

My grandfather wrinkled his nose. "I don't like dark chocolate."

"Me neither." Hyperion sighed. "So I just eat twice as much milk chocolate. That should make up the difference."

"Sounds right to me," Tomas said.

"Now watch and learn," Hyperion said, and pressed redial.

"Bonjour," he purred.

I rolled my eyes.

Hyperion rattled off an impressive flow of French. His eyes widened. "But–" He glared at the phone. "Rude! He hung up on me."

"Did he tell you when their shipment went out?" I asked.

"No, he hung up on me."

Brik flipped a burger and turned the spatula to look at his watch.

"Maybe you accidentally insulted him?" Gramps said.

"I'm practically fluent," Hyperion said. "There's nothing wrong with my French."

Tomas raised an eyebrow.

"What?" Hyperion said.

Tomas shook his head. "I'm just saying, there's a big gap between practically and fluent."

Peking quacked in agreement, and my partner glared at the mallard. Bastet smirked.

"You speak French?" Hyperion asked Tomas.

"It's not that different from Spanish," he said.

I spoke a little Spanish and a little French, and it seemed like a world of difference to me, but okay.

"If you think you can do better," Hyperion huffed, "be my guest."

Tomas took the phone, pulled his reading glasses from the breast pocket of his red shirt, and squinted at the buttons. He pushed redial and pressed the phone to his ear.

"This is Tomas Salazar from the Wine Merchants in San Benedetto. Have you shipped our order yet?"

French squawked faintly over the phone.

"It's not my fault it hasn't arrived yet," Tomas roared. "Now get off your butt, walk over to your computer, and check your damn shipping records!"

Slightly more subdued French drifted through the speaker, and Tomas nodded. He clapped one hand over the speaker. "He's going to check his records."

"English?" Hyperion said. "Your fluent French is English?"

"It's not about French or English," Tomas said. "It's about communication. They needed to hear the name of a business and an angry business owner. So, I gave them the Wine Merchants."

I shook my head in admiration. It was easy to look at Tomas, in his decades-too-old rumpled clothes and think he was past it. But Tomas was no slouch.

"But what if the Wine Merchants didn't order any wine from them?" Hyperion asked.

"It doesn't matter," I whispered. "All we need to know is when they started shipping."

"I'll find out." Tomas pulled a stubby pencil and a notepad from his other breast pocket. He set the latter on the outdoor table. "Hello...? Yes, I'm here. Yes..." He bent and scribbled in his notepad, phone jammed between his shoulder and his ear. "Okay... Okay... I hear the price is still going up... It is? Ah, ha... Yes... Imagine that. Okay, thank you." He hung up and returned my phone.

"Well?" Hyperion asked.

Tomas moved closer to the French windows. Light from the living room streamed through them onto his notebook. He adjusted his glasses and peered at his notes. "Shipping began two months ago. the Wine Merchants put in an order for six cases last year, so they should have received it by now."

Hyperion blinked. "Wait. the Wine Merchants did order some of that wine? That was lucky."

"That's... interesting," I said, thinking hard. "Six cases?"

"Yup," Tomas said. "The winery said we couldn't order any more. That vintage is finito."

Huh. Maybe my theory hadn't been so crazy after all. "I'm calling Detective Chase."

Hyperion straightened. "Tony?"

I dialed.

"Ms. Beanblossom. Tell me you haven't found another body."

"Um, no."

Bastet casually slunk toward the grill. Brik obligingly dropped a tiny piece of burger. The cat pounced and trotted back to his avian friend, triumphant. Peking shook his head in a superior, vegetarian way.

"Put him on speaker," Hyperion hissed.

"I'm putting you on speaker," I said.

"Hello, Detective," Hyperion caroled.

"Hyperion."

I cleared my throat. "I learned something odd I thought you should know about. The Wine Merchants ordered six cases of Duvrosone Bordeaux. It started shipping two months ago. Zimmerland is late on their shipment of Duvrosone to their private clients, but they did manage to get some of the wines to local clients."

"And?"

"And I was wondering if when you inventoried the Wine Merchants you found any bottles of Duvrosone Bordeaux?"

"Hold on." There was the sound of rustling papers. "Duvrosone Bordeaux?"

"Yes."

"No."

I rubbed my chin. "No?"

"There were no bottles of Duvrosone in our inventory."

"Wow. I wasn't sure you'd even taken an inventory."

"We didn't. After Mr. Carson's death, we asked his partner, Ms. Badger, if anything was stolen. She said "no," and gave us the inventory."

"Huh." That was even more interesting.

"Is that your professional opinion?" he asked dryly.

"What? No. Sorry. Thanks. Bye!" I hung up.

"The man's a genius," Hyperion said dreamily.

Gramps and Tomas glanced at each other. Brik checked his watch and flipped another burger.

"Do you have to be somewhere?" I asked tartly. I wasn't sure how Brik had ended up on my back porch, and I wasn't complaining. It just seemed with all his watch checking like he wanted to be somewhere else.

"Hm?" he asked. "No. I'm good. Burgers are ready."

The men converged on the grill. I touched the photo album icon on my phone and scrolled through my pictures from the Wine Merchants. Long racks filled with wine bottles, black labels dangling. Boxes of wine in a semi-circle beside Whitmore's desk. Whitmore, lying prone on the floor, his face turned toward that desk. I furrowed my brow. There was something wrong....

My mouth slackened. Of course. It was so simple. And terrible.

Now all I had to do was prove it.

CHAPTER 29

The guys drifted off after the burgers vanished. I went to bed. But I couldn't sleep, thoughts spin-cycling through my head. It was seriously unproductive, but I couldn't stop.

Finally, when my alarm clock flashed midnight, I got up for a cup of chamomile tea. I didn't bother turning on the lights. The moon was full. Its light streamed through my kitchen window and illuminated granite counters and the butcherblock work island.

I reached for the handle on the glass cupboard door.

A shadow stole past the window, and my breath stopped in my chest.

I froze, one hand raised.

He was back.

On tiptoes, I made my way to the living room. I sidled between the dining table and the sofa, and crept to the French doors.

Hand trembling, I reached for the porch's light switch.

A masculine shriek cut the air.

"Now," Brik shouted.

A spotlight flared.

I fumbled the door lock and ran onto the porch. Its light flicked on.

A bright beam of light scanned down the dogwood tree. A pair of men's black trousers, slowly rotating. A black turtleneck. And Hyperion, glaring. He hung upside down, one leg flailing, the other tangled in rope. His near-black hair wafted like seaweed. His dangling hands grazed the ground.

I jogged down the tanbark path, bits of soft wood pressing into the soles of my feet. "Hyperion? Brik?"

The light flashed away from Hyperion and to my face, blinding. I raised one hand in a warding gesture. "Hey! Cut that out."

"Oops. Sorry, Abigail," Razzzor said and dropped the light.

Brik emerged from behind a hydrangea.

My hands fisted, my muscles quivering. "What the hell's going on?"

"You tried to kill me." Hyperion's eyes bulged, either from indignation or the blood rushing to his head.

"I had nothing to do with– What *is* going on?" I asked Brik.

"We, uh, thought we'd set a trap for your visitor." Razzzor flicked the flashlight beam toward Hyperion.

I folded my arms over my teacup pajamas. "So *you* snuck into my yard?"

"I guess that was a little hypocritical," Razzzor admitted.

"You think?" I snarled.

"We didn't think you'd let us do it," Brik said.

"Thank you for your honesty." I knelt beside Hyperion and turned him to face me. "And what are you doing here?"

He flung out his arms in what I guessed was an I'm-the-victim-here gesture. It made him rotate more quickly. "Collecting herbs for my class. Now, can you get me down?"

"At midnight? Is there some magical reason you had to collect them at midnight?"

"Yes." He huffed. "Not getting caught."

I looked around my garden. "I guess the only real surprise is that Tomas and Gramps aren't here."

"Are you kidding?" Brik said. "Tomas would have killed Hyperion with a bottle cap."

Hyperion's shudder sent leaves rustling to the earth.

"Why didn't you just ask me for the herbs?" I said to him.

Brik reached up and grabbed the rope.

"It was more fun this way," Hyperion said.

My neighbor pulled a knife from his belt.

"Fun?" I fumed. "I thought you were connected with the murders. *You* put the hawthorn twig in my tea canister – didn't you?"

"Maybe."

"Why?"

"My magical herbs instructor said it gave it extra mojo." Hyperion eyed Razzzor. "Who's he?"

"This is Razzzor," I said.

"Huh. So you *do* exist."

"Tuck your head." Brik cut the rope, and Hyperion dropped unceremoniously to the tanbark.

He grunted. "Ow."

"You totally deserved that," I said.

Hyperion stood and brushed himself off. "I will never look at the Hanged Man card the same way again. All the blood rushing to my head was disorienting."

My nostrils flared. "You have a lot of nerve to turn this to Tarot. No more midnight raids on my herb garden."

My partner hunched his shoulders. "Okay, okay."

"You could have hurt me last night," I said angrily. I couldn't believe he'd knocked me down. It was so... un-Hyperion.

My partner's brow furrowed. "What?"

"You practically ran me over," I said less certainly.

"Wait. What?" A baffled expression spread across Hyperion's face. "Last night? Who ran you over?"

"I thought you did, but–"

"I wasn't here last night." My partner splayed his hand over his chest. "Honestly. I even have an alibi – assuming you're talking about another midnight raid. I was with a, um, friend."

I didn't want to know who his *um*-friend, was. "I don't need a witness," I grumped guiltily. Stealing my herbs, I could believe. But Hyperion would never hurt me.

"If it wasn't you last night," Brik said, "then who was it?"

"Someone snuck into your garden?" Hyperion asked. "What a nebulous horror."

"Yeah," I said. "Nebulous."

We trooped into my house. I sat everyone down, handed Hyperion a calendar, and made tea. When I returned from the kitchen, the three men were huddled over the calendar at the dining room table.

"I'm telling you," Hyperion said, "I *had* to come those nights. I was experimenting with collecting herbs during different lunar cycles."

I set down the teapot. "Did you figure out which nights were Hyperion's and which weren't?"

"They were all mine except for last night," Hyperion said. "Sorry. I didn't realize you'd noticed me."

I frowned.

"I was practicing being stealthy," he said.

"I don't like this, Abigail," Brik said.

"I called the police," I said.

"You what?" Hyperion set down his teacup, rattling the saucer. "You called the cops on me?"

"I didn't know it was you, and it *wasn't* you last night." I bit my bottom lip.

"All right," Hyperion said, "let's assume last night was the killer."

"We sort of did," Razzzor said.

Hyperion waved away his objection. "That must mean Abigail is a threat to him."

The three men turned to stare at me.

"What?" I said.

"Exactly," Hyperion said. "What do you know?"

"I don't– I mean, who knows what this guy thinks?" I rubbed my damp palms on my pajama bottoms. How do you anticipate someone who's nuts?

Hyperion pointed at me. "You know something, and you're keeping it from us."

"Yeah." Razzzor folded his arms. "I recognize the look."

"What look?" I asked.

"Furtive," Razzzor said. "Are you trying to protect me?"

"No. You're a grown man."

"Thanks for noticing," he said dryly.

"I just... I'm not sure," I admitted. "I found one of those black labels that the Wine Merchants uses in the Zimmers' wine cellar. It was for a Bordeaux, from the Margaux region, to be specific."

"So?" Brik said. "You found a wine label in a wine cellar."

"But what was James doing with a bottle of wine from the Wine Merchants? He was a distributor. He should have been selling them wine, not buying."

"Maybe it was a gift," Razzzor said.

This was all so tangled. Could I be wrong? "Look at this." I unplugged my phone and scrolled to the picture of Whitmore's office. "Look at those boxes of wine and tell me something isn't off about them." I handed Razzzor the phone.

Razzzor's brow furrowed. "They're boxes."

"But look at the arrangement," I said. "They're in a semi-circle."

Hyperion snatched the phone from his hand. "Let an experienced investigator take a look." The corners of his mouth tilted downward. "That is weird."

"What?" Razzzor said. "Now you're just saying that to make me feel like I missed something."

"The boxes are in the way." Hyperion shifted on the dining room chair, and it squeaked against my bamboo floor. "They partially block the path around his desk. It wouldn't make sense to stack them like that. Not with that big empty space in the middle."

"Exactly," I said. "It's like—"

"Boxes are missing," Razzzor said. "But that cop told you there was nothing missing from the inventory."

"He said Madge gave him an inventory list, and nothing was missing," I said.

Hyperion zoomed the photo on my screen. "Is that a case of Duvrosone?"

I nodded. "There's one case, at the top of the left-hand stack."

"Madge was lying," Hyperion said.

"But why?" Brik asked. "Unless she was trying to blackmail the killer – which is incredibly stupid – why cover for him or her?"

"Madge *was* murdered," Hyperion said. "Maybe she did try to blackmail the killer. But what are we saying? That someone – one of the Zimmers – stole that wine after killing Whitmore?"

"Why?" Brik asked. "Like you said, the Zimmers are wine distributors. They don't need to steal wine from the Wine Merchants."

"Archer told us the wine from Zimmerland was continually late," I said. "He only received his bottle of Duvrosone Bordeaux from Zimmerland last week."

"But again," Hyperion said, "why didn't Zimmerland buy their own wine?"

"That's a good question," Razzzor said slowly.

"And what about that stalker?" Hyperion asked. "He's exactly the sort of creep who'd prowl around your house."

"I know." Deacon made the perfect candidate, especially since he seemed way too interested in Deva and her death. "But I don't see why he would kill Madge."

"He could have killed Whitmore and Deva though," Brik rumbled. "Maybe Madge was in the wrong place at the wrong time. Maybe she saw him watching Deva, he panicked, and shoved her over the cliff."

Razzzor straightened from the table. "I need to go. Sorry about the Hanged Man thing, Hyperion."

He waved off the apology. "It's just another Saturday night, even if it is Monday."

But Razzzor wasn't listening. He strode to the front door and let himself out, slamming it behind him. It was just like him to get bored when we were talking about something important.

Brik cleared his throat. "Hey, guys–"

"Your best friend is weird," Hyperion said. "But at least he's real. I'll grant you that."

"Gee, thanks," I said, waspish.

Brik shook his head. "Abigail–"

"Was that really his Tesla?" Hyperion asked.

"It was," I said, "until someone pulled out its wires."

"Hyperion–" Brik began.

"You can't blame me for that," Hyperion said.

"I blame the jerk who sabotaged Razzzor's Tesla."

"Don't you two get it?" Brik asked. "Razzzor's going to Zimmerland."

Hyperion and I looked at each other, looked at Brik.

"He figured something out," Brik said. "Didn't you see the look on his face when you asked why Zimmerland wasn't buying its own wine?"

"Why wouldn't Zimmerland buy its own wine?" Hyperion said.

My hand fisted on the blue tablecloth. "Because... Remember that time you blew our profits on that giant teacup balloon?" I asked. Brik was right. Why hadn't I seen it?

Hyperion waggled his head. "I wouldn't use a pun like *blown*–"

"And I was late paying Tomas my rent, because I had to spend the rent money on supplies?"

"You were late paying Tomas rent?" Hyperion's eyes widened in horror. "He could kill you with a bottle cap!"

"I'm saying," I ground out, "the only reason you don't buy inventory to resell is if you don't have the money."

"It's true," Brik said. "I see it in construction all the time."

Acid burned my throat. "Razzzor's gone to Zimmerland to find proof one of them killed Deva. He's going to do something crazy like break in and hack their computers."

"How good is that lawyer of his?" Hyperion asked.

"We've got to stop him," I said.

"We?" Hyperion asked.

"After that stunt you pulled in my garden, you owe me."

Hyperion puffed out his cheeks. "Fine. I'll help."

We looked at Brik.

My neighbor rolled his eyes. "Fine. But if the cops show up, you're on your own."

"Sounds fair," Hyperion said. "Oh, do you mind if I grab those herbs I left behind before–"

"Yes," I growled. "Yes, I do."

CHAPTER 30

Brik unfolded himself from Hyperion's Jeep and scanned the dark parking lot. "I don't see him. What kind of car is he driving?"

"I don't know," I said. "He couldn't have gotten his Tesla fixed that quickly. And I don't see any cars but ours."

Why hadn't I paid more attention? I should have seen where this was going, and now Razzzor... I rubbed my throat. He'd be fine. This was just another ridiculous stunt, and we'd get him and bring him home.

I tried phoning Razzzor again. The call went to voice mail.

A light flicked on in the rear of the oversized, glass building.

"That can't be right," Hyperion said. "It's one in the morning."

I tasted something sour and pressed a hand to my stomach. "Razzzor." He'd done it. He'd broken in. "You don't have to come inside," I told them. "Razzzor's my friend."

"But we have a special bond since he trussed me up like a turkey at a Renaissance Faire." Hyperion strode toward Zimmerland Wines. "Besides, it's not like we're breaking and entering."

Brik shrugged.

We slunk around the rear of the low, concrete building. Razzzor's car – whatever it might be – wasn't here either, but a rear, metal door swung ajar. Pulse jittering, I reached for the handle.

Hyperion slapped my hand away. "Fingerprints." He edged the door wider with his elbow.

I exhaled noisily.

Brik and I followed him inside a dimly lit passage, cases of wine lining the hallway. Ahead, a light glowed through an open door.

Hyperion and I looked at each other. He nodded.

We walked to the door, and I pushed it wider.

A spartan office. Cases of wine stacked on the wood floor. And for an instant I was back at the Wine Merchants, and there was a body... I stepped inside, and the vision vanished.

Deacon Alstatter, in his messenger uniform, stood frozen behind the desk.

"You." Blood beating in my ears, I strode toward him. "What are you doing here?"

The bike messenger vaulted over the desk. I lurched backward. His foot struck my shoulder, knocking me into a pyramid of wine cases. A cardboard box crashed to the floor. Deacon hurtled toward the doorway.

Hyperion stepped into his path, and then Hyperion dropped to the linoleum floor.

"Hyperion!" My breath stopped.

Deacon flew backward. He smashed into a skyscraper of wine cases. The boxes tumbled to the floor, glass breaking.

Hyperion stood and brushed off his sleeve.

I extracted myself from the boxes and stumbled to my feet. "Are you okay? What happened?"

Brik stepped into the doorway.

"Just a little move I learned in martial arts," Hyperion said modestly. "No one expects you to go low. Wait. Are you asking Brik? Brik didn't throw that bike messenger." He pointed his thumb at his chest. "I did it. Me."

Brik raised his hands. "He did. He did."

"I'm calling the cops," I said and excavated my phone from my purse.

"Wait. Wait!" From the floor, Deacon raised his hand in a warding motion. "No police. Please."

"You broke into Zimmerland Wines," I said. And where was Razzzor?

"So did you," Deacon said. Red wine seeped from one of the boxes at his feet.

"Au contraire," Hyperion said. "We were concerned citizens. We saw a suspicious, open door and came to check to see if the owners were okay."

"That's right," I said.

Brik nodded.

The bike messenger scrabbled, one foot slipping in the leaking wine.

Glowering, Brik took a step forward. At the look on his face, even I nearly backed away.

Deacon stilled. "You don't understand—"

"I understand you killed three people," Brik growled.

"Three—" Deacon blinked. "I didn't kill anyone."

"Says the burglar-slash-stalker," Hyperion said.

"I didn't!"

"Then why are you here?" I asked.

"Because Layla Zimmer killed Deva," Deacon said. "It all leads back to Zimmerland Wines."

"Layla?" I asked. "Why do you think that?"

"Because she always hated Deva. She thought she and James were having an affair."

Hyperion glanced at me.

I shook my head. "Were they?"

"Of course not." Deacon raised his chin. "Deva would never do that. She loved *me*."

Brik's expression hardened. "And so you killed her."

"No. I thought it was you at first." He glared at me. "You were always sneaking around, following her…"

"I wasn't–" Okay, maybe I had been. "I can see where that might look suspicious, but… Wait a minute. Were you the one who was in my garden Sunday night?"

Deacon looked away. "It wasn't my fault."

"It wasn't your fault you snuck into my backyard?"

"I was doing it for Deva," he said sullenly.

"You do understand how this looks?" Hyperion asked. "The stalking. The breaking and entering…"

"I didn't kill anyone," he snapped.

Hyperion pointed at him. "Where were you a week ago Saturday, between nine and eleven AM?"

"I was working."

"Can you prove that?" Hyperion asked.

"Sure. My employer has a computerized log of every delivery I made."

"Then he didn't kill Madge," Hyperion said.

"No," I said. "The killer was always closer to home."

An unmistakable click sounded behind us. "What do we have here?" James asked.

We turned.

James Zimmer pointed a gun at my center.

It's funny how time seems to slow when you're about to die. I noticed the whir of an air conditioner. I noticed the gleam of reflected lamp light on James's polished shoe. I noticed the slick shimmer of the gun barrel. But mostly I noticed his finger on the trigger.

I smothered a whimper. But it was okay. I could talk our way out of this. After all, we hadn't broken in. Slowly, I raised trembling hands. "This isn't what it looks like."

"They broke in," Deacon said. "I was following them, and they overpowered me."

"You big, fat liar," Hyperion snarled.

"I am not fat."

"*That's* what you're worried about?" Hyperion asked.

Hands raised, Brik backed toward me.

"We saw a light on and the door open," I said. "And we found Deacon inside."

"I know," James said.

"You do?" I asked.

He shot me a pitying look. "Do you really think I don't have security cameras? Have you any idea how much my inventory is worth?"

I suspected it was worth a lot less than it was valued at, but I smiled. "That's a relief. Um, so, would you put the gun down now? I don't think Deacon's going anywhere."

Deacon shook his head wildly.

James's mouth twisted in disgust. "Pathetic."

Brik stepped in front of me.

James shot him.

CHAPTER 31

The gunshot echoed off the cement floor, deafening in that small space. Silence filled the vacuum as time stopped. We all stopped. James, his gun arm extended. Hyperion and Deacon, gaping. Brik—

Brik fell against the desk and slid down to the floor.

"No!" I dropped to my knees beside him and slithered out of my jacket. Not Brik. I had to fix this. I had to make him okay. *First aid.* Think, *Abigail.* What do you do when someone's bleeding?

"Stop that," James said. "And get up."

Deacon swayed. His eyes rolled up in his head, and he plummeted to the floor.

I pressed my jacket to the red stain blossoming on Brik's shoulder. His face strained in agony.

Nausea spiraled up my throat. "I'm sorry," I whispered. I was sorry for the pain I was inflicting now. I was sorry for dragging him here. And I was especially sorry for not having an escape plan.

Footsteps clattered down the hallway.

Layla appeared in the office's open doorway. Her face paled. "What...? James? What have you done?"

"I had no choice," James stammered. "You can see that, can't you? We have no choice."

"Call 9-1-1," I said to her. "Brik needs an ambulance."

She stared.

"He's been shot." My neck corded. "He needs an ambulance."

Layla shook her head. "But...?"

"Look, it was a mistake, that's all," I babbled. "James surprised us and assumed we'd broken in. And why wouldn't he? It was only a mistake." I met James's gaze. *You can still talk your way out of this. Take my explanation and let us go.*

She shook herself. "Okay. Okay." Layla turned to her husband. "What do you need me to do?"

His shoulders relaxed beneath his snowy dress shirt. "Get the office keys."

She nodded and scurried into the hallway.

I lowered my head, my stomach clenching. "Damn."

Brik laid his hand on mine. "You tried." His chest rose and fell in quick movements.

"This is a bad play," Hyperion said to James.

"You don't know what my play is," James said, his voice shrill.

"It doesn't take a psychic to know it's not going to work," my partner said. "Not that I'm a psychic."

"Clearly." James barked an uneven laugh. "Or you would have seen this coming. Put your phones on the floor and slide them over to me."

Hyperion did as he said.

"My phone's in my purse." I nodded toward it, my hands still gripping my jacket.

"Then... then get it out," James said. "And his too." He nodded toward Brik. "I'm guessing it's in his back pocket."

Brik squeezed my hand. "It's okay."

Words stuck in my throat. I slid my hand free, dug in the bag and shoved the phone across the linoleum floor.

Brik winced and lifted one hip. I reached around him and pulled out his phone, then slid that over too.

"And his." James motioned with his gun toward the unconscious Deacon.

I patted his pockets and found his phone. James was going to kill us all. He had to now. And I had no idea how to stop him.

I spun Deacon's phone across the floor, where it nudged James's patent leather shoe.

James kicked the phones into the hallway. He edged backward, toward the open door.

"Deva found out about your scam, didn't she?" I said tonelessly. *Razzzor.* There weren't a lot of people I had faith in. But Razzzor was at the top of the list. He had to be around somewhere, and he would have heard the shot. He would call for help.

My chin lowered. Unless he'd never come here at all.

"What happened?" My voice scraped. "Did she find one of your bottles of counterfeit wine?"

"No, she found my labels. I told her they were for a friend's collection, but I don't think she believed me."

"Why counterfeit Razzzor's wine?" I asked.

"It was a test. I wanted to see if I could pull it off."

"And you sold the bottle to Whitmore, who Deva dated," I said, "and to a wine bar Deva serviced. You were planning to frame her all along."

He shrugged. "Two cases. I told him I was selling them at cost, a special to try to get him to bring us on as his sole supplier. It worked like a charm. People think they know wine, but they have no idea."

"Then why kill him?" Hyperion said.

"I went to his store to check on things, make sure he'd been fooled. When

I saw he had cases of Duvrosone Bordeaux, I offered to buy them. I needed them. He sold them to me, but then—"

"He realized you should have had your own Duvrosone," I said. "After all, you're a supplier." I blinked rapidly. I knew why I was blathering on. I figured if I could keep James talking, he wouldn't be shooting. But why was he playing along? Was he trying to figure out how much we knew? Because it was too late for that. We knew he'd shot Brik. We'd seen him do it. He couldn't let us go.

"He started asking questions," James said. "We argued." His gun hand trembled. "It was an accident."

"And then you took the wine," I said. "Some bottles had Madge's black labels on them, labels you had to remove. I found one in your wine cellar. But you left a case behind at the Wine Merchants. I'm guessing that's when Deva walked into the store."

"I couldn't let her see me there. I went back for the last case, but then that bike messenger came in, and then you and Razzzor."

My spine bent, my heart racing. "But according to Whitmore's records," I said, "the wine had all been sold to you. That's why it didn't show up on the inventory Madge gave the police. She only realized later that the extra case in his office meant something was up." I paused. "It must have killed you to leave that case behind."

"It did, and I'd paid for it."

"How?" Hyperion asked. "You're broke, aren't you?"

Layla reappeared in the doorway. "Broke?"

"Temporarily," James said quickly. "It's all under control. After tonight, it will all be okay."

My gut squeezed. Whatever he'd planned, it didn't include us walking out of here. "No," I said, "it won't. You're trapped in a ponzi scheme."

"What does she mean?" Layla asked.

"We may have spent slightly outside our means," James said.

"But... the house!"

"Don't worry, we'll take care of it tonight."

"You've been taking the wine futures money to pay your expenses instead of buying wine," I said. "When your customers got impatient for the wine you never ordered, you gave them counterfeits. And you were using Razzzor's wine—which is pretty good—to fool people. It tastes like a Burgundy, doesn't it?"

Waste not, want not. He'd emptied Razzzor's wine into more expensive bottles and passed them off as Burgundies. Then he'd put cheap plonk in Razzzor's bottles.

"Those cases of Duvrosone at the Wine Merchants must have seemed like a godsend," I said. "*Real* Duvrosone. Did you give them to your best customers? Or only to high profile locals?"

"Is this true?" Layla demanded.

"And you're the one who shot Razzzor." It was a good thing his shots pulled to the left.

"He wouldn't leave me alone!"

"James?" Layla asked.

Sweat beaded James's forehead. "We'll be okay. I'm almost out of the hole."

"You killed three people," I said. "You killed Madge at Layla's party."

"Madge confronted me at my own home. We were standing near the ledge. She was being completely unreasonable."

Razzzor, where are you? "So, you shoved her over," I said. "Deva found out about the counterfeit wine, and you killed her and framed her."

"I had no choice," James said. "But it will be all right now."

"It's not all right." I stared hard at Layla. She wasn't a killer. *Stop this, Layla. You can stop this.* "Three people are dead, and you're up to your neck in debt."

"Not for much longer," James said. "The insurance on this building will cover everything. Those keys?"

"Here," Layla said numbly. "I got them." She handed him the keys.

A painful lump hardened my throat. So much for feminine solidarity.

Her husband grasped her elbow and steered her into the hall. He slammed the office door, and the lock clicked.

"Insurance?" Hyperion said. "Please tell me he's not going to do what I think he's going to do."

"We need to move," Brik rasped.

Dizzy with fear, I rattled the lock. Who makes locks that lock a person *in?* What idiot designed this door?

Hyperion hurried to the desk and booted up the computer. "Password protected, dammit."

He scanned the walls, the ceiling, and pointed at a vent, high in one wall. "There. You can get through that, Abigail."

"And how exactly am I supposed to get up there?" I sniped, fear driving my fury.

"I'll boost you."

"I'll need to get through the grate." I returned to Brik and pressed my hand over his.

"Pocketknife." Brik grunted. "On my belt."

Hyperion squatted beside him and removed the pocketknife from its casing. "I should have known you'd come prepared."

Deacon sat up on one elbow. "What happened?"

"We're locked inside," I said, biting off the words, "and Brik's been shot."

Hyperion flipped open the screwdriver attachment. Dragging a folding metal chair to the wall, he sprang atop it and attacked the grate.

Warmth seeped through my fingers. There was too much blood. Pain spiraled through my chest. "Brik..."

"It's okay," he said. "I volunteered."

I forced a smile. Contra every TV show in history, shoulder wounds are *not* okay. There are a lot of veins in the shoulder, lots of possibilities for bleeding out. My jacket felt damp beneath my hand.

The metal grate clattered to the floor.

Hyperion peered through the opening. "We're in luck. There's a storage room on the other side. All you need to do is get to the other room. He won't have locked all the doors."

But what if he had? I looked away, unable to meet Brik's gaze any longer. James still had the keys to this room. I wouldn't be able to open it without them. This was a get-help mission, not an extraction. And if I didn't get help in time…

"Go," Brik said.

"I dunno," Deacon said. "Her hips look a little big for that vent."

"Seriously?" I burst out.

Deacon shrugged. "Hey, I don't think I can get through it either."

"I can get through it," I snarled. I was getting through it and saving Brik, if I had to lose skin and break a hip.

Deacon knelt beside me and lifted my hand from my damp jacket. "Then I'll take over here," he said.

For a moment I didn't move, too startled by his gesture. Then I met his gaze, nodded and rose, taking Hyperion's place on the chair. Hyperion boosted me into the vent.

And my head nearly slammed into the grate on the other side. I drew a long breath and released it before speaking. "You forgot the second grate."

"I didn't forget it. I couldn't unscrew the screws from the back. You're going to have to push it out."

"Fine. Back me up."

Hyperion grunted and briefly released me.

I slipped backward a foot, grasped the metal grate on the other side, and pushed.

It didn't budge.

I banged on it with my fist and all I got was waffle hand. "I'm going to need to kick this out."

Hyperion sighed. "Fine. Turn around."

I bared my teeth and was glad he couldn't see. Wriggling backward, I dropped onto the chair.

Hyperion eyed me. "How much do you weigh?"

"You're going to lift me up there no matter how much I weigh," I said, "so the answer is immaterial."

Hyperion sighed. "Fine. Hold on." He looked around, found another chair and set it behind the first. He clambered onto it. "This can go wrong in so many ways." He sniffed. "Do you smell anything?"

I inhaled. *Smoke.* I stared at him, my skin turning clammy. "They really did it."

"Did what?" Deacon asked.

Hyperion shook his head, his eyes bulging. "Never mind. Abigail? We're out of time."

I turned, and Hyperion hitched his arms beneath my shoulders. "Okay, kick your feet up."

"I can't kick my feet that high. I'm going to have to walk up the wall."

"Oh, for God's sakes." Brik staggered to his feet. "You're both going to fall on your butts. Abigail, climb onto the desk and get on my shoulder."

"You were shot in your shoulder," I pointed out.

"My other shoulder."

"Okay, okay," Hyperion said. "She can sit on one of my shoulders and the good one of yours."

It didn't seem like a stable idea, but a wisp of smoke drifted beneath the office door. Possible death by fire is remarkably motivating.

I clambered onto the desk. Awkwardly, I sat on Hyperion and Brik's shoulders. They moved forward, and I wobbled, gasped. Hyperion grabbed my butt and lower back to steady me.

I yelped. "Watch it!"

"Trust me," Hyperion gritted, "I have zero interest in your ass. Now get it through that vent."

We staggered forward to the wall.

Brik braced one hand against my low back. "Hurry."

My heart banged against my ribs. I was going to land on my head. Brik was going to pass out from the pain. I was going to fail, and we were all going to die.

Gritting my teeth, I stretched my feet out, and my friends shoved my legs through the hole in the wall. My feet clanged on the opposite grate. I kicked it. "It's loosening!"

"Hurry," Brik repeated.

I kicked again. And again. The vent crashed to the floor on the other side of the wall. "It's out. It's out," I said again, unsteadily.

"Go, go, go!" Hyperion shoved me forward.

Panic arced through me. "No, wait–" I was airborne.

And then I wasn't, and a shock of pain drove through my body. I gasped on a cold, cement floor.

"Abigail? Is the door on that side open?" Hyperion shouted.

"Unhh."

"What?"

I rolled to my side and tried to breathe, but the room was choked with smoke. I lay in a warehouse-type area, stacked with boxes and with a pull-up garage door.

"Checking," I wheezed. Staggering to my feet, I trotted to the garage door and yanked upward. It didn't move.

Choking back a primal scream, I coughed and looked around. A metal latch hooked it shut.

I struggled with the latch. After seconds that seemed like hours, I discovered that if I pushed it in, the lock released. The latch scraped backward. Muscles straining, I dragged up the heavy door.

Smoke billowed past me, and a breath of cool air embraced my skin.

A Jeep screeched to a halt in front of me, and I jumped backward. Sirens wailed in the distance.

Detective Chase unfolded himself from the car. "I heard someone was shot."

"How–? Yes. Brik's been shot, but the door's locked. He's—they're all locked inside."

The detective popped his trunk and pulled out a crowbar. "Show me."

Covering my nose with one arm, I ran into the warehouse and scanned for an interior door. Black spots seemed to float in front of my eyes. I finally found the door, my eyes streaming. I yanked it open and was in the hallway.

"There." I pointed to the door. "James and Layla Zimmer did this. James shot Brik and locked us inside. He must have set the fire."

"I know." The detective rattled the knob, then attacked it with his crowbar. "Wait outside for emergency services."

I backed away on wobbly legs but couldn't leave, not without Brik and Hyperion. Smoke thickened in the hallway.

A piece of metal clanged to the floor. The door swung open. Detective Chase pushed inside.

"Brik?" I shouted.

Hyperion and Deacon emerged carrying Brik between them, and I gasped a hysterical laugh. Detective Chase hurried behind the three. I held the door for the men, then ran ahead, through the darkening smoke, my throat tightening. Glass crashed, and I winced.

I raced outside and sucked in lungfuls of night air. Blinded by smoky tears, I braced my hands on my thighs. The sirens grew louder.

Another car screeched to a halt. A door slammed.

I straightened and rubbed my eyes.

"Abigail." Razzzor pulled me into a hug. "Are you all right?"

"Brik. Someone shot Brik," I half-sobbed and pulled away.

I knew what this was—an adrenaline dump. We'd just come through a life or death situation. The chemicals that had kept me going were now overloading my system. Because Brik would be okay, and he was just an irritating neighbor anyway. I wasn't crying over him. Not really.

Brik sat on the pavement. Detective Chase whipped out a pair of hospital gloves from his pocket. Snapping them on, he squatted beside Brik and pressed one hand to his wound, while Hyperion told him about James.

An ambulance stopped beside Hyperion, the detective, and a sagging Brik. Two uniformed men jumped from the van and opened the ambulance's rear doors. Detective Chase said something to them as they pulled out a stretcher.

"He's going to be okay," Razzzor said.

"How did you–?" I shook my head. "I need to check on Brik." It was only neighborly.

"Yeah, sure." Razzzor followed me to the ambulance. We watched paramedics help Brik onto the stretcher.

"Is he going to be all right?" I asked, my voice high. I coughed. The smoke inhalation had done a number on my vocal chords.

"He's talking," one of the paramedics said. "That's a good sign."

"I'm fine," Brik said, his face taut and pale.

"Sure you are." I forced a smile.

They loaded him into the ambulance. Razzzor looped an arm over my shoulder, and I leaned into his comforting warmth. We watched the ambulance pull away.

The detective shoved his cowboy hat back with his thumb. "Now Ms. Beanblossom, why don't you tell me why you three decided to break into a wine distributorship?"

CHAPTER 32

I stared after the departing ambulance. Its taillights vanished around a bend. "What?"

And then I realized what he'd said. And sure, being alive in jail beat dead in a fire, but panic spiraled through me. "I didn't. I mean, the door was open. And James killed all those people. He and Layla are getting away."

More fire engines streaked toward us, casting the lot in flickering blue and red.

"Nope," the detective said. "We got 'em."

"You..." I sagged against Razzzor, and his arms came around me. "How?"

"We got a tip."

"A tip?" I asked. "From whom?"

"Um, from me," Razzzor said.

"You *were* in there?" I pulled away and glanced toward the building. Black smoke flowed in waves from the open garage. "But why didn't we see you?"

His nose wrinkled. "I didn't need to go inside. I hacked into their security system from my car. When I saw James pull the gun on the security cameras, I called the cops."

"Uh-uh," Detective Chase said. "I didn't hear any of that. Mr. Night? A word?" He walked toward his Jeep, and Hyperion followed.

I stepped away from Razzzor. "You hacked their security?"

Fire engines groaned and squealed to a halt, and men sprang from the trucks.

"I was trying to get into the computer files," he said. "Why would you think I went inside?"

That was an excellent question. Razzzor never did anything IRL, as Hyperion would say. He'd always use a computer instead.

"How was I to know?" I grumped. "You've been acting like such a weirdo lately." I shook my head. "Sorry, that's not fair, not after what happened to Deva."

He colored. "Anyway, his security system is tied into an external, third-party server. It automatically records when the system is on."

"And he left the system on?" I asked, disbelieving.

"Um, no. He turned it off when he went inside, which was before you went inside. But I turned it back on again."

"Do you mean everything was recorded?" I glanced down the road where the ambulance had disappeared. As soon as Hyperion was free, I was going to make him drive me to the hospital.

He smiled modestly. "Yup. I almost turned it off when I saw you go inside. But like you said, the back door was open, and James and Layla were in the front room. It didn't look like you three were breaking in, so I left it." His face fell. "It was a mistake. I should have called the cops earlier."

"How were you to know James was going to try to kill us?"

"It was obvious Deva hadn't run that wine scam, so it had to be someone else at Zimmerland. I suspected James might be in debt. That's why I wanted to see his accounts."

"I didn't think you were a numbers guy."

"I was going to send the data to my accountant. Then I saw you three break — I mean stroll — into the building. His security cameras have audio too," he said. "We got everything." He took my hand. "Abigail, when I saw him pull that gun. I thought I was going to lose you. I can't lose you."

I smiled, wry. "Then who would you game with? But you're not getting rid of me that easily." I squeezed his hand.

"That wasn't what I meant."

I dipped my head, unable to meet his gaze. "I know what you meant," I said quietly. We'd both been politely ignoring his crush on me for a long time. But it hadn't escaped me that Deva and I looked a lot alike. He had a type, and I was it. "Razzzor, I don't feel–"

"Don't say it."

"You've always been a wonderful friend."

He groaned. "Don't say we're *just friends*."

I hesitated. I did care about Razzzor. He was a good man. Kind, brave, and funny. I wished I loved him, but I didn't. Not that way. But all I said was, "I'm sorry about Deva."

"I'm sorry about your neighbor." He looked away. "You like him, don't you?"

"Ew! Cooties! He has parties nearly every night. He acts like my yard is his. He's pushy and rude."

"He took a bullet for you."

"Yeah." There was that. My gaze darted to the road. The ambulance had long vanished.

Forget Hyperion and the detective. I was going to the hospital *now*. "We've got to get to the hospital," I said. "I don't want to leave Brik alone. You drove here, didn't you?" I looked around the dark lot, but still didn't see any car that might be his.

"Don't we need to talk to that detective?" Razzzor asked.

"He's got it all on video. He can find us later."

Razzzor shrugged and led me across the parking lot. "I don't understand how James thought he'd get away with the fire. How could he explain all those bodies inside?"

We walked toward a space-age sports car.

"I think he planned to blame the whole thing on Deacon. Deacon had a reputation as a stalker, and James had thought the cameras were off. It would look like Deacon shot Brik, set the fire, and we got trapped inside." Though James had taken the gun. A missing murder weapon would have been harder to explain.

The sports car's doors swiveled silently upward.

I eyeballed it, suspicious. That did not look comfortable. "What fresh hell is this?"

"My new Lotus. It's electric."

Of course it is. I slid into the passenger side. Razzzor got in, and the doors glided downward.

There was a shout. Detective Chase ran toward us, his tie flapping.

"Should we wait?" Razzzor asked.

"What sort of horsepower has this thing got?"

"Two-thousand, baby."

I leaned forward, hands fisting. "Punch it."

EPILOGUE

All's well that ends well? Hardly. Life doesn't wrap problems in neat bows. But I wasn't complaining about messy and incomplete. Not tonight.

Smoke wafted from my barbecue. Gramps and Tomas argued amiably about the best way to grill corn on the cob. Peking snoozed on Brik's lap.

My neighbor sat, his denim-clad legs extended, a bottle of beer dangling from one hand. "Would you stop looking at me like that?" he grumped.

"Like what?" I sipped my zinfandel.

"Like I could drop dead at any minute. I'm fine, and for the hundredth time, it wasn't your fault."

No, it had been James's fault. Though Brik wouldn't have been in the line of fire if it hadn't been for me.

But tonight, I hadn't been studying Brik for signs he might faint. I'd been thinking of that kiss.

He hadn't mentioned it since that evening at the Zimmers' house. At some point, we were going to have to have a talk about it. Or keep ignoring it like cowards. I could work with either. "Then here's to your health," I said.

Gramps joined us and clinked beer bottles with me. "Abigail, can we talk?" He angled his head toward the open French door.

"Sure." I walked inside, and Gramps followed, shutting the door behind him.

"Is something wrong?" I asked.

His blue eyes seemed to darken. "It's about that postcard."

"I know I'm being petty about it, but I'd just rather not even know when you get the next one."

"She's moving back to San Borromeo."

The bottle slipped in my fingers, and I clutched it more tightly. And God help me, amid the shock and anger in my gut there was hope too. I crushed it, ruthless. "You mean she's coming for a visit?"

"She said she's moving back."

"But… You know her. That doesn't mean anything. She'll change her mind before she even gets here."

He gave me a pitying look. "I once told your mother that she'd always have a home here, with me, if she wanted it."

"She's moving in with you," I said flatly.

"I don't know," he said. "It was just a postcard. She didn't even give me a firm date."

I blinked rapidly.

"Are you okay?" he asked, expression anxious.

Hyperion leapt up the porch steps.

"It's fine," I lied, my mouth dry. "I'm fine."

"Really?"

I hugged my grandfather and made myself smile. "Really. Thanks for letting me know." I opened the door and returned to the porch. I'd get through this. I was an adult. I'd survived a killer. I could survive my mother.

Hyperion looked pointedly at my beer. "Porch drinking, Abigail?"

I shrugged. "What can I say? I'm outdoorsy." I was also celebrating. The lawsuit against me had officially been dropped. James and Layla could hardly sue me for slander now, not when they'd been arrested for murder.

"Let me rephrase that. Porch drinking without me, Abigail?"

I tilted my head toward the cooler. "Help yourself."

Bastet prowled up the steps. The tabby stared intently at the chocolate cake on the patio table. The tabby sneezed and nudged Brik's boot, meowing loudly. Peking rustled his feathers and hopped onto the porch. The two animals nosed each other, getting reacquainted.

Shooting me a worried look, Gramps returned to the barbeque.

"Where's Razzzor?" Hyperion pulled a bottle of beer from the cooler.

"He had to meet with his new backers," I said and forced thoughts of my parents from my mind.

"Backers for what?" My partner twisted off the bottle top and flicked it toward the bannister. It tumbled to the ground. "Darn."

Tomas tsked. "You'll never kill a man with that wrist action, son."

"You'd better pick that up," I said. "And Razzzor's project is top secret."

I was a little miffed he was keeping it a secret from *me*, but maybe that was a good thing. I wasn't his Girl Friday anymore. And I couldn't be more for him. Razzzor needed to stretch his own wings.

Peking flapped his wings as if in agreement.

"Did he hear the news?" Hyperion asked. "The trial date's been set for James and Layla."

"Then they're going ahead and charging her as an accessory?" I asked.

"She *was* an accessory to attempted murder." Brik scowled. "Ours."

"I'd hoped she would have turned on him." But Layla had been a hostage to her desires. She couldn't give up her status or her wealth, even if it meant sticking with a killer. "How could she have trusted he wouldn't kill her too?"

Brik looked out over the solar lights, toward the dogwood tree. "We don't always trust the right people."

"Abigail does," Gramps said.

"She's a good girl," Tomas agreed.

"Oh, please." Hyperion rolled his eyes. "Everyone knows good girls are only bad girls who don't get caught. Now what am I doing wrong with the bottle cap?"

Tomas popped another beer and demonstrated with a cap, sending it flying into the wall of the bungalow, where it stuck. Gramps shook his head and flipped burgers. Brik closed his eyes and leaned his head back on the lounge chair.

Warmth flooded the ache in my heart. The people I cared about were okay, and they'd come through for each other. Brik had come along to Zimmerland Wines to help. Razzzor had leapt to the rescue. Hyperion had kept his cool.

And I meant what I'd told Gramps. I would be fine, because I had friends. Good friends. People who counted and who I could count on no matter what came. Gratitude rushed through me, and I smiled.

Note from Kirsten:

Justice is done in the California wine industry!

This story was inspired by some very real wine shenanigans. The way the frauds in Hostage to Fortune "worked" are consistent with actual wine frauds, where the FBI got involved.

Even though the murder was solved, there's trouble on the horizon—Abigail's mother. Hyperion's going to be an important friend when Abigail's mother comes to town. And poor Gramps—he'll be stuck in the middle between his daughter (who he's not happy with) and Abigail. But I'm sure they'll figure it out... as well as another murder or two, of course, in book 3 in the Tea and Tarot series, Oolong, Farewell.

Here's a bit about that book:

When all the neighbors want you dead...

Abigail Beanblossom is finally getting into the groove of her new Tea and Tarot room. But in Abigail's mind, when things are going right, that's exactly when they're about to go wrong.

She never could have guessed, however, the mother who abandoned her as a child would suddenly return looking for tea and sympathy. Now, all Abigail wants is to escape. So, when her grandfather's friend, Archer, asks Abigail and her partner Hyperion to investigate the murder of his neighbor, the two amateur sleuths leap at the opportunity.

Abigail suspects Archer's fears of arrest are a tempest in a teapot. The victim's been renting out his mansion for noisy events and bringing the entire neighborhood to a boil. And the old money and nouveau-riche suspects are as plentiful as they are quirky.

But when Archer becomes suspect #1, Abigail and Hyperion must steep themselves in the fraught world of upper-crust homeowners associations and Instagram stars. Because this cockeyed killer is just getting started...

Oolong, Farewell is book 3 in the Tea and Tarot cozy mystery series. Start reading this hilariously cozy caper today!

Tearoom recipes in the back of the book.

P.S. There will be penguin topiaries.

P.P.S. I'd also like to thank magical herb specialist, Michelle Simkins, for two of the tea recipes and for information on harvesting herbs.

RECIPES

HAWTHORNE AND ELDERBERRY TEA

1 part dried hawthorn berries (not powdered)
1 part dried elderberries (not powdered)
1 part dried rosehips (not powdered)

Steep 1 tsp. 8-10 minutes.
This is tart and fruity and refreshing and excellent with honey – a great summer iced tea as well

Optional: If you're making a large jar, put a thorny twig from the hawthorn in there too. Scoop a spoonful, and just avoid the twig.

FOOL TEA

2 parts lemon balm
2 parts rose dried rose hips
1 part oat straw
½ part orange peel
1/8 part lavender

EMPRESS TEA

1-2 parts dried lavender blossoms
4 parts dried chamomile blossoms
4 parts lemon thyme

Steep 3-5 minutes. Parts should be small for just one cup–say 1/8 - 1.4 tsp lavender to 1/2 a tsp of the other two. Note: lavender can have an assertive flavor, and not everyone is going to love it. But it IS very relaxing. A little goes a long way, so you may want to experiment with reducing the amount of lavender.

CHERRY MINI TEA CAKES

Ingredients
10 T (tablespoons) unsalted butter
1 C all-purpose flour
1 1/4 C ground unblanched almonds
1 C sugar
1 tsp (teaspoon) coarse salt
5 large egg whites
4 tsp kirsch
30 sweet cherries, pitted, stems removed

Directions
1. Preheat oven to 400 F.
2. Melt the butter in a pan over medium-high heat. When the butter begins to bubble and pop, reduce the heat to medium. Continue to heat the butter, swirling the pan every now and then, until the butter is lightly browned. Remove the pan from the heat.
3. In a medium bowl, mix flour, ground almonds, sugar, and salt. Add the egg whites and whisk until the mixture is smooth. Stir in the kirsch. Add the melted butter but be sure to leave any dark-brown grit in the pan. Whisk mixture to combine. Let the mixture stand for 20 minutes.
4. Grease 30 cups (2 mini-muffin tins) with butter or baking spray. Dust cups lightly with flour.
5. Pour 1 T batter into each muffin cup (this should roughly half-fill the cups). Push a pitted sweet cherry into each cup.
6. Using the back of a teaspoon, cover the cherries by smoothing the batter over them.
7. Bake 12-15 minutes, or until cakes are golden brown and a toothpick poked into one of the cakes comes out clean.
8. Allow cakes to cool for 10 minutes.
9. Run a knife around the edges of each mini tea cake to loosen them and remove them from the cups.

BOOKS BY KIRSTEN WEISS

Wits' End Mystery Novels
At Wits' End | Planet of the Grapes | Close Encounters of the Curd Kind

Tea and Tarot Cozy Mysteries
Steeped in Murder | Fortune Favors the Grave | Hostage to Fortune

The Witches of Doyle Series
Bound | Ground | Down | Witch | Fey | Fate | Spirit on Fire | Shaman's Bane | Lone Wolf | Witch | Tales of the Rose Rabbit

Perfectly Proper Paranormal Museum Series
The Perfectly Proper Paranormal Museum | Pressed to Death | Deja Moo | Chocolate a'la Murder

The Riga Hayworth Paranormal Mystery Novels
The Metaphysical Detective | The Alchemical Detective | The Shamanic Detective | The Infernal Detective | The Elemental Detective | The Hoodoo Detective | The Hermetic Detective | The Gargoyle Chronicles

The Mannequin Offensive

The Pie Town Cozy Mystery Series
The Quiche and the Dead | Bleeding Tarts | Pie Hard

Sensibility Grey Steampunk Suspense
Steam and Sensibility | Of Mice and Mechanicals | A Midsummer Night's Mechanical

ABOUT THE AUTHOR

Kirsten Weiss has never met a dessert she didn't like, and her guilty pleasures are watching *Ghost Whisperer* re-runs and drinking red wine. The latter gives her heartburn, but she drinks it anyway.

Now based in Colorado Springs, CO, she writes genre-blending cozy mystery, supernatural and steampunk suspense, mixing her experiences and imagination to create vivid worlds of fun and enchantment.

If you like funny cozy mysteries, check out her *Pie Town, Tea and Tarot, Paranormal Museum* and *Wits' End* books. If you're looking for some magic with your mystery, give the *Witches of Doyle, Riga Hayworth* and *Rocky Bridges* books a try. And if you like steampunk, the *Sensibility Grey* series might be for you.

Kirsten sends out original short stories of mystery and magic to her mailing list. If you'd like to get them delivered straight to your inbox, make sure to sign up for her newsletter at kirstenweiss.com

Made in the USA
Middletown, DE
27 January 2021